Horse Tales and Hoof Prints

Horse Tales and Hoof Prints

2nd Edition

Rusty Clark DeVoid

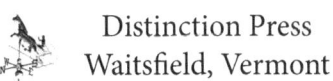

Distinction Press
Waitsfield, Vermont

Horse Tales and Hoof Prints
Rusty Clark DeVoid
2nd Edition

Distinction Press
Waitsfield Vermont
www.distinctionpress.com

Designed and typeset by Kitty Werner, RSBPress

Dedication

This book is dedicated to Professor Mary Hall. Her gentle persuasion convinced me to write the many stories sewn into the fabric of my family history. I never envisioned myself as a writer. Telling them with verve is far easier than signing them over to the scrutiny of the pen. It was her enthusiasm that allayed my fear of rejection and guided me through primitive beginnings. She always found merit and emphasized improvement. Sincere commendation fueled incentive and self worth. How wonderful it is to have someone enjoy the intrinsic value of your efforts.

Even though she's gone I still feel the warmth of her words prodding me to continue. She was a true leader.

Mary, I miss you.

Preface

MANY OF THE events actually happened. A few of these stories have been fictionalized, but the people and the heart of the tale remains loyal. Most were related to me by my father and his father. Passed on as bona fide experiences in their lives and their neighbors' lives. A regional history transported like the songs of a troubadour. Told at meeting places, county fairs, and social gatherings, they carried excitement and flavor about people who wrestled to survive and prosper.

An inseparable part of these hard-working folks were their horses. Muscles, sweat, and a strong back were vital tools for survival. Horses fit right in as obedient members of the family. A dedicated, loyal power source that helped shape a nation.

Many a tankard has tipped to a worthy animal and their story deserves telling. Here are a few of those stories. Although several experiences may be applied to one horse, the circumstances are authentic. The characters are as close to accurate as possible. And, of course, the storyteller must be allowed a measure of freedom.

Don't be quick to reject the science fiction portion. If our forebears were abruptly propelled into the present, would science fiction readily describe their reaction? They were concerned about walking to school without the concept of walking on the moon. Cell phones, wide televisions, 3D theaters, malls: How disorienting our world would be to them.

Yet some have witnessed these great transitions. In one brief lifespan, they have been forced to adapt to a supersonic age of gadgets, noise and speed.

Even in the storm of such mechanization, life's concerns, past and present, haven't changed. The land we were raised on; How can it continue to support us? What's to become of it? Will our children be all right? You'll see the common links in these stories. History is not to be disregarded. Past generation's strong definition of place and purpose is evident. Today's society lunges forward, hungry for progress. But it is necessary to stop occasionally and look around. Consider the past, where we've been, and where we're going. Use this as a gauge to see if we truly are making progress.

Rusty Clark DeVoid
Hinesburg, Vermont

Contents

The Town Constable

THE DAY WAS hot and the air was thick. Small dust clouds scampered out of the way of the horses hooves as she ambled along. The horse plodded down the center street of town pulling the empty carriage. People went their way, showing no concern.

Stepping off the board walk, Andrey intercepted the horse and tied the reins to a post. He plunked back down in the chair there in front of the barber shop and leaned back. It was a good spot to rest a while and measure up this town.

The horse was moving on. She had pulled the reins loose with her teeth.

Andrey was about to go after it when the man beside him spoke. "What are you intending on doing?"

"I'm going to tie up that loose horse."

"You just sit still and watch. You're new in town. Otherwise you'd understand."

The horse stopped in front of a shop and waited. As people went by they would speak to her and she nodded in response.

"Why would you want to tie up the town constable?"

"That's a horse."

"That's Ben Stokes' horse and that's the town constable. Sally is just waiting for Mercy Stokes to do her trading. Does that every Saturday. Done it for so long that folks don't marvel no more. Everywhere Ben or Mercy goes, Sally pulls up in front and waits."

"She's got a special nose for trouble, too. One Saturday two men come busting out of the saloon over there. They was yelling and trading blows in good shape. Sally wandered over, shouldered one of them to the ground and put her big foot on him. There he was, laying in the mud, thrashing and cursing. His fighting partner didn't want to mess with anything that big so he stayed out of it. Sally refused to let that fella up until Ben come along."

The man stretched and rolled the match stick to the other side of his mouth. "Ben took a lot of joking over that. People said that no one argued with him because of his horse and not his strength. It went on like that until one town meeting night. We was all over there at the school when we heard an awful bunch of squealing. Someone came in and told Ben that his horse had gone crazy. Ben said there was trouble and ran out. We all sorta followed to see what it was. Ben no more'n stepped into his carriage when Sally bolted out of town. A few of us mounted up and followed. Just as Sally turned onto Jim Albright's road we all knew what it was. Everyone could smell the smoke. Jim had left his young'uns home that night. They was old enough to take care of things. Well, seems as though they forgot to damper down the stove and the chimney got too hot."

The man replaced the chewed matchstick with a new one. "When Jim saw it was his place, he put the whip right to that little filly of his. Her legs stretched out there like a prize pacer. But it warn't no use. Sally got there first. Ben had the buckets full from the well and was heading up the ladder before anyone else arrived."

He analyzed his progress on the new matchstick before continuing. "The town meeting was there-to-fore postponed until the next night. One of the first pieces of business was to appoint Sally permanent town constable.

"Yeah, when you see Ben or Mercy, you'll see Sally. And wherever you see trouble, you'll see the town constable."

It was right about then that the innkeeper's dog charged across the street. It ran around Sally, growling and nipping her heels.

The man grabbed the stranger and hauled him back into his chair. "Just stay out of it. Sally has that dog figured."

The dog barked and jumped until the innkeeper came out and hollered to it. It turned its attention toward its owner for just a moment. That was a mistake. The next thing the dog remembered was picking itself up from the steps across the street and counting the number of sore ribs that had appeared out of nowhere.

The young man sauntered over to Sally and pulled out a big juicy apple. Sally sniffed it and turned her head.

A tall, lean man with huge hands and weathered skin walked over and ruffled Sally's mane.

"You must be new here. Everybody knows Sally won't eat a thing unless Ben or Mercy says its okay. Yep, she's quite a critter. When the mill caught fire, she roused up the fire patrol afore anyone from the mill could get up here. She's got a nose for trouble, ain't cha, Sally."

Sally nickered in reply.

"She can tell a lot about a body afore they even says a thing. One day a dressed-up dude happened into town with a buggy full of stuff. He no more'n backed down off of his seat onto the ground when old Sally here had a holt of his back side. She tore his britches in grand shape. Wouldn't turn loose of him until the sheriff arrived. That dude ranted and cussed about his fine suit being ripped and all. I suspect he lost a little skin, too, but he warn't about to show anybody. Well, did he put up a fuss when the sheriff told him to leave town afore the sun cast his shadow. It was some time later when we heard he'd swindled a few good folk in the next town up the trail. A regular flim-flam man we suspect. And old Sally here knew it, too."

Mercy Stokes appeared on the boardwalk steps. "Telling lies about my horse again, Avery?"

"Oh, no, ma'am. I was just telling this stranger here about Sally getting a holt of the best part of that swindler. It's the truth, ma'am. I was there when it happened."

Mercy pulled herself up onto the seat, and without a word, Sally pranced off toward home. They were a good distance from town when Sally's ears perked up and she quickened the pace. Mercy suspected trouble when Sally broke into a determined trot. She turned off the main road and headed for Hal Pritchard's place. The house was white and stately. Hal had a penchant for tending the house and letting the barn get tattered.

Sally flew by the front porch and down the path toward the meadows. Mercy hung on as the little carriage bounced crazily over the ruts. Down beyond the stock pens Sally galloped. The carriage vaulted the brook, throwing Mercy into the back with the goods.

When they approached the meadow, Mercy saw a problem. Hal's bull had the little Albright lad imprisoned on a boulder not much bigger than he was. The little guy had been fishing and tried to take a short cut across the meadow.

Hal should know better than keep that half-blind creature. He was a mean one, even as a calf.

He'd been warned numerous times, but Hal argued that he was good breeding stock. He had failed to heed good advice, and now there was serious trouble. That bull was blowing and pawing and working himself into a frenzy.

The little boy stood on that rock with only his fishing pole between him and sixteen-hundred pounds of angry muscle.

Mercy fretted about what to do. She certainly couldn't outrun that bull, even if he was almost blind.

Suddenly a blood chilling screech pierced the air. Sally was two hundred yards up the outside of the fence line. She stood on her hind legs with both front feet paddling the air like a prize fighter. The carriage shafts strained in their sockets.

The bull turned to the challenge. Sally stomped and snorted as he appraised the intrusion.

That shrill scream was too much to let pass. With ground-shaking hooves, the bull stomped towards his challenger. He was slow to approach with just his nose and ears to guide him. Behind him, the little boy sprinted toward the gate so fast that a lightning bolt couldn't catch him.

The bull approached the fence, swaying and blowing froth. When he got close enough, the buggy whip lashed out with a vicious crack, taking a chunk of hide with it.

"Take that you formidable beast," Mercy growled. She leaned back against the carriage. "I've a good mind to give the same to your owner."

Sally lowered her head to the little lad. He hugged her with arms that barely reached around her nose.

"Get up here in the carriage with me and I'll take you home." Mercy held him tight to calm his shivering fear.

Sally didn't have to be told where to go. She trotted right up the road to Jim Albright's house.

When Mercy arrived home, Ben helped her unload. "What did you do, play checkers with these groceries?"

"Sally took me on a rescue mission," she replied. "That man, Hal Pritchard, has been told many times about that blind bull of his. It had the Albright boy pinned on a rock in the pasture. Could've killed him, too, if Sally hadn't heard it. That man needs some sense pounded into him. The way he keeps that house so trim. And all those flowers. Have you seen his barn? It's a disgrace."

"All right, Mercy. Don't get all worked up. I'll speak to the man."

"He'd better do more than just listen or I'll take the whip to him, too."

Ben grinned as he pulled the wisps of the bull's hair from the whip's lashes. Without any children of their own, Mercy fretted about everyone else's young ones. Oh, she knew her place, but that didn't prevent her from loving them with fresh donuts and good advice.

With the breast plate and harness hanging on their hook, Sally ambled into her stall. Ben rearranged her top knot while she chomped her oats. "Ya did it again, eh, girl. I don't know what we'd do without you."

Monday morning Sally was ready as usual. The sound of the barn door latch found her lined up with the harness rack. She always stopped at the front steps so Ben could fetch his lunch bucket and a goodbye kiss.

Sally let Ben off at the mill and trotted the carriage up to the livery.

Andrey took a big bite of apple as he watched the horse skillfully back the carriage into its shed. She waited patiently for Joe the livery keeper to come out and release the shafts so she could go inside.

He turned away from the store window and pawed through the soda crackers.

"Them's all the same," the storekeeper said. "You don't have to look'um all over. They're all the same size."

"That horse over there. Ben Stokes' horse. Is she for sale?"

"Sally? You'd stand a better chance of asking Ben to sell

his only son. That is if he had one. Besides, Sally is a community horse. Why there ain't a soul around that she ain't helped. No, Sally is as good as Ben's child."

The storekeeper opened a jar and took out a licorice stick. "I know that for a fact cause I stood right here and watched him. It was the winter of '98 I think. One morning it was so cold a pickle would've froze right in the barrel. Sally brought Ben to work as usual. A body could sorta feel that something was gonna happen. Well, sir, a little later on it commenced to snow. It snowed so hard that ya couldn't see the hitching post out that window. It just kept coming down. Later on the mill workers came in here and they was a dragging Maude Ryan with um. Said they found her wandering down the street almost froze to death. We thawed her out enough so that she stopped shivering and her jaw stopped dancing and she told us what happened."

He bit off a hunk of licorice and used the remainder for a pointer. "She said Orlen had been out to the barn when the blizzard hit. She got worried when he didn't come in so she decided to go out and check on him. Well, she couldn't see the barn cause it's a good ways from the house, so she fetched a length of rope from the cellar and tied one end to the porch post. That's so she could find her way back, ya know. Well, old Orlen warn't in the barn so she worked her way to the hen house. Orlen warn't there either. Well, by that time she was fit to be tied with worry. So Maude made up her mind to come to town for help. She stumbled along the fence lines till she found her way here. Yes sir, she sat right over there on that box of Salvatore and told us all.

"Everybody knew it was useless to go out there. Why those fence lines she followed here were buried by then. Everything was white. And with that mean wind biting your skin and that cold snow stinging your eyes, a body

17

couldn't find a thing, ya know. Why a man wouldn't be able to find his hand if it warn't hitched to him."

He paused for another bite of licorice. One elbow on the counter, he leaned over closer. "It was right about then that Joe from the livery come busting in. He said Sally was gone. Ben turned whiter than the snow. I watched him, I did. He stood right by the stove there and froze up like a block of ice."

"No one knew what to do but wait it out. A man don't stand a chance in a storm like that, ya know.

"Well sir, everyone sorta bunked out on whatever looked comfortable. Everyone except Maude and Ben. Maude hugged the stove and fretted about Orlen. Ben paced the floor, wringing his hands. Yes sir, he paced between the door and that pickle barrel until well past dark. I thought he was gonna wear a furrow in my floor. He didn't look at anybody for fear they might see the tears in his eyes. Yes sir, it was like his own child was out there in that freezing cold."

With the candy gone, the storekeeper looked for something else to wave. The feather duster would do. It flourished around as he spoke. "It was well along into the night when we heard an awful commotion out on the porch. When they opened the door, all the snow from out in the street come right in here. It was piled up in front of my counter here this high. Well sir, coming right in with the snow was Sally. And she was a dragging Orlen Ryan. She sure looked awful white with all that ice and snow caked on her. It was thicker than the fat on a winter hog. And there was Orlen with his arms hooked through her harness. His coat was all tore up, maybe from a fence or two, but he was here. We cut the harness to get him loose. He was so stiff that unbending his arms might've snapped them off.

"Well sir, it took some maneuvering, but we got them both over there next to my stove. That warn't no easy trick, getting a horse over there, ya know. Her heavy corked up winter shoes put some monstrous gouges in my floor.

"Old Orlen was frostbit some, but he managed all right. Didn't lose nothing important. When he finally came around, we cooked up some beans for him. Maude had to feed him, ya know. His hands shook so bad he couldn't find his mouth. Kept dumping those beans in his shirt pocket. Maude hovered over him the rest of the night.

"Ben was busy, too. He pulled off all that ice and snow with his bare hands. Nobody heard him complain about it. Not once. He run his fingers through her mane and tail, pushing out the stuff. Then he lifted each foot between his legs and rubbed it hard. He used one of my good knives to dig ice out of her feet. I made him pay for it, too. It was a brand new knife.

"Well sir, I guess things was all right then and everybody slept well. All except for Ben. He combed that horse and fussed over her until sun up. Never slept a wink. Except for the wind, that was the only noise for the whole night. Just someone chunking up the stove and Ben Stokes' brush sliding through Sally's hair. Well, there was the rattling of Orlen's teeth, too, I suppose.

"Well, sir, I can tell you real straight that Orlen Ryan ain't no poor man. And between him and Jim Albright, old Ben Stokes won't ever have to buy any winter hay for Sally. Those two will see to that ya know.

"Yup, Sally did what no man could. Even to this day nobody knows how she knew Orlen was out there or how she found him. Don't know how she found her way back to town either. Even Orlen don't remember. Too bad more people don't have that kinda horse sense."

The storekeeper stopped the young man just short of the door. "What is your name stranger?"

"Andrey."

"Well, Andrey, I suppose you'd like to pay for them apples you ate."

Andrey pushed his coins across the counter. "You must've made a good chunk of money that night of the storm."

"I did, all right. Those fellas cleaned me out of blankets and gloves. Ben bought two new blankets for Sally on the spot."

Andrey leaned over close to him. "Did you charge them for the heat from your stove, too?"

Over at the livery, Joe said that he could use good help and hired Andrey immediately.

"Just one thing," he warned. "Sally knows when it's time to leave so when you see the door open you just go out and hook her up. She opens the door by herself but forgets to close it. We can give her that much."

It was well into the winter before Andrey got his first taste of Sally's intuition.

One cold mid-afternoon, she seemed unusually nervous. "What's the matter, girl?" Andrey cooed. "Do you smell trouble?"

Her ears tipped forward and she bobbed her head.

Andrey grabbed his coat. Sally already had the door open. She was nosing a coil of rope that hung on the wall. Andrey knew better than question good horse sense. He shouldered the rope, jumped on her blanketed back and they bolted out the door.

He hung on hard as Sally ran like a storm wind toward the mill pond. The bitter breeze pulled at his hair and scraped his cheeks.

When Sally stopped he could see the trouble. Ike Wilkes had been ice fishing. The big pond was well frozen over at the shallows but not in the center. Ike's white hands clung desperately to the rim of the hole.

It took three tosses for the rope to fall within his grasp. Andrey pulled but the ice was too slippery to lift Ike from the water and the rope was too short to reach the shore line.

Sally eased herself out onto the ice. It was dangerous. If she slipped or fell through it would spell doom. Her shoe corks dug deep into the frozen surface and Ike eased out of his predicament.

The mill workers were surprised to see Andrey helping in this huge icicle in the shape of Ike Wilkes.

Winter turned into spring and everything went as usual. Sally made her regular weekday trips to town and once on Saturday. The new grass was getting tall and flowers blossomed everywhere. Corn sprouts were up in the field and the sun was warm. Mercy hummed to herself as she worked in her kitchen. Ben would be up for dinner soon. Fixing fence seemed like an endless task.

She heard Sally whinny. It was nothing unusual. She had the run of the place as long as she stayed out of Mercy's flowers.

Suddenly, Sally broke into a screech and started throwing herself around in a wild tantrum.

Mercy damped down the stove and tossed aside her apron. Maybe that horse had gotten into a nest of bees. She put aside that idea when Sally went racing toward the meadow where Ben was working. Mercy ran like an angry tornado, her skirts billowing out behind. She found Ben crumpled up in the grass. He didn't respond to Sally's gentle nudges.

Mercy fell to the earth beside him and Sally headed for town.

It was the innkeeper who saw Sally thunder into town all sweat and lather. She nearly broke the door down to Doc's office. It didn't matter if he was with a patient. She wanted him now.

Doc's buggy rattled into Ben Stokes' yard and down across the meadow in pursuit of Sally. He found Mercy sitting in the grass with Ben's head in her lap. It was too late.

All the neighbors got together and helped Mercy with the barn and fences. Ben's absence was especially hard on Sally. Oh, she continued to bring Mercy to town every Saturday but during the week she would be wandering the streets and hanging around the livery.

Everyone tried to convince Mercy to move into town but she held out.

Meanwhile, Sally continued with her rescue missions. Ike Wilkes had another run of bad luck.

He slipped with his axe while cutting wood and would no doubt have bled to death if Sally hadn't come along and given him a fast ride to the Doctor's office.

When fall closed in Mercy, finally reconsidered. She couldn't slaughter the hog alone and the garden produce was rotting before she found the time to process it. With no wood pile and the taxes due, she put her land up for sale.

It wouldn't take long to find a buyer. It was prime territory and the promise of a new road coming through added value.

Autumn was in the full of its color. Leaves swirled out of the way as the carriage went by.

The smell of apple cider wafted on the breeze. Wood smoke curled up from every farm. People were slaughtering hogs and making soap.

The streets were busy when Sally plodded into town.

Mercy was in the carriage but she wasn't sitting on the seat. She lay all scrunched down in the foot well when Sally pulled up in front of Doc's office. They pulled her out and Joe led Sally down to the livery. Everyone says that Mercy knew the end was near when she harnessed Sally. She must've collapsed on the way to town. Doc made the final pronouncement right there in the street.

It was Andrey who found Sally. He had just come back from helping the Doc with Mercy when he found her. She was down on her knees, still between the carriage shafts. She never got up again.

The whole town seemed to be in a hazy fog that day as the word spread. Nobody said much at all. Something important was missing.

It was Sally.

The next Saturday was a big day. Folks came from all over. There were more people at the Stokes' auction than the property could hold. Carriages lined the road for a mile in both directions. There was even a couple of those new automobile contraptions. Everything went for a premium price. Sally's harness brought a better price than a brand new one. The Albright boy got Ben's best fishing pole. Hal Pritchard's wife captured the carriage. She said she bought it just for the Whip. She firmly announced that Mercy threatened to use it on Hal and if he didn't straighten out she was going to see to it that it happened.

When all was settled, the towns people used the money to buy a big bronze statue of Sally.

They set it right in the middle of the new town square. The road around it is known as Stokes circle.

If you happen to pass through a town with a statue of a stately horse with no rider in a small central park, you'll know why it's there. The plaque at the base reads *Sally, Town Constable*.

Things have changed a lot over the years, but there's one thing that won't change. Sally will always be there. A lot of folks have forgotten all about her but you won't forget her now that you know her.

The Best Town Meeting Ever

GRANDPA MADE CERTAIN he was in trusted company before he'd tell this story. He'd shift his position so he could see the door. Then after a long reminiscent smile he'd start his usual way.

"Well, sir. That day was cloudy, wet, rainy, cold, and miserable. I hated to take Molly out in such weather but grandma wouldn't miss this day for anything. This was her chance to tell those town officials what she thought. They weren't running things very well and they were going to know it."

Grandpa described Molly's harness as he outlined the proper procedure for placing and adjusting all the straps.

"Used a breastplate you know. Didn't need a pulling collar cause the carriage only weighed about half the horse so it warn't a big strain."

Molly knew just how to step between the shafts so Grandpa could attach the carriage. He put the bonnet up and loaded the blankets. One for Grandma to cover her legs with and one under the seat for Molly so she wouldn't get the shivers while waiting outside. It might take quite a while for Grandma to speak her piece. She was known to keep these meetings going well into the night. There were very few that hadn't fallen under her close scrutiny.

When the carriage pulled up in front of the porch Grandma climbed in, positioned the soapstone foot warmer and covered her finery with the blanket. With a quick "Git," Molly slogged along toward town.

"Can't you hurry up?" Grandma asked. She didn't want to be late. She had to have a good seat so everyone could hear. "That's all they've been doing is wasting money," she sputtered, preparing herself for the confrontation.

"Couldn't go any faster," Grandpa stated. "Mud was deep and he didn't want to hit a rock. Might break a wheel." He was no doubt wondering what kind of fracas she would cause this year. Last year it was the seventeen dollars Mort spent on the cemetery grounds. That was a lot of money and the fence was still in poor shape. Mort countered with his decision to add a ditch in the rear section. "Everyone deserves a dry bed to rest in," he said. "Apportion more money and he'd be glad to fix the fence but he warn't gonna do it for free."

The year before that it was the road fund. She kept going so long that Silas Chambers jumped up right during her dissertation and said, "I propose a vote." "Second that," came from all over the room. The moderator shouted, "All those in favor?" "Aye," echoed through the hall. "All those opposed?" The room was silent. Grandma just stood there like an angry statue. The gavel dropped with a clack. "The ayes have it," and the meeting quickly adjourned. Grandma fumed about that for months.

With a slow look around Grandpa continued his story. "She got quite upset when I pulled right up in front of the town hall. Thought that was what she wanted, seeing how it was raining. Guess she didn't like all the men standing on the porch, watching her get out of the carriage. Thought they were just there to see the size and shape of all the women's bottoms. And maybe some ankles, too. Don't know where she ever came up with that. It's hard to talk in a group amongst all those chairs inside. Besides, those that want to smoke can light up."

Grandpa continued, "I didn't want to go way around the lot and come back to let her out in the other direction. Then I'd have to turn the carriage around again to put it in the back lot." After a brief discussion Grandma decided to get out of the carriage front first. She threw back the blanket and leaned forward to clear the bonnet.

Grandpa paused for a moment, as if he were viewing it all over again. "Just about then, Molly decided to adjust her position and the carriage jerked. Grandma just disappeared. Musta missed the foot pad and went face first in the mud. Got up huffing like an old steam engine," he mused. "Wiped herself off and glared at the men on the porch. They was all looking the other way. All except for Mort. He blew a little smoke from his pipe, folded his arms and said, 'Well I guess every now and then even the devil gets his due.' Just to add to matters, Molly chose that moment to look back and snort.

"When Grandma turned around where I could see her, I must admit, I'd never seen anything like it. About then she didn't give a lot of regard to how she got back in that carriage."

With a quick "Git" they were headed the mile-and-a-quarter back home again. Very little was said on that excursion but Grandma's determination wasn't about to be thwarted.

"Now Mort and Silas figured on the worst so they quickly went about expediting matters. They must've saved it purposely, for the timing was perfect. Just as Grandma strode into the town hall in clean garb, the gavel clacked. 'Meeting adjourned,' the moderator announced and Grandma's angry huff was shrouded by the shuffling of chairs."

Now Grandpa gives a satisfying nod to the validity of his story and adds, "Don't know how those men on the porch held it in but they did. Must've been a lot of chuckling done later. Yup, that was from then on known as the best town meeting ever."

Child Whisperer

DAN SPARKS CAME out of the store just as the Doc was passing by. He waved. "Morning, Dan."

Then he looked up at the young girl sitting on the wagon. "Morning, Rosie."

She just sat there, wringing her hands, staring at something distant.

"Wave to the Doc, Rosie," Dan said.

She forced a gesture in his direction and returned to her deep uninterruptible thought.

"Not much progress," Doc admitted.

Dan just nodded and fastened his goods into the wagon.

Doc sighed. "There's another lad down in Trace with the same affliction. The physician down there telegraphed me about it. We're both stumped. No-one's come up with an answer yet."

Dan gestured toward a disturbance down the street. It sounded like an outside auction.

"That's some traveling salesman. Just arrived. Trying to sell some cheap junk," Doc said.

Dan mounted the seat and shook the reins. Rosie's head turned. She watched the salesman as they passed by. Was it his rapid talk that captured her attention? Or possibly his flourishing gestures? What ever interested her, it was the first time she had ever focused directly on something. On anything. Dan saw it and it frightened him. Could an overweight, fast talking, itinerant salesman steal the attention of a hapless youngster? Could he lure her away? Maybe it was his constant talking. Perhaps this was an answer to release Rosie from that inner shell.

On the trip home Dan strained his voice attempting to sell Rosie the neighbors fence posts as they passed by. He tried gestures, rapid speech, monotonous chatter. Nothing swayed her at all.

Maybe it was the shiny cookware on display.

Dan stopped the wagon near the porch. "You can get down, Rosie."

She descended slowly, feeling for the steps with her feet. Never releasing her gaze at some distant object, as though at any moment it might disappear forever.

"Take this parcel into your Ma," Dad ordered.

Rosie mounted the steps, crossed the porch, and waited at the door until her Dad opened it.

"Put it on the table, Rosie."

She set it on the table and stood there waiting. She understood what others said. She did small chores in the barn. Put her plate in the sink after meals only after being told. She recognized shapes, voices, people, and colors.

Her parents talked to her constantly. Ma read to her, sang lullabies and kissed her good night in unwavering hopes that something would somehow crack her captive shell.

On the next trip to town Dad again tried the constant banter. He praised the roadside flowers, described the trees, pointed out brooks, spoke of the fish, and explained the rocks.

Rosie played with the ribbon on her dress and stared at the floor.

Some confusion in the street forced Dan to stop. He walked forward to estimate the problem when the sheriff called him over.

"Help us get this man over to the coroners."

There lay the itinerant salesman stretched out beside his wagon. Doc made the final pronouncement and now it would take several men to transport the body.

They fashioned a carrying blanket and lugged the heavy, limp body down the street.

When Dan returned, traffic had cleared, leaving the sheriff evaluating the situation of what to do with the man's belongings.

"Maybe I'll park this load over behind my office till someone claims it," He said. "Nothing here worth stealing."

Dan casually agreed and turned toward his waiting wagon. Fear grabbed his heart. Rosie was gone. She never got off without his implicit instructions. Even falling asleep there. Responding to nothing but his voice. What enticed her to move?

His frantic search quickly ended when the Sheriff pointed to the front of the salesman's wagon. Rosie was standing in front of the salesman's horse straightening his forelock and rubbing his cheeks.

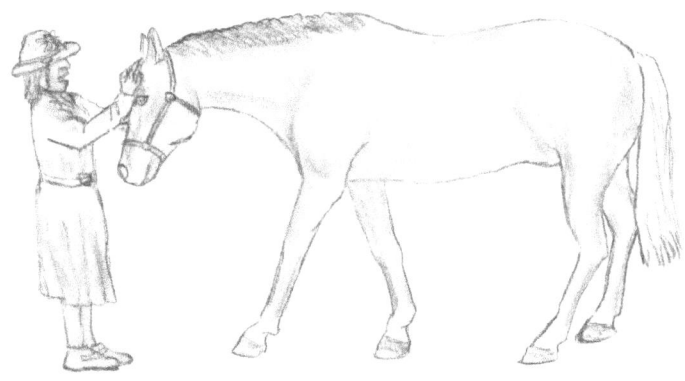

Dan's heart wrenched again. Her eyes were focused on the horse as she talked softly. He just stood there, paralyzed. In all her life she had never spoke. Never cried. Never whimpered. Now there were sounds, an audible response emanating from a once silent world. His daughter's voice, heard for the very first time

They weren't comprehensible words. Some might call it gibberish, but that was just fine. It very well was a language all her own and it sounded so sweet. The horse nickered in response. It knew what she said.

The Sheriff tapped Dan's arm. "Why don't you pasture that horse at your place. At least until someone claims him."

Without any direct orders Rosie lead him over, sat on the back of the wagon, holding the reins and swinging her feet all the way home.

When Dan told his wife she hurried out to see. Rosie led the horse around the area, introducing him to his new home. She did just as her father did, only in her own language. She explained the grass, complemented the trees and praised the flowers to a horse that followed her every step.

Ma and Dad watched in tearful delight and astonishment. Until now, they had no clue as to the effect of their years of effort.

Finally, Rosie led him into the barn. Fixing his forelock, she patterned her mom by singing a short lullaby in her unknown language, and kissing him good night.

Once out of his sight she returned to the captive world of suffocating silence.

As the days coursed by, Dad and Ma sorted through her conversations with the horse and came to the conclusion she had named the him Neigh Neigh. They followed each other through the field. She stood by him as he grazed and rubbed his shoulder when he drank. He waited at the gate whenever she went to the house. He didn't need a bridle or a halter. On rainy days she stood with him in his stall and looked out over the top of the split door. The only time she left him alone was at night when he was in his stall.

Two months later the Sheriff arrived with a stranger. They both dismounted the carriage and appraised the surroundings. Ma and Dad met them at the door.

"This here fella says he is a relative of the deceased salesman and is laying claim to the horse," the Sheriff said. "Says he'll leave her here for the sum of twenty dollars."

Ma's heart sank when the stranger flashed a neatly folded document in front of their faces. Dad's countenance changed from desperation to rage. Still, he went and fetched the horse.

The stranger smiled. "Ain't she a fine specimen."

"This she is a he," Dan growled.

"Still worth twenty dollars," the stranger snapped.

While the trio vied for position, Ma went inside to the china chest and fetched her Gramma's tea pot. A twenty dollar gold coin fell into her hand. A wedding gift from generations past. She and her husband had vowed to use it only for something special. Could she separate herself from it now? So many emotions rushed through her head it made her stomach churn. At least it was bargaining power. She would have to measure her devotion at the final moment.

When she stepped outside she knew what her decision would be. Neigh Neigh lay on his belly on the lawn, feet tucked under him. Rosie knelt beside him, an arm around his neck, singing him a song. Ma was convinced they were saying goodbye.

The men noticed her gaze and stopped abruptly. Everyone listened to Rosie sing her own special song. A song her

Mama sang to her every night. Ma never knew she heard it. It was a ritual that added hope for a better day tomorrow.

"See?" The stranger chirped. "I told ya she was worth twenty dollars."

Even Ma could see the protruding veins on the husband's neck.

"Now let's be reasonable," the Sheriff replied. "You just hear me out. That there birth certificate you're flashing around may establish your last name being the same as the deceased, but that don't prove kinship."

The Sheriff's arm back-stroked toward the road. "Mr. Harrison, just north of here, ain't claiming kinship to a president. And Mr. Adams in town ain't claiming to be a relative to this nations founding father."

Knuckles on his hips, the Sheriff drew a confident breath. "You're gonna need more proof than what you got there. And even if you do come up with proof, Mr. Sparks here has been boarding your animal for quite some time. According to local standards for boarding, you may owe him money."

Ma tightened her grip on that coin in her pocket.

"Well!" The stranger huffed. "The county court will have something to say about this."

"They sure might," the Sheriff replied, swaying with confidence.

Red with rage, the stranger turned toward the road with a strong step.

"You'd better hurry," the Sheriff yelled after him. "When I get back I'm gonna put an impound on that wagon and everything on it."

The whole group watched the stranger stomp out of sight.

"Think he'll come back?" Dan asked.

"He ain't coming back," the Sheriff huffed. "That paper

he has looked awful new. How many birth certificates look all that good. I suspected that guy right from the start. I just had to give him a chance to prove it."

Ma stood there, bewildered. "There isn't any Mr. Harrison around here."

The Sheriff smiled, gesturing toward the road. "He don't know that."

Thumbs confidently locked in his belt, the Sheriff turned toward Dan. "You got any chores I can help you with?"

He quickly accessed Dan's questioning look and fought back a Cheshire cat grin. "If I was to leave now, I'd catch up with that fella right quick. Then I'd be forced to be neighborly and stop and give him a ride. If I'm here a while, he'll have to walk all the way back to town."

Ma could just feel that treasured coin settling restfully back down into her Gramma's cherished porcelain tea pot.

"I've got a chore for you, Sheriff," she chirped. "There's a whole pan of corn bread in the kitchen just waiting to be buttered."

"Now I'll have you know I took a whole course in that very subject back in sheriffin' school. Come on, Rosie. We have some work to do."

Later that afternoon, when the Sheriff returned to town, he found the storekeeper pawing through the dead salesman's wagon. "Looking for something special?"

"Just bought all this stuff from that stranger. Said he was a relative and had rights to it."

"What'd you pay for it?"

"Ten dollars," the storekeeper replied. "Said he wanted thirty so I offered him fifteen. Said he'd settle for twenty so I offered him ten. Then he wanted some for the horse and wagon. You should'a seen him turn red when I told him that included the horse and wagon."

"Well," the Sheriff drawled. "Did ya get a bill of sale?"

The storekeepers arrogance quickly faded. "No. Guess I didn't," he admitted. "Figured the guy was straight."

"Did he tell you what relation he was to the dead man? Father? Brother? Cousin? Or where he was from? Or how old he was?"

The store keeper shrugged sheepishly.

The Sheriff waited a while to let the point sink in. "After he took your money, which way did he go?"

The storekeeper pointed toward the train station.

There he was, sitting in the train station trying to hide behind a newspaper. The Sheriff didn't have to enter. He saw no need to. In a few minutes this fella would be out of the area and no one would get hurt.

Through the window he caught the ticket agent's attention, pointed to the stranger and nodded. Relieved yet still concerned, he pulled at his chin. There was no need for others to get hurt by this conjurer. How could he track him?

Ahhh, there was the answer. A disheveled old rail bum, a small fellow, leaning back in a chair till it propped against the wall. He probably looked quite a bit younger three shaves and four haircuts ago. Overdressed for the summer, he no doubt wore all he owned. Tinney was a full-time hobo and a part-time thief.

"Tinney," the Sheriff said, kicking the chair. "Tinney, wake up."

Tinney jumped to his feet, sending the chair for a wild dance. "What? What? I ain't done nothing. Oh! Sheriff, it's you. Just passing through Sheriff. I ain't done nothing."

"Tinney," the sheriff replied. "You never have done nothing. That's why you're here. Now I've got a job for ya."

"Sure Sheriff, sure. Anything you want."

"That stranger in there just bought a ticket to Trace. Now don't get obvious and go in and look at him cause he'll suspect he's being followed. Just get on this next train and see where he goes. You don't have to know everything. Just figure out what he's up to and report back to me. I know he's got some sort of scheme going and I want to know what it is.

"Sure, Sheriff, Sure. Old Bengy's down there in Trace. He knows everything."

Tinney stared up at the Sheriff, looking through his eyebrows. The Sheriff drew out a rum-soaked cigar and sniffed it. He could just imagine the aroma, as it slid under the Sheriff's nose. He was quick to tuck it into a safe place.

"What about ole Bengy?" Tinney asked. "He's out of work ya know."

He snatched a second cigar out of the Sheriff's hand.

"Now you make sure Bengy gets that. There's a telegraph office right over there and I might just inform him you're coming." The Sheriff dropped a dollar into that same wiry little hand. "Traveling expenses you know."

"Sure, Sheriff, sure. I understand. I'll do a good job. You'll see."

The Sheriff patted his shoulder. "I know you will. I'll have a fine reward for you when you come back. Now take your time and do a good job."

The Sheriff wondered as he walked away, just how trustworthy Tinney was. He could keep going and disregard the assignment, considering it too much work. And just how authentic was this Bengy fella. It sounded good but leave it to an old rail runner to have a slick trick to add a little extra. No big loss in any direction. This would weigh Tinney's accountability and keep him out of the area if he didn't follow through.

No one else came around to claim the salesman's property so that incident was laid to rest. Dan Sparks could confidently be considered the owner of a horse. Neigh Neigh followed Rosie everywhere. He would've come right into the house if the door was wide enough.

Dan saw no need to take two horses to town. Rosie's horse was used to pulling a wagon. As long as Rosie went along, Neigh Neigh served nicely.

One late October day, on the way home, It started to rain. A hard, cold, penetrating downpour. Dad wrapped his coat around Rosie, hugging her in close to minimize the shivering. He felt a little ashamed of himself. This was the first time he'd even considered hugging his only child.

Home finally arrived and he hurried her inside for dry clothing and a chair next to the kitchen stove. Ma formulated a hot soup while Dad went back out to put the wagon away.

A moment later he came back in. "The horse won't move without Rosie," he said in answer to Ma's inquisitive look.

She tossed him Rosie's wet coat. Soon he returned. It worked. Neigh Neigh dutifully followed Rosie's coat into his dry stall.

Later that night Dad looked into Ma's worried eyes. Rosie coughed and sneezed constantly. Her breathing sounded like gravel rolling around in a jar. Nothing stopped her shivering. Dad decided to get the Doc. A good night's rest wasn't possible so why waste the time trying.

Ma rested fitfully next to Rosie's makeshift bed of chairs and blankets, by the stove. Loading the stove was the only thing that drew her from replacing a hot compress and holding her hand.

Stomping boots on the porch and a cold breeze brought

Doc into the kitchen. After shaking off and wringing out, he studied the ashen form.

Pulse, temperature, heart and chest. Doc put away his stethoscope. "Pneumonia I suspect. Keep doing what you're doing right now. Hot soup and tea is a good remedy. Give her one of these pills night and morning. Hopefully her lungs will clear in a couple days."

Doc pushed his soggy hat back into shape and glanced at his patient one more time. "I'll be back to check on her."

Even with all the poultices, elixirs, and compresses, she made no improvement. Her bed right next to the parlor stove and the room unbearably warm didn't help. She breathed with raspy gurgles while Doc shook his head in anguished defeat.

After an all-night vigil, Dad looked down at her limp and desperate form. She was looking right at him. Her mouth moved slightly. He read her lips. She was saying "Neigh Neigh."

Pulling blankets tight, he carried her to the barn. Neigh Neigh's head was out the stall door waiting for her.

She raised a weak arm and he put his head down where she could rub his ear and pat his nose. Barely audible, she sang a slow, labored lullaby. The horse nickered softly in between scratchy gasps. It took a long time and she was almost finished when her hand slid down his nose and fell limp by her side.

Who could possibly know what was in Neigh Neigh's heart as he watched Dad carry her away. He hung his head, wedged himself in the corner of his stall and didn't come out for days.

It went from rainy and wet to fiercely cold as winter pushed the thermometer into a tailspin plunge.

Tinney rushed into the Sheriff's office, chased by a frigid wind. Huddling up to the stove, he shivered so much he couldn't talk. The Sheriff let him stand there absorbing heat until his jaw stopped dancing. No wonder he was cold. An old plaid shirt showed through the elbows of a tattered jacket. His pants exposed another pair underneath at the pockets and knees. Thin socks peeked out through the front of his street shoes. Even his gloves were missing fingers.

"Don't look like you belong outside in this weather, Tinney."

Tinney shuffled around looking for a place he could hug the stove and not get burned. "Woulda been a long ways south but had, had a job to do."

The Sheriff handed him a pint of Old Mother Earth. "This might warm you up."

It raised a huge sparse-toothed grin. After a long contented swig, Tinney looked away, sneaking the bottle into a trusted pocket, as if it were his all along.

Pulling off what was left of his gloves, he draped them over a chair, moved it closer to the stove and sat down. "You suspected right of that fella," Tinney reported. "When I left he was trying to convince a rich old widow he was a long lost nephew. She don't have much family and her memory ain't good so there's no one to deny it."

The Sheriff locked his desk. "Make yourself at home Tinney. I'll be back soon."

He couldn't pull his coat tight enough to stop the intruding wind. Firing off a telegraph to the Sheriff in Trace, he forged a path to the market for extra supplies.

When he returned he found Tinney stretched out on a hard cell bunk. He'd done some serious damage to that bottle of Old Mother Earth.

About daybreak, Tinney responded to the aroma of hot

coffee and biscuits. He sat up and checked on the bottle. It was safe in what was left of the inner lining of his coat.

It took several cups of coffee and a half dozen heavily buttered biscuits to bring Tinney into a satisfied position. That's when the Sheriff pushed a box toward him.

Tinney nearly choked when he pulled out a new pair of fur lined boots.

"They're your size," the Sheriff said. "You didn't complain when I borrowed one of your shoes yesterday. Those gloves of yours came up missing so I felt obligated to replace them."

Tinney just sat there caressing those boots like they were a couple of abandoned kittens. A used coat and a pair of pants some teenager outgrew made him look more sociably acceptable.

Later, at the train station, the Sheriff slipped Tinney a pack of rum-soaked cigars. "That aught'a keep you till you get to a warmer place. If you need a job, come on back. This area could use a private investigator."

He watched Tinney swing up into an empty freight car. His left arm pinning that bottle in safely. He looked happy. Maybe it was the boots. Or maybe it was one of the few times he felt worthwhile. What ever the reason, the Sheriff felt content and it didn't matter if Bengy was a real person or a contrivance.

As warmer weather gradually wrestled winter out of the area, town folk appeared on the streets more frequently. Dan Sparks showed up one day, looking for Doc. He found him at his office tending to his clients.

"Doc," he said, "I gotta do something. That horse is wasting away. He eats hardly nothing. Ma washed some of Rosie's clothes preparing to give them away. They were hanging

41

on the line when that horse broke through the fence. There he was rubbing up against her clothes."

"So what can I do?" Doc replied. "I ain't too good at treating horses."

"Didn't you say there was a boy down in Trace with the same affliction?"

Doc nodded.

"Maybe I could take the horse down there and see if it would help him."

Doc thought long and hard. There were a lot of things to consider here, including a patient's right to privacy. "I'll see what I can do," he replied cautiously.

It was a week later that he handed Dan Sparks the address. They prepared for the trip with the purpose of saving the animal, but now Dan was apprehensive about his decision. Letting go of the horse was letting go of a tangible piece of Rosie.

He and Ma discussed it at length without really attending to their own individual feelings. Was this other person equipped to stable a horse? Should they leave him there if the conditions were less than ideal?

Finally, with Rosie's coat hanging on the back of the wagon, they set out for Trace. Neigh Neigh dutifully followed along.

Dan knew he was at the right place when he pulled in. They had decided to go right on by if the situation didn't appear correct, but there was no need. A young man sat on the porch of a well-kept house. He was about Rosie's age and had the same empty stare that tore at their hearts for so many years.

A large stable dissolved the concern about Neigh Neigh's care and company. Only one other issue lay ahead and that the horse would decide.

Dan and Ma introduced themselves. "Looks like you've got room for another horse," Dan said.

"What's your son's name?" Ma asked.

"Matthew," the man replied.

They all watched Matthew stretch out his hand to the approaching horse. "That's the first time he's ever moved on his own," the man said.

Dan didn't mention that it was the first time the horse had left Rosie's clothing.

They all had coffee on the porch, watching Matthew welcome his new friend. Everyone's heart danced when Matthew giggled at Neigh Neigh's nudge. The man and his wife saw new beginnings. Dan and Ma saw reflections of their daughter.

"It's a blessing," Matthew's mother exclaimed. "What do we owe you?"

Now that was a part Dan and his wife hadn't discussed. In fact they hadn't even considered it.

After a long silence Ma solved the dilemma. "We just want the horse to have a good home."

Dan nodded in agreement and they soon set off on the journey home. It was a long thoughtful trip. They managed to leave the horse there with a good feeling. Now came the clothing and personal belongings. A few things would have to stay.

Dan suddenly realized they hadn't told them the horse's name. Ma assured him that Matthew would rise to the challenge. It may very well be his first personal decision.

A few weeks later a letter arrived. They both anticipated it but dreaded it as well. Reservations always ghost a person's thoughts.

They chose a position at the table preparing for special

news. Ma opened it with a shaky hand. She read it slowly, as if it were from Rosie.

Matthew was making superb progress. The horse was looking better and responding to Matthew's commands. Then she drew a calming breath and swallowed hard. She pushed the letter forward so her tears wouldn't stain it and read the final line. "Matthew has named the horse Neigh Neigh."

Home

It was a good day to go to town. Things were well caught up around the farm and they had a long list of needs. Not nearly as long as the list for fall canning, or when the girls were home. Four daughters demanded a lot of mending and making. A relentless demand for new and bigger stuff.

No doubt future grandchildren would keep Lucy's needles busy. Frugality demanded a lot of labor and dear little Lucy would use the summer to threaten Old Man winter with an arsenal of socks, mittens, and scarfs.

It took four pulls to start the old T truck. It was getting a little tired but what wasn't now-a-days. After much fussing with lunch, all the trade goods, and her hair, they were ready. Clarence picked up little Lucy's stool, threw it in the back, and they left in a cloud of summer dust.

There was something going on at the fairgrounds and Clarence knew he would have to come back and check it out while Lucy was buying her yarn, fabric and thread. If you wanted to call that buying. She had to weigh every selection in her hand. The texture and quality of each item was critical even down to identical spools of thread.

Lucy avoided these masculine gatherings as most women did. They couldn't place any practicality in smoking and telling lies.

Now Clarence felt it necessary to get the local news— who was running for office, what winter was going to be like, who died, and where the new electric lines were going. The men would make predictions as to what brave young lad was going to step forward to be the new milk inspector. But not in front of Clarence. Word got around quickly about Clarence throwing young Vilas Spencer out of his barn. He stayed in the milk house and took his samples. He hadn't washed his boots before going to the next barn so he wasn't to be trusted. That's how disease spread, you know.

His truck fit right in amongst the other old iron. Neatly arranged parking just wasn't necessary.

"Need a car, Clarence? That truck is getting old." It was Eric Court, the area's smooth dealer.

Always looking for an opportunity to his advantage as long as it didn't involve much work. "I'll give you ten dollars for the old heap of bolts. You shouldn't need it now that Adam's Feed is delivering grain. I could even arrange a trade for a nice car. Now wouldn't Lucy appreciate riding in a Reo?"

Clarence just kept on walking toward the crowd. At six-feet, four-inches he could see right over the top so he stayed in the back. Not only to stay out of others view but he preferred being inconspicuous. Lucy would say that he was trying to pull live bark off a dead tree.

The crowd was hovering around the auctioneer as he tried to raise bids from a sour audience.

A pile of well-used harness, kegs, and buckets waited their turn, along with a side-hill plow, trunks, and household stuff. It explained why Eric was here. Some of this was no doubt his.

Nothing interested Clarence, but some strange desire, an unexplainable attraction, took him over by the delivery vehicles still bearing a few items yet to be viewed.

Clarence heard the disturbed whinnering and turned toward it. There was Eric Court yanking at the halter, trying to get a horse out of a trailer. The animal refused to cooperate. Clarence knew the problem immediately. "I'll give you eight dollars for that horse right where he is."

Eric scoffed. "Eight dollars and your truck." A few more heavy yanks and the horse moved forward, measuring the ramp with every step.

Clarence continued on and doubled back a little later. He wasn't about to give Eric any hint of his interest.

The auctioneer introduced the stallion and had the bidding up to a tidy ten dollars when Clarence waded through the crowd. He slapped the stallion on the rump and sidestepped the vicious kick. Eric's slight frame flapped on the thrashing halter.

"You can get in some serious trouble pawning this animal on someone, Eric."

Eric finally got the beast calmed. "You just surprised him."

When Clarence waved a hand in front of the horse's face, it didn't respond. The auctioneer fell silent and the crowd melted away, leaving Clarence holding the halter.

It's not easy for an experienced trader to suddenly realize he's been taken. Someone had got the better of Eric and it had come to light in front of the whole crowd. "Eight dollars and your truck. You've got a deal."

"I said eight dollars, Eric, and that's all."

There was no arguing with two-hundred-sixty pounds of determination and a hand the size of a shovel blade.

Clifford came trotting over, knowing by Clarence's grip on the halter that the deal was made.

"I'll deliver him for a dollar-and-a-half, the same as I charged Eric to get him here."

Eric winced at the exposure of his loses.

Clarence smiled. "Just hold him here until I get back with Lucy."

"Done deal," Clifford replied.

He knew in front of which store to stop. He set out the stool, loaded her merchandise, and helped her in. The short trip back to the fairgrounds lent time to prepare for the corrosive reaction. How could he tell her what drew him to the animal when he didn't know himself? Who could understand the bonding that took place when he first saw the horse? How can anyone explain the force that joins man and beast?

It did look a bit strange and conspicuous idling out of town with a slow-stepping horse tied to the bumper of the truck. When the stallion set his feet and stopped, it lifted one rear wheel of the truck, making it spit dirt. Clarence got out and loosened the halter rope, talking to the animal. It shivered at his touch. Instead of blows there was a reassuring voice. Gentle yet firm. A few more pats along the shoulder calmed any concerns. Clarence started the truck and they proceeded on.

"So what are you going to call your horse," Lucy fretted, "stubborn?"

"No. But Stubby will do."

Clarence pulled up in front of the house, fetched Lucy's stool, and helped her unload.

"Still don't know what you need of a horse. Especially a mean one," Lucy huffed.

"Lucy," Clarence said with a firmness that wasn't to be ignored. "He's blind."

Stunned, she watched him lead the horse away. They were the same height and no doubt the same temper. Who else besides a hard-headed Irishman would work a farm with a team of mules. Mules were all attitude but they would do anything Clarence asked. Maybe he needed something to train, to focus his attention, now that the girls were gone. Maybe he just had a passion for rescuing things. What else would fit better than an ill-tempered, unwanted, abused, blind stallion.

As summer ebbed, Stubby spent most of his time learning the layout of the pasture. He was getting used to his stall, and the sounds and smells of the barn. Clarence's voice and big gentle hands were as normal as grain and water. And as always, Clarence would straighten his top knot and tug at his ears. "Remember now, ears forward in my barn."

During the busy fall haying, Lucy would occasionally start the barn chores while Clarence was bringing in a late load of hay. On one of these occasions Clarence's heart almost stopped. He saw Lucy backing out of Stubby's stall with a water bucket. He knew a word would startle them so he waited until she was clear and the door closed. "Lucy I don't want you in there. You're only the size of a mouse. If that horse kicked, you wouldn't come down for a week."

"Oh, don't be silly, Clare." She caught herself. What would be her reply: that he wasn't mean? That settled matters. Stubby was part of the group.

There was confidence in Stubby's step when Clarence led him around. He stepped to the same rhythm as Clarence's barn boots. Gentle tugs at the halter gave direction. A slight tug down meant expect a drop, up for a rise, and back for a shortened stride.

This morning they went a different direction than the pasture. Stubby matched the clumping of the barn boots as usual, until Clarence stopped him. He knew the smell of fresh air and the heat of the sun so outside was just ahead. A nudge down on the halter and they negotiated the drop nicely. A few steps later Clarence said, "Whoa," and the halter went limp. What a frightening experience. After a long silence Stubby shook his head and sniffed the ground. He was alone in a world of silence. What used to be desirable was now unnerving. An hour passed before Stubby dared to take a step. More snorts brought no results. He moved ahead a little. His ears snapped to attention when he heard Clarence say, "Whoa."

This was a necessary trial and it took a while for Stubby to absorb the confidence that a familiar hand would return. He would, on occasion, be left unattended but not forgotten.

Winter made its chilly rounds and Stubby got a little practice at pulling the snowplow. Nothing broken and some good training with the "gees" and "haws."

Now spring gave way to some pasture time. Noises from the house would bring Stubby over to the fence to meet Clarence plodding to the barn. "Remember now," Clarence would say as he passed, "ears forward in my barn." Stubby ears rolled forward in reply.

This winter Stubby would help skid out the winter wood supply. From the kitchen window little Lucy watched for them coming along the snowy trail, blowing frosty breath, Stubby stepping to the same cadence as his master. When the log came to the rise in the trail Stubby would lay into the harness with confidence. He had the distance well gauged. Clarence let him go and he brought it right up in front of the cutting bench.

This was a good reason for a snort and a mane shake. Every job well done called for a good snort and a mane shake.

Stubby knew the whole regimen. Taking the box sled down the back pasture to dump the trash. He stopped in the same place with a snort and a mane shake. The end of a work session meant a stop in front of the harness rack, lift each foot for a hoof clean and check, then a warm stall with sweet hay. It was always the same except some days were hot, some days were wet, and some days were cold.

The milk truck came and went. The grain truck came and went. The seasons came and went.

There was always a warm stall, fresh grain, and Clarence.

Then came that unusually hot summer. Clarence knew something was wrong. Haying seemed to take forever. He struggled with the winter wood pile.

The doctor did not have good news but who would expect disaster to strike with such veracity. A brucellosis test took all but three of his herd. They couldn't be sold. It was a complete loss. Clarence was convinced that the milk inspectors were the carriers.

Three cows weren't much good and with Lucy left with the chores it just couldn't be done.

The mules were no match for tractors so they went cheap. That left Stubby in the barn alone.

Clarence would go out when he could, turn him into the pasture and stay with him for a while. Most afternoons he'd bring him back in, serve his grain and tug on his top knot. "Ears forward now."

Stubby's ears would roll to attention until the barn door closed.

Clarence heard Clifford's truck arrive. A while later he heard the knock at the front door.

Lucy was in town so he got up, and forced on his coveralls.

"Sorry, Clarence. I didn't want to disturb ya, but we can't get that horse in the trailer. He just won't go."

Clarence did his best to stand straight as he took Stubby down to the pasture to get a cool drink from the brook and a pat on the rump.

51

Clifford watched them come back. Did he notice that they were matched step? If he did nothing was said. Three more tries and Stubby still wouldn't go up that ramp.

"Okay, fella," Clarence said, "We will be walking this trail together. Now remember, ears forward." Stubby's ears responded like a marching band to a raised baton. Clarence snubbed the rope at the front of the trailer. His hand traced the entire length of the animal on his way out. He never looked back.

With memories of he and Stubby walking through the snowy wooded trail, log in tow, frosty breath, Clarence Wheeler fell asleep.

Simple Dreams

BEFORE SHE COULD even read the word, she knew what she wanted. She would point to it in the Sears & Roebuck catalog. Other children were wishing for dolls or velocipedes but not a Stanhope special at $62.50. Some wondered if she was a bit touched but it's not bad really, to have a big dream at a young age.

Determination is a virtue and she started right out with plenty. Through the years she worked at everything from picking berries to laundry. Child caring, sewing, anything that would help with her dream.

Every time a new catalog arrived, she would quickly check it to see if the price had gone up.

Finally, in her last year of school, while working at the local mercantile, she had enough. Waiting for it to arrive seemed longer than saving the money.

That fabulous day was still welded in her mind. Twelve years and the wonderful Stanhope special was here. Shiny black with a thin gold stripe. A sturdy leather top and soft cushioned seat. What a handsome unit it was. The two men that took it out of the freight car winked at each other. "You'd better get a husband cause you don't have a horse to pull it," they chided.

Then her father pulled his surprise. He lead out a proud-stepping Morgan. At fourteen hands, he was just the right size for the new carriage. She remembered his exact words.

"Every lady with such conviction deserves a trusty mount."

It was love at first sight. The horse looked strong, confident, and ready to serve. She knew his name in an instant. "Joshua," she squealed and gave him his first big hug.

Of course Mr. Cooper at the mercantile would credit her for the harness and everything was set.

Even now, from her rocking chair, she remembered that first ride. Joshua accepted the carriage with devotion. It was his and he knew exactly what to do. After a few trips he didn't need reins. She would harness him and go back inside to change into church clothes. Whatever it was he recognized about the routine wasn't important. He just knew, and he would prance away to church. She read her bible on the way.

Her father said Joshua had pride and pride wasn't a virtue. Yes, he was a high stepper but it wasn't bad really. One can have confidence and that's not wrong.

After church, Joshua would take her through the countryside on an excursion of his own invention. In the spring, Mrs. Harper's daffodils were spectacular. Joshua occasionally followed the river where there were fields of fresh grass edged with lilacs. Apple orchards were bleached whiter than Megan Forester's sheets. Forsythia bushes dominated the front of Lucien McKay's home. A roadside stream made a good stopping place for a cool drink and a rest in the shade of a big willow tree. Gillen's pond always had a flotilla of mallards harvesting its boundaries.

Hazen's Notch roiled with refreshing scents of balsam and cedar. Queen Ann's lace and brown-eyed daises dominated the roadsides in summer. Joshua would stop occasionally and nibble at a few. Just to get the flavor, of course. The same was true with the Jerusalem artichokes down where the road runs close to the river.

Avery's Lookout was a special spot in the fall when the valley blushed with color.

People marvelled at Joshua's travels but it wasn't bad really, to get that roaming spirit satisfied occasionally. Everyone needed an opportunity to get out and look around at the countryside. To see where all those alluring fragrances came from that were riding the wind.

When someone waved or approached the carriage, Joshua stopped so they could chat. The reins lay on the dashboard spike. When they stepped away Joshua would proceed without a command. Some thought it extraordinary, but actually there was nothing odd about it at all. The farmers had voice commands for their teams. One could hear them whoa and giddap, or gee and haw. Those who saw Joshua go by unguided would watch wonderingly, but it didn't matter. Joshua always arrived home before dark.

Whenever they met one of those wheezing gasoline dragons, Joshua knew what to do.

He would stop and hold his ground until the dust demon was well out of sight.

When her dad died, mother was soon to follow. They were challenging times with far too many difficult decisions. Joshua knew just where to take her for thinking and coping. Even in his own advancing years, he braved the ascent to the top of Hazen's Notch. It was a striking autumn day, exploding with color. It brought to mind the good times. Wonderful times to be remembered, savored, cherished. Two of societies biggest sins are disregarding the past and not being content with a few simple things. It's not bad really to have a lot of possessions but what is the point of it all? The only thing we can rescue from this world is our integrity.

Dad always said, "The only trustworthy things in this world were God and a good horse."

Our creator knows we need examples like them, for how else would we learn humility, to be content with ones lot in life, grow old with grace, and die with dignity.

It was a few days after her mother's funeral. Church services were just finished when one of the Johnson boys approached the carriage. He took the reins from the spike and handed them to her. He even called her by her first name. She remembered the lingering touch of his hand. Maybe it was just a kind gesture. It wasn't bad really to suggest companionship. All these years and his look of surprise still rested in her memory. She put the reins back on the spike. Then she smiled. "Joshua knows the way." There was no intended impudence in her manner. Just inner strength.

With the farm sold, she and Joshua moved into town. A small nook in the business section made a neat little hat shop that supplied their needs nicely. The young man who represented her supplier must have been impressed. Each time he visited, he stayed a little longer. Occasionally leaving an extra roll of shiny ribbon.

Once, he stayed so long he would have to run to meet the train. He hurriedly announced his plans to launch his own store with a large array of different departments. He needed someone to manage the hat and bonnet section. Her skills would match his needs nicely. Would she be willing to come with him? The profits would be enormous.

There's nothing bad really with being ambitious. To some people the adventure of it would be alluring. Even the scent of wealth. But the question hung in the air. Was this a business contract or a proposal?

Quick decisions just weren't in her. She wasn't sure really, what propelled her answer. She just remembered saying it. "After Joshua leaves." That was what she said.

He looked so confused. Maybe he thought she was going to vault into his arms, leaving past and present to chance. Joshua was her charge, her loyal friend. Deserting a trusted companion was unthinkable.

Within a few seconds he gathered his wares and rushed out. She never saw him again.

The next sales representative was a rather corpulent gentleman of extended years.

Two years later, Joshua went his way in a simple and dignified manner. The shop slowly faded as hats lost their style. The hardware store next door needed the extra room.

Now she was limited to sitting here on the porch and rocking. It wasn't bad really, for Joshua still took her for wonderful rides in her dreams. Even now she could hear Turner's Brook playing along the rocks; feel the cool breeze in that little pull-off shaded by the big willows.

"Would you like to come in for your tea, ma'am?"

She turned her head slowly. Such a young girl. A clean white dress with a bibbed front. A small folded cap pinned in her hair. Even her shoes were white.

"Oh, no, dear," she replied. "Joshua will be here soon."

"Are you expecting visitors, ma'am?"

She didn't have to answer. How would a young girl understand? She just closed her eyes and waited. It wasn't too long before she heard it. Joshua's hooves pounding the earth in that sturdy rhythmical stride. Behind him was her carriage. Her shiny black Stanhope special. He stopped right in front, ready to take her to some wonderful place where the grass was rich and the flowers were bright. Even now she could smell the balsam and fresh leather.

There on the porch, the rocking chair stopped rocking.

Stay the Way They Were

He was slow at pulling up his suspenders. Arthritic hands were reluctant to obey even the most meager commands. Everything seemed to be a struggle. Why couldn't things just stay the way they were?

He gathered up his usual breakfast purely out of routine. A little cereal in a bowl. There was no milk in the ice box. Not even any ice. A small amount of water would have to do.

He sat there at the table in the only chair in the kitchen. It was chilly. Even the stove was cold.

G would've had it going by now. Her given name was Gertrude. Ugly name. That was gone soon after she started school. Everyone knew her as G. Even signed papers with a G. When asked what her given name was, she always replied G. That was it.

At this time of day she would be avidly orchestrating the many daily duties of cooking and cleaning, rattling dishes around in the sink. Now the sink was empty and the stove was cold.

A sliver of light touched the worn table top in front of him. It came from G's most prized possession, a small cut glass flower vase sitting there on the window sill where she could monitor the progress of some choice cutting. She was always fussing over an herb or prolonging the life of the last blossom of the season. Now it was empty: trolling small shafts of light in hopes of reclaiming lost attention.

In the backyard, G's herb garden wrestled with an ever expanding weed population. What was always so neat and trim looked crowded, harassed by intruders.

"Sorry, G," he mumbled. "Just so many things to do. Besides, I wouldn't know the good stuff from the weeds."

He opened the barn door and stood there stunned. Where were the cows? Every stanchion was empty. Mice scurried away from the last droppings around the grain bin. A scattering of brief memories traced through his mind. He tried to pull them together but all they would form was a hazy unfinished picture puzzle. He had sold the cows weeks ago. Or was it just days ago? What stood before him was stark emptiness. That's what space was without life. Emptiness.

He walked around trying to fill in the blank portions of events. The most tormenting part was, how many times had he been out here to check on an empty barn? Had he forgotten to take care of his herd when they were here?

The horse's harness hung, limp and dusty, on the wall. Jake! Where was Jake? He hurried to the window. There he was out in the pasture.

He went outside, closing the door on the missing parts of his life. Even if they did return, some would quickly evaporate again and the history of it all would soon look like lace in the wind.

An apple off the old tree. That's what Jake needed. When the horse heard him whistle, he ambled along the well-worn path to the gate, missing him by a solid twenty feet. He whistled again. "Stone blind, ain't cha, fella."

Jake maneuvered along the fence and fetched his treat. The man ruffled Jake's mane. *Why couldn't things just stay the way they were?*

Now it was a sad morning. Very sad because it reminded the man of his resolve. The great decision. Just like the empty barn. Just like the empty house. He had started a project a while back. Who knows how long ago. Now it was time to finish it before it passed out of mind again.

It took a long time to find. He couldn't remember where he had put it last. Uncooperative hands struggled to strap it on.

Jake obediently followed, head low, big hooves clopping along slow. He followed the man across the field they had cleared, through the wood lot they had harvested, by the brook they both drank from, to a little clearing at the back of the property. There was the man's excavation. The shovel was still here. Good thing because he'd forgotten it.

Now it was time for a pat on the shoulder, a pull on the ear, and a few words of forgiveness. Birds flew out of the trees. Deer snapped to attention at the sharp crack.

It was dusk when the hole was finally filled in. He sat down and leaned against a tree. Too late to try to go back to the house. He'd no doubt get lost in the dark. The stars were bright and the night was cold. "Why couldn't things just stay the way they were?" he muttered.

There in the forest, he fell asleep, waiting for the dawn that would never come.

Winners Run Wild

Two YOUNG MEN leaned on the fence, watching the horses and discussing their dilemma. The conversation stopped when the fat man showed up. That's what everyone called him. Few knew his given name. He was the fat man and that's all.

He shoved his belly into the fence far enough to get his elbows on the rail. "You two got this situation figured out?"

Neither one moved.

"Can't run Eastern Pride with a hoof like that, now can we. So where do we find an entry worthy of representing our fine stable?" He rolled his cigar to the other side of his mouth and wrapped it in a cheek. "How about that one over there?"

One of the young men frowned. "He's just an antagonist."

"He's capable of finishing the race, ain't he?"

"Max ain't gonna be happy," the second man muttered.

The fat man backed away from the fence and yanked hopelessly at his belt. "When serious competition comes to town, folks don't expect the local boys to hang their heads and hide. That horse is now officially called Grey Lord and you're riding him. He'll finish the race if you don't push him too hard at the start. Maybe this will show Max that I need more to work with than Has-Been nags and Wanna-Be jockeys."

About two miles south of the stable was a small tenant

farm run by a young couple. They were just finishing supper. Gloria had to lean back in her chair to put the envelope in her pocket. "My cousin's team is coming to town. Says he'll be riding his horse at the track."

Nate nodded and stuffed his mouth with the last slice of bread.

His mother sat sipping her tea. The squeak of the rocking chair stopped.

"We should go see him." Gloria said.

"Saw him at our wedding just a year ago," Nate replied.

Gloria pulled the thread-bare apron straight and patted her bulging tummy. "Says his horse is the fastest of all. Even sent me a dollar to bet on him so I can win."

Nate stared at his plate. Amazing, how a few seconds had changed his life so dramatically.

Maybe for the better. Horse racing was a lot of traveling around. Always away from family. At least he had that run. That mighty run. That one chance to know what it was like.

Gloria pushed herself out of the chair and started gathering up the dishes. They had no electricity so the work had to be done by dark. "We could use the money with the baby coming. Besides, he came all the way up here to be at our wedding. We should at least oblige him by watching him race."

Nate shook his hat and shrugged. There was still plenty to do before sundown. "I guess."

"Said if the baby was a boy we could name it after him if we wanted to."

Nate yanked his hat down hard. "Son's gonna carry a biblical name and that's all."

Gloria felt the thud of the screen door all the way to her heart.

With a thrusting start, Nate's mother struggled to her feet. Arthritic hands grabbed for the cane. "Don't worry 'bout it girl. You just took him by surprise is all." She set her tea cup in the sink and stared out the only window in the kitchen. "He lost his Daddy, the whole summer's crop, and his dream all in one. Gonna take him a while to heal."

The day promised to be hot and clear as they walked the path to town. Nate led Gloria up a little side path to look-out hill.

"Where did it happen?" she asked.

Nate pointed off toward Frenchman's Mountain and a little road that twisted down, turning abruptly at the bottom, next to the school house.

"Where were you?"

Without breaking his distant stare, Nate pointed to the ground.

Gloria watched him for a while before she spoke. "When did you realize there was trouble?"

"When the truck came into that first turn up there. I heard the diesel over-winding. Then Dad laid-to on the horn."

Resting a tender hand on her belly she mentally measured the distance to the school house.

Not in feet, or miles, or strides, but in disappointments. She thought of her yet-to-be-born infant. To lose something that precious in an unexpected instant. A sudden immeasurable gap. There must have been a lot of tears that day.

"Do you miss him?"

Nate didn't answer.

"We'd better not go," Gloria said. "This may be just too much for you."

Nate grabbed her hand. "Hey, I made my decision. I'm a farmer now, and a family man. We're gonna make it together right here. Now let's get along so we won't be late."

A good crowd of competitors had come from far away and the bleacher stand was crowded.

Nate elbowed his way through the pack and found seats for him and Gloria. She tried to get comfortable. Without maternity clothes, at least her apron tied high covered the bulge.

Soon the horses strutted out onto the field. Gloria's cousin rode a light stepping, long-legged mare named Southern Stride. Near the end of the procession Grey Lord ambled out onto the track to line up at the gate. He had neither light step or bulging flanks. Even his rider didn't seem too enthusiastic.

When Nate saw Grey Lord, he stiffened so quickly that Gloria thought he'd seen a snake.

"That's Norris," he whispered.

"They just said it was Grey Lord. Or something like that."

"No. That's my horse."

Gloria winced. "What?"

"That was the horse I had to sell to save the farm."

From the bowels of his wallet Nate pulled out a small patch of paper. He unfolded it and tried to flatten out the wrinkles. "Here," he said, pushing the ten-dollar bill into Gloria's hand. "Get to the betting booths and put this on —what was it?—Grey Lord to win."

Nate started digging his way through the crowd. "Hurry, before they close."

The booth attendant watched her smooth out the bills.

"Grey Lord to win," she said.

He could see she wasn't of comfortable social means. "He's a one-hundred-to-one shot, ma'am. Are you sure you want to do this?"

Gloria stared at the money. That was the most she'd ever had at one time. Now it lay there as frail as an autumn leaf on a mountain stream. She looked down at her hands. "Grey Lord to win," she muttered.

Soon she had only a piece of paper no larger than her gate pass.

When she got back to her seat, Nate hadn't returned. She wedged herself in and tried to relax, but couldn't. Where was he and what had they done? In a flash of excitement, all that money was gone. Well, ten dollars wasn't the end of the world.

The horses were at the starting gate. Where was Nate? Why hadn't she just put aside that silly letter from her brother. Was this sport so strong it held grown men in it's addictive grip?

The gate opened, the loud speaker blared, *They're off!* The horses bolted away. All but Grey Lord, that is. He twisted, turned and snorted. Totally confused.

Arms folded across his corpulent front, the fat man watched. He knew the problem. The horse had run this track many times, but without the sound system. It was the noise.

The loud speaker blared. *They're into the first turn with Southern Stride in the lead.*

Grey Lord whinnied and stomped. Then he heard a voice over the crowd. It was his master's voice pinching his ears. He hadn't heard it in so long. Grey Lord ramrodded to attention. His master was calling him. He heard it clearly now. Long and stretched out, he heard *"Nooooorris, ru-uuuuuuun."*

His heart burned hotter than a blacksmith's forge. My God, not again. That loud blaring was the diesel. The shrill voices of the children notched deep into his very soul.

Norris stood high on his back legs, front feet thrashing the air. Then he sank down. Down so far his rider's feet almost touched the ground. Down so far his tail whisked the dirt.

The crowd quieted for no one had ever seen such a thing. Few would believe their eyes. Few would believe when later told, for who had ever seen eleven-hundred pounds of flesh launch into the air.

When Norris touched down his rider slammed into his neck. He bounced around and finally regained his seat.

The competition was coming out of the second turn when Norris leaned into the first. The jockey had to lift his leg to clear the inside rail. Norris came out wide and strong, hoofs driving hard. He had to warn them. The blaring diesel was getting louder. He had to get there first.

Pinned to his back tighter than the saddle, arms pumping in unison, his rider urged him on.

They ran with strength. They ran with purpose. They shared that energy; that force that bonds man and beast.

The fat man prided himself on being able to watch a race, even a photo finish, without flinching. He would lean back, fold his arms across that mountainous belly, roll his cigar from side to side, and not move until the winner's circle was filled with sweaty flesh.

When Norris thundered into the second turn even the fat man was standing.

With his rider hunkered down, they both were pumping, pumping, pumping. Every muscle fired with all its vital force. Norris could hear his hooves beating out; warn them, warn them, warn them. He would not be late again.

Out of the third turn he started passing the back of the pack. He didn't care about the other horses. The children; couldn't they hear the diesel? It was getting louder. It was

getting closer. He had to get there first. He pounded into the fourth turn just behind the leaders. They were packed on the rail. Norris had to go wide. So wide his hooves were hitting, yes, taking chunks from the outside fence. His lungs were on fire and sweat burned his eyes. They weren't moving over. He had to warn them, warn them, warn them. The children were so loud. He was close and so was the diesel truck.

One of the jockeys turned to look back. With his shifting weight, his mount moved a little to the side. That small gap was enough. Norris charged through, blowing sticky froth. Everything was blurry. His heart threatened to burst. He heard the children cheering and his rider rose up. Did he make it this time?

As the last of the contenders galloped by, the fat man looked around. Had anyone noticed? He just realized he wasn't sitting in his box seat. He was leaning on the rail.

The blaring diesel stopped. There was no grinding crash. No screams. No fire or heat. Norris slowed.

His legs were rubber. He staggered and swayed. Blinded by his own sweat. He knew who was in front of him. The voice he hadn't heard for so long. His master was speaking consoling words and rubbing his neck. Yes, he had warned the children. This time he beat the truck.

His master led him to the grassy infield. They gave him a cool drink of water and a wreath of flowers. The children were safe. His master was pleased. It all felt so good.

A while later Gloria came up with a handful of money. The fat man nodded in approval and the jockey handed Nate the reins. He didn't need them. Nate clicked his tongue and Norris followed him away.

"Won't Max be mad you sold him?" the jockey asked.

The fat man thumbed the money. "Not when he sees this. Besides, that ain't no thoroughbred. He's just an ordinary horse with a special purpose and only that man who just bought him knows what it is."

"That's still some horse," the jockey said as he watched them go.

The fat man spit and nodded. "Not many people ever get to see a horse run like that."

Something else happened that day that may never happen again. The fat man put his hand on the young man's shoulder. "And not many jockeys get to ride them. You did a good job there."

One of the stable workers came running over. "Those visiting fellas are still talking about it. They won't be back soon after counting their losses. No, sir."

"Warn't no losers today, son," the fat man said.

"What about all them that bet on their Southern Stride?"

The cigar rolled to the other side. "This day is gonna be talked about for a long time. Even those who lost their bets still got more than they paid for. Nope, no losers today. None at all."

They were a ways down the road when Nate turned to his wife. "I'm sorry," he said, his voice taking a solemn curve.

"What for?"

"For spending all our money on a horse. I guess I wasn't thinking." There was a long pause.

"But we do need a horse on the farm."

Gloria lifted one side of her apron. "It's easy to hide things under a bulge like this."

Nate gasped. "You saved out some?"

"Well," Gloria said. "I had my own dollar to bet, too."

With a quick swing, Nate pulled her in tight. "You bet on Norris?"

"No, I bet on you."

"First we stop and get you a brand new dress."

"Not now," Gloria said. "I won't be big like this very long."

Nate knew there would be other times she could use it. Plenty of other times.

Tragic Pursuit

THE STOREKEEPER WATCHED through the window as the lad jumped down from the wagon, the way a child leaps from a tree limb.

"How's it going, Homer?" Sam asked.

"Just fine, Sir," the boy answered. He had to stretch a bit to reach over the glass-fronted counter. "Fifteen sacks of seed corn, please," he said as the coins rattled across worn oak.

"You'll have to load them yourself," Sam said. "Ethan isn't home from school yet and I've got these other people waiting."

He wrote out the receipt in big letters and handed it to the lad. "Move your wagon out back and start loading. I'll send Ethan out as soon as he gets here."

Sam shook his head in disbelief as he watched through the window. Homer had to pull himself up the side of the wagon until his belly cleared and tumble into the box. He wasn't tall enough to use the wheel hub as a step.

A short time later a tall young man in bibbed overalls walked in.

Sam nodded toward the back. The young man slipped the strap of books from his shoulder, rolled up his sleeves, and stepped out the back door.

When the last customer left the store, Sam pushed aside the curtain that hid the connector hallway between the store and the house and dropped the store keys in the wooden box on the shelf.

Elmira was moving pots around on the stove when Ethan came into the kitchen. The young man punched the handle on the water pump and grabbed the soap. "I wish Homer would learn to read. He was loading cracked corn instead of seed corn."

"I wrote the receipt in large letters hoping he'd compare the shapes to the ones on the sacks," Sam said as his leather apron collapsed neatly on its peg. He took Ethan's place in front of the water pump. "I would've been more specific, but I didn't want to embarrass him in front of all those folks. I couldn't go out and show him with Mrs. Beatty hovering around the ivory buttons. She must have gypsy blood in her."

Drying his hands, Sam watched Elmira arrange the simmering pots on the table. "It ain't his fault he's lacking. We'll just have to help him the best way we can."

It was two weeks later when Hattie came into the store with Homer in tow. Sam looked up over the rim of his reading glasses. "How's the planting going, Homer?"

Hattie's chin jammed forward. "Everything is going just fine, Sam."

"How many acres you got under seed, Homer?"

"That's none of your business," Hattie replied.

No one else was in the store, giving Sam a little verbal freedom. He set his glasses aside. "Well, Hattie, if you expect Homer to do a man's work, maybe you should allow him the opportunity to speak for himself."

Hattie's whole frame slammed to attention as Sam continued. "I specifically addressed Homer and my questions weren't of a prying nature." Sam wiggled his pencil in

Homer's direction. "How old are you young man?"

Homer stretched. "Fourteen."

Sam appraised him slowly. "You don't look a day over twelve."

Hattie threw a sack of flour on the counter. "You have a lot of nerve, Sam," she growled.

"So do you," Sam replied calmly. "Sending a young lad into town to do a man's job. Why don't you take on a hired hand until Homer gets some size and education?"

Hattie frantically pawed through her purse. Frustrated that she couldn't speed up matters by finding the correct change, she slapped down a paper bill.

Sam adjusted his glasses and wrote out a receipt. His voice was low and authoritative. "You and the lad can't keep up with that farm Hattie, no matter how hard you push him."

Hattie spoke through clenched teeth. "Your nose is getting pretty long, Sam."

The register drawer opened with its usual ka-ching. Sam made change slowly. The bills slid into a neat pile in front of Hattie.

"Homer," Sam said, "if you get tired of that farm, you just come on down to town. You'll get a room and a job any time you want…and it'll be a job you can handle."

Jamming the money into her purse, Hattie grabbed the bag and threw it at Homer. It surprised him, but he managed to hold on to it. "We don't have to shop here," she snarled.

Sam shrugged. "No, you don't. You can go all the way to Shepardson, if you please. Then you can take advantage of their good nature."

Hattie shoved Homer out the door and slammed it, sending the bell into a frenzy. Elmira slipped from behind the curtain that separated the store from the hallway. She eased over to the window. "You were pretty brazen with her."

"That woman is a tyrant." Sam said, unsetting his jaw. "I hate to see her treat that boy like that. It's not right."

Elmira settled back from the window. "I hope you didn't make it worse for him. Besides, you can't protect a child that's not yours."

"All I did was offer him an opportunity. There's nothing wrong with that."

Elmira knew that Sam wasn't wrong. There wasn't a soul around that didn't want the best for the lad. However, there weren't many who wanted to deal with that woman either. It wasn't easy when love tugged at the heart and fear stood in the way. Everyone had their own responsibilities to look after. A person could end up being sorry for either way they took.

It was the next evening. Sam and Elmira were finishing up the supper dishes when they heard the tapping on the store window. Sam guided the lantern through the curtained hallway and along the crowded store aisles. When he held it up to the front door, Homer's face appeared in the pallid light.

Sam pushed back the curtain. "The pump is over there. Elmira will set you up with supper." When Homer had pushed down every bit of food on his plate, he looked up and smiled.

"Thank you. That's the best meal I've had in a while."

"You're welcome, Homer," Elmira said. "It's a pleasure to feed a growing man."

She said it with her back to him. It was hard not to stare. His hands, those shoes, and the ring of dirt around his neck. It seemed atrocious but maybe it wasn't really that bad. She had known worse situations. Far worse.

Sam tugged the cash box out from behind the wood storage bin.

At the hotel, Kent answered the solid rap on his back door. "Thanks for responding at this late hour," Sam said. He pointed to Homer. "Could you give this fellow a room and a bath? He'd prefer a room in the rear." A coin clicked down on Kent's table. "He'll need breakfast, too. I'll send Elias over for him in the morning."

Sam's heavy hand fell on Homer's shoulder. A gentle nod meant things were going to be all right. But in his heart Sam knew they weren't. The lad couldn't possibly be aware of his circumstances. Homer wasn't prepared for what lay ahead. Sam didn't feel prepared either, but at least he knew the tactics of his adversary.

The sun was high and hot when Sam saw her storm into town. He nodded to Elmira. She put down her dust cloth and flowed behind the curtain just as Hattie charged through the front door.

"What have you done with my son, Sam?"

"Can't you be little easier on my front door, Hattie? You're gonna break it clean off."

Hattie set both fists into her waist. "Where's my son?"

"I thought you weren't gonna shop here anymore."

"You've kidnapped my son and I want him back."

Sam glanced at the front door to be sure no one was entering. "First of all, I wouldn't do such a thing and, second he ain't your son."

"That's a lie," Hattie huffed.

"If you can produce a birth certificate or adoption papers proving he is, then I'll believe you. Until then I'll have to go by what Tom told me."

Hattie huffed up like an angry volcano.

Sam took a fly swatter and slapped at an imaginary fly. "Can't trust what you say anyway. You told everyone you were helping him with his school lessons at home. Well, he can't even read the label on a bag of seed corn. Maybe the school board should decide to test Homer and see if you're doing what you say you are."

Elmira pushed the front door open wide and Clayton came clumping in. Red suspenders strained to reach over his barrel chest and hold work jeans in the vicinity of his waist. Trunk-like legs tapered down to meet a pair of size- fourteen shoes. A badge hung askew on a faded, sweat stained shirt.

Hattie jabbed an arm at Sam. A finger tickled the air. "Sheriff, arrest this man. He kidnapped my son. He's holding Homer. I know he is."

Clayton stepped around the pickle barrel, pretending to be aroused by the aroma. He pulled a lemon-drop candy from it's jar and tossed it into his mouth. Leaning against the counter to block the two feuding parties, he stuck his thumbs in the suspenders, moved the candy to one cheek, and cleared his throat. "Where's the boy, Sam?"

"He's not here."

"Suppose I search for him."

"You can look anywhere in here or in town and you won't find him."

Clayton moved the candy around and stared at Hattie. "Have you checked down at the train station? Maybe he took the same route Tom did two years ago."

Hattie's eyes turned to liquid lightning. In three stomps she cleared the front door. Fortunately, Elmira was still holding it open.

Clayton slid back over to the candy jar. His huge hand snatched two more lemon drops. "I think I'd like to talk to Homer. Is that possible, Sam?"

He turned to find a fishing pole laying on the counter. Clayton snatched it and held up the candy. "For the boys," he said, disappearing through the door.

Heavy feet plodded along through new grass. The spring sun traced a track of sweat clear down the back of his shirt. Finally, he reached the shade of a group of alders. They moved aside to the swing of his arm and a refreshing damp air hovered on the other side. Clayton slowly navigated the rocky terrain of the old river bed to the other side where the river still flowed with verve.

"You fella's been here long?" Clayton asked, easing himself down on a large rock. He pulled out a handkerchief and unfolded it. "I just happened to have these with me."

Tucking away the empty handkerchief, he shifted a bit, picked up his fishing pole and gave the line a flick. The three sat quietly as their lines cut through the gentle current.

After Ethan finished his candy, he reeled in his line. "Well, I'd better get back and help Pa." He was well out of sight when Clayton spoke. "Homer, have you been fishing much?" Homer shrugged as he stared at his pole.

"Well, you ain't gonna catch nothing that way. Here, I'll show ya. Now you just put that line right over near that big rock. Fish hide in the shadows, see. You've got to take their lunch right over to them. That sorta invites them to have lunch with you."

The pole wiggled and Homer almost dropped it.

"Now, slow down, slow down," Clayton said, pushing at the air. "You don't want to yank the hook out. Just ease him over here and you can have lunch together."

He chuckled as the boy pulled it in and then watched it flopping around on the grass. Homer had a twinkle in his eyes that Clayton had never seen before.

"Yep, she's a beauty. Now, I'd better get busy and catch one for myself. I can't very well show you how to cook one fish, now can I?"

Clayton looked cautiously up and down the stream. Then

he leaned over close to Homer. "I'm gonna use my secret method and I don't want you to tell a soul. Not even Elias." He pried his shiny badge from his pocket and tied it on his line. "Good thing fish can't read," he giggled.

Clayton fiddled with the fish dangling from freshly cut sticks. He poked at the fire under them." Where you going from here son?"

Homer shrugged.

"Would you like to stay around?"

"I guess," Homer muttered.

"How old are you?"

"Fourteen."

Clayton touched one of the fish with his finger. "You know, son, I'll be honest with you if you do the same. I'm here to help and that's the truth."

Homer hung his head. "I'm only twelve."

"Well, Homer, I can easily tell you everything I know 'cause I don't know very much at all. Heck, I just showed you all I know about fishing and it ain't even dark yet." He handed him one of the skewered fish. "The next-to-the-last important thing to remember about fishing is to watch out for the bones. Ya pick the meat off with your teeth and use your fingers to search for the bones. I know it don't make sense but it works."

Homer sat back to enjoy his handsome catch. "So what's the last thing to remember?"

Clayton smacked his lips and raised one finger. "If you have no luck and you haven't caught a thing and you're really hungry, don't even consider eating the bait."

Homer eyed the worm can. When he looked up, Clayton had the biggest grin he'd ever seen.

There was a soft rap at the back door into Sam's kitchen.

"Elmira, I've got a visitor for ya."

She set the pot aside, "Come on in, Clayton. You and Homer can wash up over at the pump." She tossed her apron over a coat peg and pulled out a measuring tape. It quickly slapped around Homer's waist and down one leg. "Those are the same clothes you had on yesterday and the day before." She sputtered, disappearing behind the drape and into the hallway.

"Well, that's a fine looking outfit," Sam said as Elmira spun Homer around for inspection. "Now let's see how fast a fine young man takes to learning. Clayton says you catch on real quick. Elmira has some books upstairs that she's been anxious to show someone. I think you could handle the assignment."

It didn't surprise Sam when Hattie came crashing in through the rear kitchen door right during supper. It quickly depleted the thrust of her mission when Homer was not at the table. "I want my son, Sam. I'll go to the county seat and have you arrested, I swear."

"Kinda hard doing all them chores alone, ain't it, Hattie. Would you like some supper? You should be hungry."

Hattie pushed herself up to her highest stature. "I'm not here for hospitality. And certainly not from you."

"I'll find your son and send him up tomorrow with Ethan. They can help you catch up on things."

Hattie's chin tightened sharply. "I don't need your help, Sam. I just want Homer back."

"You ain't gonna get my help, Hattie. Homer and Ethan will be up tomorrow morning to do the farm chores. And if Homer doesn't want to stay, he can come back with Ethan. That's the best for all. Now go home and they will see you tomorrow." Sam brushed his hand toward the door.

Hattie surveyed the table with wild in her eyes. The kind

of wild that would get excitement from doing something outrageous.

Sam put his hands on the edge of the table. His words came out in a low assertive growl, "Now don't be doing something you'll be sorry for."

After a while, good judgement won. She stormed out into the night, slamming the door.

"That woman sure is hard on doors," Sam sighed.

Swaying along in the wagon seat, Homer's slight frame tightened as the farm came into view. He sagged a little, as if returning to some expected punishment.

Ethan pretended not to notice. "What's that windmill doing on top of the house."

"Pa built that. It pumps water from the cellar cistern up to a tank in the attic. Then it runs down to taps in the kitchen and bath."

"What about the one on the barn?"

"That one runs Pa's forge."

Hattie's face appeared in the window as they passed the house. "Where do we start, Homer," Ethan said, stopping in front of the barn.

Homer wiggled down. "I think we'd better fence off that plowed piece. I'm supposed to plant corn there and we'll have to keep the cows out."

Ethan hauled the wire from the barn while Homer gathered tools from the shed. Then they loaded posts from the lower end of the field. They drove posts most of the morning. It was a good thing Ethan was there. That maul was far more than Homer could handle.

As they stretched the wire, Ethan watched in amazement. Homer used a strange looking pair of pliers. He gaged and tightened it, then flipped them around and set the staple.

They were enjoying the day until the clang of the dinner bell drifted across the meadow.

Homer's stature shriveled.

A reassuring hand fell across his shoulders. "You don't have to go up there if you don't want to. We will just stay right here and keep working."

Homer shook his head. With a big inhale, he gathered up his courage.

"She can't do much anyway," Ethan said as they eased up onto the wagon. "That's why I'm here."

Ethan pulled the horses over in the shade of a tree. Hattie had a table set outside. That was a relief. Neither of them wanted to be in the confines of the kitchen although the idea of water taps were intriguing to Ethan.

Homer jumped down, yanking his britches up and his hat brim down. He eased down at the table, hat brim shielding him from that venomous glare.

Ethan took off his hat and bowed his head. No one moved while he said his silent prayer.

Homer followed suit. Except for the hat. That remained welded in place.

When Ethan looked up Hattie was staring at him. Or was she studying him as one would size up an opponent. He cleared his throat. "Can I please have some salt?"

She didn't move at first. Finally with an air of disgust, she went back in for the salt shaker. The two young men cleaned their plates in record time. Ethan daubed at the corner of his mouth and snatched his hat. "Well, we'd better get back at it." Homer led him by two steps.

Hattie made no move to interfere. It was a relief, yet worrisome. She wasn't one to let an opportunity for wickedness to pass.

Ethan watched with intense curiosity as Homer worked

those interesting pliers. "Where'd you get those?" he asked.

"Pa made'um. He was always inventing something. He said this wire grabbing part was a new feature."

Looking puzzled he said, "Ethan, what's a feature?"

Ethan straightened up from his work. "Well, I guess he meant that it was something special." Satisfied, Homer nodded. He flipped the pliers around and went to drive another staple. His swing went wild and smashed his finger. The pliers slipped from his hand. With a groan, he fell to the ground in a knot.

Ethan grabbed his handkerchief and tried to catch Homer's small twisting frame. "Let's see that finger. I'll take care of it."

"Noooo," Homer moaned. "My stomach."

Ethan cast a horrified glance at the house standing stark and threatening in the distance.

Hattie was nowhere in sight. He yanked the wire out of the wagon, threw the posts aside, cradled Homer and laid him in the bed. Mounting the seat in a single lunge, he whistled the horses into action. Suddenly his greatest fear stood right before him. Hattie was blocking the roadway. He yanked the team to a stop. "Something is wrong with your son. I've got to get him to town."

"You aren't leaving," Hattie growled, grabbing the side reins.

"You let go of them, Miss Hattie. I'm leaving."

"I said you aren't."

A sudden jolt of pain struck hard enough to stop her in mid-sentence. One arm folded across her waist. She struggled to keep her balance and make her way along the horses flank to the wagon.

Ethan planted a foot solidly on her shoulder and shoved. She lay there on the grass in a pitiful lump.

Ethan jumped down from the wagon. "Come on, Miss Hattie," he said pulling at her arm. "Get in the wagon."

She flailed at his grip. "You did this to me."

Frightened, Ethan charged back to the wagon and took off. He looked back several times as they rocked and swayed over the bumpy road.

Through the big store front window Sam saw them come thundering into town.

"Homer is sick," Ethan shouted, wrestling the team to a stop. "Hattie was sick, too, but she wouldn't come along."

Sam pointed to the doctor's office and jumped on board.

Doc hurried to prepare a place. His stethoscope ran smoothly over the lad's skin. Homer winced when Doc pushed on his stomach.

Sam ran for the door. "Your nurse is off today. I'll fetch Elmira to help you."

The doctor folded his stethoscope just as Sam and Elmira came charging in. "Sam, I'm going to need—"

"Heavy cream and salvatore," Sam snapped, holding up the ingredients. "The anecdote for arsenic poisoning." He gave them to Elmira and laid a gentle hand on Homer's head. "What happened, Ethan?"

Ethan spoke with a quivering lip. "Hattie served us lunch. I wondered why she went to the trouble of setting up a table outside. At first I thought she didn't want us in the house, but then I noticed that all three plates were arranged with special care. We had two slices of tomato and hers had only one. I felt a bit uneasy about it so I asked for some salt, and while she went to fetch it, I slid one of my tomatoes onto her plate and swapped with her. I figured it wouldn't hurt even if I was wrong. I guess I should have given her plate to Homer."

"You're an observant young man, son," the doctor said.

Sam rose slowly from his chair, his eyes locked on some distant object. "You said there were two plates alike. Homer ate his and Hattie ate yours." He turned to Ethan. "Where's Hattie, son?"

He shivered and swallowed hard. "I left her curled up on the grass. I couldn't get her into the wagon. I tried. Honest I did, but she refused."

Sam's stride toward the door was blocked by Elmira. "Sam, you can't go up there. You have too much contempt for that woman. She's desperate. There's no telling what she'll do."

He touched her cheek. "I have to go. She's sick."

"She's sick on her own account," Elmira demanded. "I'll get the sheriff to go along with you."

"No, that'll take too long." His hands dropped to her shoulders. "I know her better than anyone. Now you stay with Homer and the doctor."

Sam leaped onto the wagon and snapped the reins. It was getting dark fast. He pulled up in front of the store and ran inside. He slipped behind the counter and grabbed the double-barrel shotgun. A heavy blanket draped over his arm covered the gun nicely. With a lantern in hand he ran out.

Elmira shouted to him from across the street. "What are you stopping for?"

85

"A lantern," he said swinging it high.

"What's the other thing?"

"A blanket," he called back. "She'll need some cover on the trip back."

The reins snapped, Sam whistled, and the wagon lurched toward the setting sun.

"Sorry, girls," Sam muttered to his horses as they fell into a rhythmical trot. "You should be home munching oats instead of chasing after some devilish woman. I just can't understand people nowadays. They insist on making life miserable for everyone. That woman can't even get along with her own folks."

Sam swayed with the seat as the wagon battled the bumps. He had to slow to a walk as daylight faded. Finally, the team pulled up in front of Hattie's house. Everything was darker than an old coal bin. She wasn't on the lawn where Ethan left her. The lantern's light made wiggly shadows of everything. Sam's boots sounded like dropping planks on the porch. His fist on the door thundered through the night. "Hattie, I'm here to help. Now come on out and I'll take you to the doc's." There was only the squeak of the windmill on the roof.

She might have struggled to the barn and tried to milk a cow for the heavy cream antidote.

Lantern light glinted off the shotgun barrels as Sam pushed them through the barn door. He wasn't about to step into any snares. It was enough just risking his good reputation being out here alone.

The weapon led the way into every stall and manger. Hattie wasn't there. He poked his light through another doorway into the rear of the barn. Odd shapes flanked the walls. He surveyed Tom's machine shop. A heavy sigh filtered from a dark corner. Sam's hair did a salute as he slammed the lantern and cold steel toward it. A breeze had flirted with the windmill on the roof that ran Tom's bellows.

The muffled sound of a horse's whinny came from outside. It was one of his horses. A strange light flickered in the kitchen window. Lantern light doesn't dance like that. The house was on fire.

Sam ran for the house, crossing the porch in two strides. "Hattie!" he yelled. Only the low ugly growl of the fire answered. He shouldered the door, then kicked at it. Stepping back, Sam cradled the gun across one arm and yanked both triggers. The latch disintegrated. One solid kick severed the door. Scorching heat billowed out. Layers of old linoleum fed the fire and fresh air drove it into convulsions.

Sam hurriedly moved the team well away, then sprinted for the barn. If he could find a ladder, there was still a chance of getting in an upstairs window. He frantically worked his way through the hay shed. Finally, he found it hanging on two nails next to all the harness.

The barn door had swung partially closed, so he had to stop and set the ladder down. Just as he reached for the latch, it moved toward him. Shifting orange fire light cast a shadow of a huge form.

Driven by fear and self preservation, Sam swung hard. Bone struck bone with a sickening thud and the ominous figure slumped over with a sonorous groan.

Sam fell back into the darkness.

"What are you doing, Sam? I think you tore off my ear." Clayton rolled to his knees. "Oh, it hurts."

"You tried to sneak up on me," Sam barked. "Now shut up and hold open the door."

With big feet slapping the ground like bags of rocks, Clayton tried to follow. "Wait a minute, Sam. Tell me what's going on here?"

Sam jumped on the bottom rung of the ladder. "Hattie is still in there," he yelled above the roar of the blaze.

He couldn't go in through the window. Sucking in a deep breath, he reached in, feeling around. His hand hit something. Was it the soft flesh of an arm? It wouldn't move. Drawing back out, Sam took in a deep breath of hot air and threw his upper torso in. Every muscle strained but the object wouldn't move. He tried once more before the searing heat forced him to retreat. Window glass shattered with a clamorous smack, letting the voracious monster out of its cage.

Sam stumbled over to the wagon and plunked down, his head in his hands. Searing heat wrinkled the night air, driving the windmill on the roof into a frenzy. Smoke curled out between the cracks in the slate roofing. Paint blistered and browned.

Clayton leaned against the side of the wagon. "I've got a question for you, Sam," he said, holding up two small objects.

Sam didn't want to look at Clayton and he didn't want Clayton looking at him. He parted just enough fingers to see what he was holding. There in that big hand in front of him lay two spent shotgun shells. Sam stiffened. The lacerated porch door, his only defense, had just gone up in flames. Maybe Clayton had arrived early enough to see the door laying open. Maybe he hadn't. He surely would've been close enough to hear the roar of the gun.

"Are you thinking I killed her?"

Clayton didn't answer.

Sam vaulted to his feet, turning a half circle in mid air. "Well, don't think it," he roared, "or I'll make your ears a matched set. I didn't have to come all the way up here to do her in. All I had to do was stay in town until morning. The poison would've most likely got her. Besides, if I told folks what I know about her, she would've had to leave town a long time ago. It was for Homer's benefit. She would've taken Homer and left if she suspected folks knew about her. She and Tom were never married and Homer ain't her son. He ain't Tom's son neither."

"Well," Clayton drawled, "It seems kinda strange that you were taking to Homer."

"I don't need a son. I already got one. I promised Tom I'd look after the lad and I have," Sam snapped, and headed toward the barn.

"Where are you going?"

"You'd better follow me. I might be trying to escape."

Steam and smoke billowed through the roof. The windmill collapsed like a bird smitten in flight. Clayton got as close to the fire as he could and threw the cartridges in.

Sam took a long time to come back. He brought some hay and arranged it in front of the horses. Finally he returned to the wagon bed, stuck a straw in his mouth, and wiggled to get comfortable.

Clayton waited until he couldn't take it anymore. "So if Homer ain't anyone's son, then who is he?"

Sam threw away his straw. "A while ago I was down at the train station picking up a late shipment. Tom happened along and volunteered to help. As we worked he told me his story."

He pulled his knees up and hugged them. "Tom was a wheelwright and a good one. A group of travelers came along and hired him to fix their wagons. It was a lot of work and they weren't willing to sit around so he agreed to travel along with them. In among them there was a young girl with her baby. She didn't have a husband so the group didn't treat her very well and that bothered Tom. Then a few of his tools came up missing and no one knew why nor where. As time passed more tools disappeared. Tom got tired of it and decided to leave. He asked the girl to come along and late one night they left. He figured the best route to take was back through the towns they passed. That group surely wouldn't return there for fear of being arrested."

Clayton rubbed his crimson ear and watched the back porch roof collapse, sending up a battalion of sparks. They fell safely away from the barn.

"A while later," Sam continued, "the girl must've got homesick because she slipped away one night, leaving Tom with the baby. He wasn't about to chase after her so he kept traveling this way. One day he came upon a young woman walking along the road. She said her folks had died in a terrible fire and she was moving on. Said her name was Hattie. Their purposes seemed agreeable so they stayed together. They stopped here and took over this farm."

Sam stretched over the side of the wagon to check on the diminishing pile of hay. "It didn't take a lot of figuring to see why they got this farm so cheap. It wouldn't produce enough to return the seed he planted but it was what Hattie wanted. Tom had a good workshop and some land to set up a business. Hattie was determined to have a farm and they argued about it a lot. Tom told her that he would build and invent things and buy her a big mansion, but she insisted on farming. She said he'd better not think of leaving either because nobody was going to leave her ever again."

The roof collapsed, pulling the gable ends into the inferno. Two walls fell, showering the night air with sparks. Both men watched for some renegade ember that could ignite the surrounding area. Sam shook his head and sighed. "What a waste."

When the danger was passed, he continued. "One day," he said, "Tom came in from the field. He put his tools in that shed over there. He noticed one of the wall cabinet doors was ajar. It was one of those doors you had to lift and slam just right to set the latch. The can of arsenic he kept for the potato bugs was all clean while everything else was still dusty. That night at supper, he didn't eat. Hattie nagged him to eat, so Tom pretended to get angry and said he would eat it in the barn. He went out and gave it to the dog. Soon after the dog turned sick and died. Right then and there Tom struck out for town. That's when I met him at the train station. He said he was leaving and not coming back. Didn't say where he was headed. Asked me to look after Homer."

Sam swallowed hard. "I guess Homer didn't get a very good start. I kinda feel sad for the little guy."

Clayton rose slowly and motioned Sam to follow. He pushed the lantern into the tool shed toward the open cabinet door. There among the things on the shelf was one round clean spot where some object had recently been.

Through the shed window they saw the last of the structure sag into the foundation. Clayton stared, almost mesmerized. "I guess the devil got her fire."

Sam stared blankly at the rippling waves of heat. "Maybe she wasn't in there."

Clayton winced in disbelief. "You said she was."

"When I got here, I beat on the front door. I didn't hear anything so I checked the barn. That's when the house caught on fire."

"Then why did you go sticking yourself in the upstairs window?"

"That's what makes me question," Sam said. "I thought I felt an arm. I couldn't see a thing so I'm not sure. But I do know my own strength and I could slide Hattie across the floor even if she had passed out. Whatever I had a hold on, wouldn't budge.

"Yup," Sam said, staring at the fire as if it were giving him the answers. "This is all making sense. Tom picks her up on the road. Says it appears she's running from something. Maybe this isn't her first fire."

"So what started the blaze?"

Sam shrugged. "She could've set a trip mechanism. When someone rattled the door it would tip over the lamp onto the stove. She was clever enough to use some gadget Tom had made. She could be miles from here right now."

"She was poisoned. Remember?"

"It could've been an act. Or a small dose, just big enough to make a youngster sick."

"Well, what's the matter. She ain't here bothering us anymore."

"Where's your logic, Clayton? She may well have killed Homer. And what about Ethan? She did tell Tom that no one was ever going to leave her and that's what Tom and Homer did. So if this isn't her first fire, this isn't her first attempt at murder either."

Clayton led the way back to the wagon. "We'll check the area at first light. About now I gotta get some rest."

It was almost morning when the flames died down. Sam rearranged himself under the horse blanket he borrowed from the barn. He eyed Clayton to see if he was sleeping. "Homer's gonna have a rough time keeping the farm."

Clayton's nodded a little. He knew he had to listen to some complicated concoction that couldn't be easily solved.

"He ain't Tom's son and he ain't Hattie's son. And the two of them were never married so how can Homer lay claim to something he's not heir to?"

Clayton made a low guttural grunt. His concern right now was more in getting some rest. The best solution to this problem was to throw all the interested parties in jail and leave them there until they settled their differences.

"You know I talked with Tom before he left." Sam heard a heavy sigh somewhere between acknowledgment and disgust. "He said something kinda strange. Said if something ever happened to Hattie, have the lad dig the old well a bit deeper. There's sweet water down just a little further." He pulled at his chin, deliberating on the matter. "Homer told Ethan that the house had a good spring right there in the cellar. Said the windmill on the roof pumped water up to a tank in the attic where it could run down to taps."

After a long silence, Clayton muttered, "So?"

Sam flipped his blanket aside and slid off the wagon. "Tom wouldn't say it for nothing."

The sun was full up when Ethan arrived. He found the two men sitting on the wagon engrossed in an armload of books. It was a relief knowing they were safe. A strong imagination kept him awake all night. Hattie could be a formidable adversary even if there were two of them. "How's Homer?" Sam asked.

"Doing better," Ethan replied, staring at the hot bed of coals where the house used to be.

"Where's Hattie?"

Sam looked at him and glanced toward the smoking ruins.

Ethan edged over close enough to feel the skin-searing heat. Close enough to accelerate his pulse. What would it be like to be trapped in such a furnace of fury?

Clayton tilted his notebook toward Sam. "Look at this. A fishing reel with a casting brake on it." He held up a calloused thumb. "That would prevent this."

Sam whistled in amazement. "This one has some sort of engine in it. Even the parts are all labeled."

"What happened to your ear, Clayton?" Ethan asked.

He pushed an elbow toward Sam. "You'll have to ask him."

Sam closed his book and stood up. "Clayton kinda took me by surprise.

"Well, we've done all we can here. Ethan and I will look after the animals before we head back. I'll take these books to Homer and tell him what happened."

Clayton waved and slogged over to his carriage.

Ethan trailed alongside his father toward the barn. "What's gonna happen to Homer now?"

Sam's arm fell on Ethan's shoulder. "The future doesn't look too good right now, does it. He's going to need our help. Especially yours. Just think, you get to be a big brother."

"How can I be something I don't know how to be?"

"I guess a person can be a big brother without realizing it. All you have to do is be real good at being yourself. Does that make sense?" Sam opened the barn door. He ruffled his son's hair as he passed. "You're gonna be a fine one. I just know it."

Elmira heard the wagon pull up in front of the store. She yanked off her apron and headed for the door.

Sam eased his sore frame to the ground. "Could you put the horses away, son? I've got a little work to do."

The door opened before he reached it. Elmira was stunned to see his red face, scorched shirt, and singed hair.

"Where's Hattie?" she blurted.

"She won't be bothering anyone anymore," Sam said while rummaging behind the counter. "I want you to come

94

with me. This won't take long."

He looked up at Elmira, pale and transfixed. Staring at him, but not hearing at all.

Suddenly she found Sam right in front of her, his hands on her arms. "It's all right," he said, hugging her to his chest. An entire night of anguish had to be vented. She finally settled back, daubing at her nose.

"Now find me an envelope and lock up the store. No one is here right now, so hurry."

She shut down the kitchen stove, threw aside the potholder, and patted at her hair. She could see Sam in the mirror, working with the envelope.

He turned the key in the door just as a group of women mounted the steps. "What's the meaning of this?" one of them asked.

"For those who can't read," Sam said, "It means just what that little card says. CLOSED."

One of them tossed her head. "Well, I never."

"You're right Mrs. Beatty, you never have, and no doubt you never will."

Elmira stiffened. She hadn't known Sam to speak so forcefully to anyone. Especially in the presence of others. Well, except for a special occurrence when Hattie raised his ire. And true though, that was in private. She took his arm to cross the street.

Sam overheard Mrs. Beatty murmur through clenched teeth, "You'll pay for this, Sam." She never was one to say things loud enough for all concerned to hear.

Sam turned with a casual air. "Before I pay you, Mrs. Beatty, maybe you should be paying me. I'm tired of repeatedly carrying over your credit. I expect full payment by the end of the month or I'll be forced to put the matter in Clayton's hands."

"What's got into you, Sam," Elmira asked, catching stride with him.

"I'm just tired of people pretending to be more than they really are. She was demeaning me to benefit her position and I'm not playing her petty little social games."

Doc was out of his office when they arrived and his nurse, Clara, seemed reluctant to let them in.

"I just want to talk to the lad in private, Clara," Sam said. "I know he's your patient but a few words isn't going to hurt him. Besides, I'm sure he's anxious to know. We won't take long." Sam closed the bedroom door.

"You're looking pretty good, lad," he said, attempting to calm the fear written on Homer's face.

"Do I have to go home?"

Sam glanced at Elmira, reached back and snapped the door open. "I said in private," he yelled right in Clara's face.

This time the door closed with a confident thud.

Sam pulled a chair over to the bed. "No, you don't have to go home, son. You are home." He set a stack of notebooks on the bed and pulled out an envelope. "When you and Ethan drove off, Hattie, she was sick, just like you were." Sam flipped and creased the envelope several times. "Sometime during her affliction, she must've tipped over the lantern." Sam looked straight at Homer. A serious sadness deepened his voice. "The house caught fire. I tried to save her, but it was too late. Hattie died in the fire. I'm sorry, Homer."

With the difficult part over, Sam eased back in the chair. "When your father left, he asked me to give you this letter …when the time was right. Well, I think that time is now."

"You saw my pa leave?"

"Yes. I was at the station the night he left. He talked to me before he got on the train. He was awful sad about it, but he thought it was the right thing to do. He never said where he was going. Just gave me this letter, climbed on the train and didn't look back."

Homer went limp. "He made it. Good. I heard him and Ma arguing about the farm. She said no one was going to leave her and live. I didn't know if he'd made it or not. I didn't dare ask anyone neither, cause Ma would surely find out and think I was planning something, too."

Homer swallowed a big lump in his throat. "I guess it's safe to tell you now. I found the dog in the barn. He's buried down near the end of the field so Ma wouldn't know." He twisted over close to Sam. "I'm glad Pa made it. And I'm glad Ethan is real smart, too. If he hadn't swapped plates with her, she'd a got both of us just like she tried to get Pa."

"Well," Sam gulped, turning the letter over once more for good measure, "Tom left this for you."

Elmira resurrected her composure, plunked down on the bed, and snatched the letter from Sam. "I'll read it to you, Homer. I know you'll have a little trouble with reading right now but real soon you'll be good at it. This letter says that in his absence, Tom leaves all his present possessions to you. It's signed by your father, Tom Ferguson."

"But I heard Pa tell Ma the farm was no good. That it never would be."

Sam thumped the notebooks. "That's where these come in. They are part of Tom's possessions he left behind. I brought only a few, but there's a lot more. Tom says here that there's something in the soil called molybdenum. It makes grass sparse, cows skinny, and metal hard. In here he describes how to work the stuff. There's a lot of valuable ideas in these books. Some patentable stuff like those fence pliers Ethan showed me.

"That sure is a lot to think about. I guess, right now

though, I'd be interested in that offer you made of a room and a job."

Sam smiled. "Sure is. But right now you concentrate on getting better." They each gave the boy's hand a little squeeze. They looked like a team. A good team that Homer would enjoy being a part of.

On the way back to the store, Elmira clung to Sam's arm. "Did you hear him, Sam? All this time that poor little soldier hasn't known whether his father was alive or dead. And I only had to suffer through one night, not knowing about my husband."

"I'm sorry, Elmira. I just couldn't leave the fire un-attended."

"Amazing," she said, pinching his arm. "Tom Ferguson's handwriting is very close to yours."

Sam tightened his grip on her waist. "Coincidental, I'm sure."

Hard Times Are Coming

ELIAS FILLED HIS cup with the last of the coffee and put the pot in the sink. He stared out the window, sipping the brew, and watching the sun spread out over the field, turning it as tan as fresh-cut lumber. It was the summer of 1929 and in all his sixty years he hadn't seen it so dry.

"Well," he said, "I think I'll go over to Frank's and finish the garden."

Sadie inspected the patch on her apron, tied it on and smoothed out the wrinkles. "Don't know why you bother with that place so much. With this dry spell, I'd think you would be gathering hay."

"Cause I said I would. It's the neighborly thing to do. Besides, the extra garden stuff has been handy."

Sadie put the iron back on the shelf. "Just made me more work."

Elias set down his cup, easing back his nerves. They had had this discussion before and it hadn't turned out well. "I ain't about to throwaway all that stuff when we can sell it or use it ourselves. When Frank gets back, if he wants his vegetables I'm sure he'll pay you for your time."

He pulled his sweat-stained hat from its hook. "Friends don't treat friends poorly."

Sadie huffed and jabbed at the water pump handle as the screen door squeaked shut.

"And don't worry about the chores," Elias hollered back.

"I'll do um when I get back."

It was a two-mile walk to Frank's place and the temperature was rising quickly. Frank hadn't said how long he was going to be gone. Here it was stretching well into summer. There was still hay down at his own place and plenty of things needed fixing but good friends don't abandon each other quickly. His sister just didn't understand that. Elias knew he couldn't handle Frank's place in the winter. He'd just have to close it up, dispose of the chickens and let it rest. It already looked well rested. Frank never was much for farming. He spent all his time in his shop, tinkering with some machine.

When Elias turned into the yard he saw the tracks. They came from the shed where Frank kept his Model T truck. The shed was empty and the shop was littered with pieces of something Frank had been working on. The place was a mess. Whoever came in was looking for something special.

Someone had been in the house, too. Frank's only kitchen chair was askew. An empty can of beans sat on the edge of the stove. A dirty pot lay in the sink. Maybe it was Frank. He could've returned and stepped out again. Elias dreaded the four-mile walk to town to report this to the sheriff. That ornery character would pretend he had some pressing affair, then show up after Elias had walked all the way back. Everyone suspected Halsey was slow of mind and needed time to think how he could make a situation work out to his advantage.

Elias picked up the hoe and started for the garden. There was no need of wasting a lot of sunshine.

He would be going into town with his own produce tomorrow. He would report the incident then.

The tomatoes were picked and the last of the potatoes were seeing a cover layer of fresh dirt when Elias heard the *chut chut* of a Model T in the distance.

It was Frank. He pulled in the yard and right up to the front porch on what would've been lawn except it was now brown.

Relieved, Elias put down the hoe. Now he wouldn't have to be over here so often. Of course, Frank would want his tomatoes. That would be a disappointment. With so little rain, tomatoes were at a premium.

Elias sauntered over and put the basket of tomatoes on the porch. "Howdy." Frank didn't interrupt his work. "Help me get these sacks inside."

A low drone in the distance turned Elias's attention. "Hey look, Frank. It's one of them Curtis Jennies."

Frank still wasn't swayed from his task. He just replied, "Yup."

The last time an airplane passed over Frank waved at it, exclaiming that he was going to build one of those things. "Why ain't you excited?" Elias asked.

Frank grabbed another sack. "I guess I seen too much."

When Elias came out from carrying in the last sack, Frank was leaning on the side of the truck, staring off toward the river at the end of the meadow. "There's gonna be a big bridge over there, Li. Gonna span that whole river without even a post to hold it up."

Elias studied him with a suspicious eye. Something had happened to his friend. Something drastic.

"How do you know that?"

Frank straightened. "Oh, I guess I seen too much. That's all. Come on inside and help me. I've got a lot to do."

"Can't. Sadie expects me home for supper and I promised I'd do the chores."

"Your sister knows how to take care of things. Help me finish here and I'll take you home."

Elias was torn. He'd never disappointed Sadie before. Why was Frank putting on such a rush? He had to know more. Maybe he could help his friend mend his mind.

Frank put a big stack of envelopes on the table. They were sealed and stamped but they had no addresses on them. "Here," he said, pulling up his only chair. "Put these addresses on those envelopes. And don't mess up. Stamps are expensive." Then he went into the adjoining room with a sack.

Elias could hear him in there pawing through papers. Occasionally he would bring out another bundle of envelopes to address.

They worked on into the night; Elias at the table under the only light bulb in the place, and Frank in the next room with an oil lamp.

Elias addressed letters to people and institutions all over the East Coast. Some of them sounded important. Maybe Frank was in some sort of trouble. Or maybe he was seeking financial backing for an invention of his. He hoped

Frank wasn't involved in something that would run him afoul of the law.

It was concern rather than curiosity that made him do it. Elias addressed one of the envelopes to himself and threw it in with all the others. It was only a way of knowing how to help his friend without questioning his actions. Even close friends weren't supposed to get nosy and pry into ones personal affairs.

Elias finished the last one and tried shaking some life back into his wrist. His eyes ached from the harsh glow of the bare light bulb dangling from its own cord.

The moon was high and the air heavy as they bounced along the dusty road. When they arrived, Elias' heart was still jostling. It wasn't from the ride either. He'd never known his friend to be so disgruntled, so distraught, so angry with everything. Frank had cursed out every bump in the road. Bumps that had been there since they were kids. Unhappy, that's what he was. Something had stolen his pleasantness. Something very bad.

He tried to prevent the screen door from squeaking but that was a futile effort. With Sadie's bedroom right off the kitchen every noise flowed right in.

"Elias?"

"Yup."

"Your supper is on the back of the stove."

Every movement seemed so loud. The tin plate rattled and the frying pan clanked. Even the fork scraping the plate fractured the familiar stillness.

When Elias set his dishes in the dry sink, they complained with a raucous clatter. "Sorry I was late," he muttered. "I hope you weren't worried."

There was no answer.

Creaky floor boards marked the course to his bedroom.

Sagging into the complaining iron bed, he pulled the only thin wool blanket over his tortured soul.

Daylight arrived quickly. The unwelcome sun scurried in through the shadeless window like an early rising child. With Sadie rattling around in the kitchen, no one could sleep late anyhow. Elias pulled on yesterday's trousers, ran his fingers through what hair he had left and dragged himself into the kitchen.

He pumped a little water into a basin, adjusted the mirror over the sink, took down his razor and started carving off a two-day stubble.

"What's them tomatoes on the porch?"

"Frank said he didn't want them. Said he wasn't going to be around long enough to use them."

"Where is that man off to now? He's worse than a butterfly. How are you going to keep taking care of that place for him?"

"Won't have much trouble during the winter. Besides, Frank was talking about leaving permanently."

Sadie hewed off a thick slice of bread and put it in the pan of leftover bacon grease. "So run down he ain't gonna get a good price for it."

Elias toweled off his face and stepped to the table. He pulled out his chair. The chair his dad sat in, its numerous paint chips and cracks exposing the many phases of its life.

Sadie shoved breakfast in front of him. "That man is up to no good."

"What makes you say that?"

"All that flittering around and not paying attention to business. Now he's speaking of running off. I tell you, it smells of trouble."

"Well," Elias drawled, using the bread to wipe his plate clean, "maybe he's patented one of his inventions and now he's looking for money to make it."

Sadie huffed and plunked down in her usual spot. "When has anything he's come up with had any value?"

"Sadie, I'm surprised you give the man so little accounting. You were sweet on him at one time."

Sadie huffed again. "I weren't sweet on him at all. Who would want a man that spent all his time in that shop beating his senseless head on a piece of iron?"

"That's probably what they said about Henry Ford, too."

They both pushed away from the table. Sadie picked up the plates and headed for the sink. "What are you going to do today?"

Elias reached for his hat. "I'm going to get that hay I got down. It should be dry enough by the time I get Dina hooked up. Then I'm gonna go to town and do the trading."

On the way to the barn, he stopped at the well to fill the water jug. The old oak bucket went down a long way before it splashed. This dry spell was great for haying, but the cistern was almost dry. If it didn't rain soon he'd be lugging more than just drinking water.

When Dina heard the barn door latch rattle she knew what was coming. She plodded over to the harness rack without a word spoken. She also knew the routine in the

field. Elias didn't have to say a thing. When he picked up a fork load of hay, she would pull the wagon abreast of him. And always on the windward side so the dust and chaff wouldn't come back on them.

Elias wiped away sweat, uncorked his water jug and took a long drink. Catching the jug under his arm, he cupped his hands and let the jug tilt forward. Water trickled down his wrist into the bowl of his hands so Dina could drink, too.

When she finished Elias leaned forward, putting his head on her head. There they stood, in contact with the earth and each other, letting their thoughts pass back and forth. This was living. Working together. Sharing their water. Sharing the land. It was totally incomprehensible why Frank would want to leave something like this. With a partner like Dina, who would want to replace her with some machine. Mort had one of those tractors. A spark from the exhaust pipe had set his field on fire. Willard had a tractor, too. He was putting gas in it when something hot ignited it and blew him right off that thing.

Elias pulled his hat back on. "Grass is cheaper than gas, ain't it old girl. Don't know what I'd do without you. Better than any hired hand. All they do is bust up equipment."

Dina nickered and followed him to the barn. With the hay put in and Dina in the field, Elias sat down to lunch. Fried tripe, beans and corn bread. Now what man would ever want to scamper away and leave that behind. Something was surely wrong with Frank.

Sadie had the trade goods packed and ready. With a list of needs, Elias shouldered the knot and headed for town. He passed the meadow where Dina grazed on the few remnants of green grass. She was getting along in years. What would he do when she died. He couldn't afford another horse.

One of those automobiles went by, stirring up a mountain of dust. He used to walk to town and back without seeing one. Now five or six a day went by.

Nelson's Creek was a relief from the midday heat. Big trees hugged the river, shading the road and the water. Elias stepped over a rock and down through a little cut in the bank, to the water. He dipped his hat in and pulled it back on, letting the coolness trickle down his neck. To the right was the tree he and Frank used to climb up and dive from. The diving branch was gone but the rest of the behemoth still stood firm. This area was always good fishing. They'd pulled some whoppers out of here. He hadn't been fishing in a long time. Maybe Frank could be convinced to join him just one more time.

The rest of the way to town was open, hot and dry. When the wind blew just right you could smell the balsam grove all the way across Basset Flats. That grove was a handy marker. Especially in the winter when snow covered the road, even above the fence posts.

The storekeeper was happy to see Elias. He was almost out of eggs and Sadie's butter always brought a premium price.

When the weighing and packaging of the salt, flour, and thread were finished, the storekeeper announced that Elias was seventeen cents to the good. "Is there something else you'd like Elias?"

He thought about putting it aside for a new pair of boots, but a few gumdrops would be a real treat for Sadie and a plug of tobacco for Dina. She loved the molasses in it.

Elias picked up the load and headed for the town common. He could fill his jug from the faucet there. That's when he saw the banker lining out the sheriff. He was threatening Halsey with a rolled-up newspaper, waving it around and poking him with it.

When he spotted Elias, he dragged Halsey right over.

"Elias, you're caring for Frank's place. Tell Halsey where he is."

Elias set down his load and appraised the two. "Why? Is Frank in some sort of trouble?"

"Halsey wants to ask him a few questions."

"Like what?"

"That's not your concern."

"That don't seem quite right, Victor. You want me to answer your questions but you won't answer mine. If Halsey is so concerned, he'll do the talking."

Halsey was stunned. He looked around to see if anyone else noticed his embarrassment. Elias came to his rescue. "I don't know where Frank is. You know I'd tell you if I did. Now what's this all about?"

Victor's demeanor sagged a bit. "It's about this," he said, snapping open the *Boston Globe*. A heavily underlined ad read, *How to become wealthy in one month. Send five dollars.* Then the ad listed a Boston post office box.

Elias wet his lips. Five dollars. That was a weeks wage. "What's Frank got to do with anything in Boston? That's a long ways away."

Victor yanked the paper back. "This is Frank's ad. I know it is, and he doesn't know anything about complicated financial structure."

"If he doesn't know about such things then how could it be his?" Halsey nodded in approval.

Victor aimed the paper toward the bank. "He came in a few days ago and cleaned me out of twenty-dollar gold pieces. Then he dropped off sacks of letters at the post office. Now where'd he get all that money?"

"Well," Elias drawled. "If he was at your bank with a lot of money, why didn't you ask him then? Now you're sending out the sheriff to do your work."

Victor huffed.

Elias picked up his load, signaling the end of his cooperation. Before he left, he winked at Halsey. "I think Victor got pinched."

Elias didn't look back to see the results of his comment but he did hear Halsey promise to look into the matter as soon as he finished with a few pressing details.

All the way home Elias agonized over the situation. He was so deep in thought that he passed right by Nelson's Creek and the old swimming hole without even noticing. He was turning in his own yard when Frank came along in a cloud of dust. "I need your help again, Li."

"The sheriff and the banker are looking for you. They say you're up to no good."

Frank shook the dust off his hat. "I ain't doing nothing illegal."

Sadie appeared on the front porch, her apron playing in the hot breath of a summer breeze. "What are you up to Frank? Are you stealing Elias again? You know there's work to be done."

"I ain't seen you in a while, Sadie. You're still as pretty as ever." He turned. "Are you coming, Li?" Elias looked at each of them, wondering where his allegiance should be. "You'll have to wait till I do my chores. I let Sadie down once. I won't do it again."

Later, when Elias came inside, Sadie handed him a wrapped sandwich. "Now you be careful. That man is up to no good. You don't need trouble. Besides, I need you around here."

"Yeah," Elias drawled.

Sadie gave him a sinister glare. "He may be a friend but blood is thicker than water."

Elias nodded and let the screen door close slowly.

At Frank's place the two worked well into the night, stuffing and addressing letters. Frank was as cautious as ever that Elias didn't get to see the letter's contents.

All Elias could think of was five dollars for every one. It seemed so incredible. It bothered him that his old friend would do something like this. But if this wasn't illegal then there wasn't much a person could say.

Finally, the last letter was sealed and neatly stacked. Frank reached for the pile. Elias's hand held it down and didn't move. The unspoken word. An explanation was due.

Frank skidded out a wired-together rocking chair from the parlor and sat down. He tested it slowly to be certain the repairs would hold. It took a few sighs to organize his thoughts.

"I seen the future, Li. I seen too much. It ain't gonna take long to change this whole country from the land of milk and honey to the land of bilk and money. Everybody is gonna be greedy. People will do anything for money. Anything.

"Oh, some will call it progress. They will drive on smooth macadam roads all the way from the Canadian border to Boston without stopping. I suppose you could call that progress if you don't think of what you're missing."

Frank pushed his rocker a little harder for emphasis. "Everything is gonna be big too, Li. Big planes, big trucks, big buildings. Everything. Houses, bridges, cars. More cars than I ever seen. More than I ever want to."

Elias sat there staring at him. Frozen somewhere between amazement and disbelief.

"I ain't making it up, Li. I got this idea and built a machine. At first I used a rabbit. When I turned it on, the rabbit vanished. A couple hours later it was back. After a while I got brave enough to try it on myself. The rabbit wasn't hurt and I had to know where it went. Well, I must've figured the power wrong cause I found myself seventy-odd years in the future. It was scary, Li. Real scary. Big buildings everywhere. A hundred floors high. And everybody's in a hurry, too. They try to do so many things and go so fast they don't have time to look at themselves."

Frank's voice sagged a little. "They've conquered about everything too, Li. They've conquered everything but themselves."

Frank slowed his rocking and sighed, knowing he had gone far enough with that topic.

"Why," he continued, "those cities are so big a man could get lost for days. They stretch out for miles. Nothing but cement, brick and macadam. Ain't no trees anywhere. No grass either. I don't know how people breathe. And there's a hotel on every comer, and a restaurant in between. Seems like they're all busy, too."

Now Frank closed his eyes and shook his head. "Don't know what I'd a done if hadn't met Jason.

"He was one of them luggage totters they call bellhops. I went into a hotel to stay the night. I had to do something since I didn't come back right away." He leaned a little closer to Elias. "They wanted two hundred dollars for that one night. Can you imagine, Li? Two hundred dollars just to sleep there once. All I had was a twenty-dollar gold piece. I was in a real fix till Jason came by, saw that gold piece and offered me five-hundred dollars for it. Said it was a collector's item. All I knew was that I was out of trouble. Yup, Jason was a real nice young man. He sorta looked after me. Kinda restored inside me just one candlelight of hope for the human race.

"Well, when he showed me my room I nearly fell over. Got your own bathroom in every room.

"Running water and one of them televisions. It's like a radio with a moving picture of who's talking. Everything was all right till I looked out the window. I was on the forty-third floor. Everything below looked about as big as an ant. That whole city stayed lit up all night. Every street and every building. The noise never stops either.

"At breakfast the waiter brought me some fruit. There was a strawberry in there. Seems you can get anything you want anytime, anywhere."

Frank shook his finger at Elias. "Now, I gotta tell you. You remember the ones we used to pick up on Warren's hill? If we found one the size of a dime it was a treasure. Well this one was as big as a silver dollar." Frank's voice jumped half an octave. "There warn't nothing to it. Flat I say. It was what they call synthetic. Well, it was a sin all right. People eat that stuff and wonder why they're sick. There ain't nothing good left in the food. Nothing at all. Everything worth a hoot has been taken out and replaced by something synthetic.

"I got to see one of them clothing stores, too. Big enough to cover a whole town. Had to have signs to find your way around. People in there buying up that stuff. Three and four of everything."

Frank folded his arms in his lap. "It was the second day I was there it happened." He closed his eyes, as if he didn't want to see the image he was about to paint. "Some fugitive from an asylum flies one of them big planes right into one of the tall buildings. There was fire and smoke everywhere. Then another plane crashes into the building beside it. They both collapsed like a house of cards." Frank's face sagged and his voice started to shake. "There was two thousand people in there, Li."

He leaned way back as though he was studying the sooty

grease marks the oil lamp smoke made on the ceiling. The words came from a tight throat. "You know my youngest brother was in the Great War. Said they would pound a city into rubble with their big guns. Then they'd go in and clean up. Never said much about what he saw. I guess I know why."

The creak of the rocking chair stopped. It took several breaths to regain his composure. "I worked on that big pile of rubble. They called me a hero, Li, but I warn't no hero. I was just there because I had to be. It was sensible and decent. I didn't have to worry no more about food or rooming. They fed us anything we asked for and we stayed for free right close by. Then, one morning I found myself back here.

"Jason told me about this get-rich-quick thing. It's all legal, too. I priced it high to single out the rich ones. I didn't want to mess with the common folk like us. I figure if those high and mighty are greedy enough to buy what I got, then I'll give it to them. Now I know what they're gonna do. They're so anxious to be rich, they deserve what they get."

Frank leaned over closer to Elias. "You got any money in the bank? If you do, get it out. Real soon there's gonna be a big depression. The stock market's gonna hit bottom. Nobody will have any money. Lots of people are gonna be hurt by it. Lose their land cause they can't pay the taxes."

An invisible fist grabbed Elias's heart. Lose the land? No money for taxes? How could he lose his land? He was the land. The land was him. There was no delineation. Grandfather, father, and he, the son.

"Those in the city will starve," Frank continued. "Some of the farmers will ride it out without too much damage."

Elias wasn't hearing any more. He wasn't sure he was

breathing. He wasn't even aware of Frank staring at him, wondering where his attention was.

"Well, I'd better get you home, Li."

Frank's words echoed through the room twice more before Elias recovered. He helped Frank load the few things stacked on the porch. They tarped them over with the oilcloth from the kitchen table. "So where are you going?" Elias asked.

"There's only a few places that won't be affected by the war." Realizing what had slipped out, Frank stopped and straightened. "There's gonna be another war, Li. Bigger than the Great War. A lot bigger. The whole world will be dragged into it. All for power and money. I told you they'd do anything for money, didn't I? None of the destruction will happen here in the states but it will pull the best from it. The youngsters you see in town will be leaving and only a few will be coming back. It takes a lot to pay for war. A lot of suffering. A lot of crying. A lot of tears. Be thankful you don't have young'uns, Li."

Frank pulled on the crank and the truck woke with a chug.

"How long you gonna be gone?" Elias asked as they lurched along.

"Going for good."

"What are you gonna do with your place?"

"Thought I'd sell it to you, Li. You can lend it out to someone young and strong. That way it won't cost you nothing to keep."

Elias's throat tightened. "How much you want for it?"

"We been friends for, what, near fifty years, Li? Good friends deserve good deals. You can have it for one twenty-dollar gold piece. It's worth twenty times that."

Elias stared at the dash in hypnotic distress. *This was the last he would see of a lifetime comrade. That was bad enough, but twenty dollars?*

Frank stopped the truck back near the barn so they wouldn't wake Sadie. Elias motioned for him to wait and headed for the house.

The screen door opened quietly. Elias had oiled it for just such an occasion. He knew now where all the squeaky boards were, too. There in the old chimney hole between the kitchen and the parlor, that abandoned hole for the smoke pipe of a long-gone parlor stove, was an old tin box. He moved aside a metal cover and took it out. He stole back outside and there in the moonlight laid a twenty-dollar gold piece in Frank's hand.

"Good thing you've been saving," Frank said, weighing it gently. "It's an old one, too."

"It belonged to Pa. Wages for fighting in the slave war. Sadie and I have been hanging on to it just like Pa did."

Frank nodded and put it in his shirt pocket. Then he rummaged around in the back of the truck.

"Here, give this to Sadie. It's a music box my brother brought back from Europe. I won't be needing it. I'm sorry I couldn't be the kinda man she wanted."

They both stood there, four weathered hands on that same box, touching hearts, trading unspoken memories, feeling the unsayable, sharing their hurt.

"You'd better stay here tonight," Elias said. "The sheriff will be looking for you soon."

Frank tugged a blanket from the truck. "I'll share the barn with Dina." Hanging it on his arm, he looked up at the moon. "I destroyed the machine, Li. People shouldn't be doing things like that."

There in the pallid light, Elias watched his friend walk to the barn. He looked like a battle-weary soldier plodding home.

As quiet as a house mouse, Elias put the music box on the table and went to bed.

Sleep seemed impossible. Youngsters that raced around on their bicycles and played in water puddles, gone forever. Hard times coming. Those with no money losing their land. What would he and Sadie do without this farm? Gramp's farm, Pa's farm, their farm. And the twenty-dollar gold piece. Sadie would be mighty upset. He didn't know why he'd given it to Frank. He really didn't want the place. It would be another burden. Maybe he just wanted his friend to have something to remind him. Something to ease his scarred mind. He had helped Frank recover from his brother's death. Dodging all those bullets in Europe, only to come home and die in the woods when a load of logs rolled on him. It would've been easier if Frank hadn't been the one to find him. They had leaned on each other then, and now Frank had something to hold in his hand and think back. Maybe Sadie would understand that. Maybe.

Fatigue finally won out and his eyes closed. But not for long. The backfire of a car some distance away, woke him with a start. The sun was just peeking over the horizon and the sound of a motor got steadily louder.

He had his pants on and suspenders up when someone knocked at the door. Sadie wasn't up yet but there was no doubt about her being awake. There on the kitchen table, beside Sadie's music box lay the deed to Frank's farm with a twenty-dollar gold piece on top of it.

Elias slipped it back in its hiding place and stuffed the deed in his pocket. The knock came again.

"I'm coming. I'm coming."

Elias looked out through the screen door. Halsey was standing on the porch. He pushed his way outside. Frank's truck was gone.

Halsey stuck his thumbs in his belt and huffed out his chest. "Where's Frank, Elias?"

"Let your eyes tell ya. He ain't here."

"I was just over to his place. I followed his tracks all the way over here. So where is he?"

"You have pretty good eyes Halsey, to see them tracks this early."

"Well, that's what I did."

Elias stretched some life into his limbs. "Then I suggest you go back out to the road and follow them same tracks south. He stopped here last night and said he was leaving and not coming back. I ain't seen him, nor his truck since."

Halsey's chin jutted out. "I might just check in the barn?"

"Go ahead. Be careful though. When Dina gets woke up this early, she kicks." Elias went back inside, letting the screen door slam for emphasis.

Sadie came into the kitchen in her nightgown just as the sheriff's car shuddered out the drive. "What was that all about?"

"Looking for Frank."

"Should've known."

"Well, he's gone, Sadie. Gone for good. Left this box for you."

Sadie pulled her apron from its usual hook. "Mailman left off this letter for you yesterday. You and Frank took off before I could give it to you."

Elias recognized his own handwriting. How had that ad read that Victor showed him? How to become wealthy in one month? He ripped it open. There in Frank's hand it read, *Put an ad in the paper just like I did.*

Elias's mouth curled into a gentle smile. Then he remembered the deed. It was signed and legal. He kinda wished he hadn't oiled the screen door hinges. He would've heard Frank enter and said goodbye. Or maybe thank you would've been better.

"What've you got there?" Sadie asked, briefly interrupting her caressing the satiny smooth box.

"The deed to Frank's place."

"What are you going to do with that?"

"I'm gonna mortgage it. Gotta have something to pay for my trip to Chicago."

Sadie heard him, but the statement was too far-fetched to entertain.

Yes, Chicago would be far enough away that they hadn't heard yet. Plenty of wanna-be-rich people there, too. He could tell Victor he was planning on buying a tractor. That would be acceptable. Then, when he got back he'd change his mind, give the money back and not buy the tractor. After all, hard times are coming.

That Summer

IT ALL STARTED that hot summer day. Or should I say, the summer ended that day.

The mowing machine chattered away, shearing the field, into neat windrows of thick fragrant timothy. Dad rode the seat, reins in his lap watching the grass fall. Not much to do except add weight. Without him on the machine its wheels would slide, unable to drive the oscillating knives in this thick grass.

At the end of each row he stepped on the pedal, raising the long cutter bar. A definitive clatter of empty knives told the horses to side step in unison, line up with the side row, and start again.

The cutter bar dropped. Dad sat back on the seat. Tom and Jerry clopped along, their huge bodies swaying gently. Everything looked good. Sunny weather, tall grass, well-operating machinery.

Dad was watching that new pitman arm working the heavy load when he heard the muffled thunk. A sound that reached has ears and stabbed his heart.

Jerry stumbled, then bobbed, trying to jump.

Dad hollered "whoa" out of instinct alone. In just two steps he was in front of his precious team. Jerry held her front foot high. Her eyes wide with fear and pain.

Dad's hands ran up and down her thick leg. His fear

turned to burning anguish. That woodchuck hole there in the ground under her belly had gotten both bones.

No man is ever prepared for this. What to do? What to do? His mind raced for answers. He couldn't panic. He had to make a plan.

Tom twitched and shook himself. He knew something was wrong.

Dad yanked off his belt and strapped Jerry's front legs together so she wouldn't apply weight to the break. Then he released all the harness. Tom's nervous prancing could knock her down. Now came the difficult part. He had to leave her standing there in the field alone.

Courtney heard his father yelling. He stepped to the barn door and saw Tom trotting toward him with Dad running along behind, holding up the evener. "Go down in the field," he screamed. "Go down and hold Jerry still."

"What for?" Courtney asked.

Dad stopped Tom in front of the wood sled. "Just go." He couldn't bring himself to say it. An injury of this magnitude meant disposing of the animal. Dad quickly chained Tom's harness to the sled. It was made to roll logs onto so its low profile would be helpful. He frantically searched the barn for the tools and equipment needed to execute his plan. Two axe handles, rope, blankets, liniment, and rags were dumped on the sled.

Dad rode the sled back. When he arrived Jerry was laying on her side. "How'd she get down," he shouted.

Courtney looked frightened. "She just sat down on her back side and flopped over. I couldn't stop her."

He preferred the blankets being under her but first things first. The leg had to be aligned and splinted before any major swelling set in. That would severely hinder the placement of the bones.

Courtney stood beside him. His voice quavered. "Do you want me to get the…"

"Get the axe handles and those ropes," Dad snapped.

Splinting the leg was no easy task. Just her foreleg weighed seventy-five pounds. "Okay, Geraldine," Dad cooed. "Lay still."

The team were brother and sister, named after his great aunt and uncle. Dad's father gave them to him when he got the farm. Dad just couldn't deal with the name Geraldine so he shortened it to Jerry. Only on serious occasions like this would that true name come out.

Her massive leg lay on Dad's lap as he rubbed it and wrapped it in rags, securing them with his shirt. Then he tied the axe handles on each side, checking the alignment of the knee. He loosened and retied the splint knots several times. It looked strange having such a big animal putting implicit trust in something one-tenth her size.

Dad and Courtney spread a layer of blankets as far under her legs, shoulders, and thighs as possible. Tom eased forward on the ropes tied to her good legs and she slid over onto the pile of blankets. Then ropes tied to the corners of the blankets allowed Tom to ease her backward, up onto the sled. Dad put the vertical log-holding stakes into their pockets and lashed an outrigger to each of them. They resembled the mast of a sail boat. Then he tied her legs to the outrigger so they wouldn't drag. Jerry seemed rather relaxed, almost enjoying the ride to the barn floor.

Ma and Courtney did the evening chores while Dad fashioned a lifting device. Block and tackle, harness and straps, chains and blankets, worked their way into the mechanism.

A one-ton straight lift was easy. A ton of nervous fragile horse on her side took some engineering. Even a lowly milk stool figured into the design. Temporarily lashed to her front leg, it prevented her from drawing it under for support as the contraption slowly lifted her up.

Late that night Jerry hung from the hay barn rafters in a belly and shoulder sling. Her rear section still held its own weight.

Dad sat on the milk stool rubbing the bared leg when Courtney came out with supper. The splint needed adjusting as the swelling gained.

"How's it look?" Courtney asked.

"Lotta swelling. Lotta heat."

"Coming in soon, Dad?"

"Yeah. Let me wrap her up."

It was before dawn when Courtney thought he heard the kitchen door squeak. Was that the metallic click of the rifle bolt closing? Just a dream. Just a dream. Sleep took over until the stove griddles rattled.

"Where's Dad?" Courtney yawned, pulling up his suspenders.

Ma gave a huffy grunt. "Go get him. He's in the barn."

Courtney looked over at the empty rifle rack and vaulted out of the house. The barn door flew open. The peg where the shovel hung stood barren. Then came that sharp crack way down in the field. Courtney ran like a wild wind. He stopped to cross the fence when he saw Dad drop the dead woodchuck into it's hole and bury it over. He waited there by the fence and they walked back together, discussing how to handle the workload without Jerry.

Their carriage horse, Molly, handled the dump rake and tedder. Tom pulled the hay wagon as long as the loads were moderate. Everything seemed to take longer than normal.

Dad fashioned a special hinged splint for Jerry. Padded

wooden slats conformed to her leg. Adjustable fabric straps secured it.

He would let her sling down until her feet touched while he did morning chores. He said it was good for circulation. Then the splint came off for a visual check and a poultice pack. Infection was a big concern. When the splint was back on he repositioned her support straps. At lunch time she'd get another reprieve from the sling. Dad said it allowed her innards to work. He didn't know the technicalities of lymph movement and blood circulation. It just made sense.

Supper gave her another opportunity to stand while she ate and drank. Dad would change the blankets on her sling and comb her down. He said it let her skin breathe so she didn't get sores. Simple intuition made up for a lot of science.

Then one night Dad was changing Jerry's sling blankets when he heard Tom thrashing around in his stall. Maybe he was jealous of all the attention being heaped on his sister. Dad went to tend to Tom but he wasn't about to be soothed. He wanted out of his stall so Dad backed him out. Tom lined up on the door to the hay barn and went right through an opening only big enough for a man.

Dad was frantic. Jerry was out of her sling. He didn't want to yell for fear it would make her jump. He followed and found Tom standing beside his sister just as they would be in full harness. After they had conversed in their own way and enjoyed each other's company, Dad took Tom out through the big doors and back to his stall. Tom quieted nicely, satisfied that his sister and teammate was doing well. After that incident, visitation became part of the schedule.

Summer was over before Jerry finally came out of the

barn. Dad had her putting weight on the leg previously but this was her first walk around. Every few minutes he had his hands on it checking the heat. Then came short walks in full harness. Each day ended in a hoof check and a leg rub. Dad put the milk stool down and Jerry would lay her big foot on it.

He knew all was well the afternoon he put the milk stool in front of her and she put her good foot up on it. That was one of the few times anyone heard him laugh. He slapped her on the shoulder. "Well, Geraldine, I guess you're going to be all right." She would have her strength back for winter logging and spring sugaring close behind.

Dad accomplished what few men had. But it wasn't for notoriety. His team was here for him and he was here for them. Partners, comrades, loyal friends. A real team.

From that time on, Jerry couldn't leave the barn without Tom. If there was a one-horse job to be done, Tom did it. Jerry didn't mind his absence at all but Tom assumed a protective role. He would always be beside his sister. If you took her, you got him, too.

It was the next fall when Dad took a load of potatoes to town that the store owner made a comment. "You did

a good job there," he said. "Just a half step down from impossible. Which one of them had the broke leg? I can't recall."

Dad dropped onto the wagon seat and shook the reins. "I can't recall either," he said as his big team strode out of town.

Higher Education

THEY BOTH TOOK refuge under the awning at the rear of the beer tent. A cutting summer sun turned the fair grounds into a barbeque pit. Here, they were out of the sun and out of the crowd.

Everyone came to the county fair. Everyone except Ma. Everet and Dad were tired of acknowledging all the neighbors. How's the family? Good haying weather. Hot today. Been a dry summer. Back here no one felt slighted and they were entertained by the loud laughter and lies a load of alcohol could wash out.

There was still time to see a few other things before Dad went back to buy some silky chickens. Colored eggs should bring a premium price at the market.

Skirting the farm equipment and ducking under a few tent ropes brought the pair out near the auction block.

They moved closer to get a good view. The auctioneer corralled the attention of a large audience with his rapid banter. "Eighteen, do I hear nineteen?"

When Everet saw the horse on the auction block, he was mesmerized by such a stately animal. His head hung and Everet could instantly feel his crushed spirit.

When the horse saw Everet his head raised. Their gaze locked. There was no turning away.

"Eighteen going once."

He yanked at his father's arm. "Dad, Dad, I wanna buy that horse."

"What do we need of a horse?"

"Please, Dad. Please."

"Eighteen going twice."

"I'll pay you back. Honest I will"

"Nineteen. Do I hear twenty?"

He'd never seen his son act like this. Jumping around like a child in need of a bathroom.

"Nineteen going once."

"He can help us log that steep part of the sugar woods where the tractor can't get. We'll sell wood. I'll pay for him. You'll see."

"Nineteen going twice."

The horse was nodding at him. A slow rhythmical nod.

"Dad, please. You gotta help me. I got two dollars here." Everet waved it in front of his father.

"Son, you don't know anything about horses. Where ya gonna keep him? Besides, what'll Ma say if we bring home a horse we don't need?" His hand rose in a high gesture and the auctioneer pointed at him.

"There's twenty over there. Do I hear twenty-one?"

Everet literally vibrated with excitement. Dad winced and shook his head in disbelief. Maybe someone else would bid higher and get him out of this mess. Then he noticed the two of them staring at each other. Their heads nodding in unison.

"Twenty going once."

Everet was almost as tall as he was. He suddenly wasn't a youngster any more. Maybe this wood cutting idea had some merit. Extra income had been his goal.

"Twenty going twice."

Silky chickens and colored eggs were just a pipe dream, a mere whim compared to firewood. Everet had the size and strength to carry it through.

The auctioneer opened the card with the reserve bid on it. Bidding fell injuriously short of $100. He looked over toward the sideline. The man in the grey fedora nodded almost indiscernibly.

The gavel snapped. "Sold for $20."

Everet shoved the two dollars in his dad's pocket and pushed through the crowd.

Dad just stood there, watching his son vault onto the horse and wave. "See you at home Dad. I know the way."

Someone tugged on his arm. He looked down expecting to see a youngster. There was a hat about even with his elbow. It tipped back to expose a sparse array of teeth clamping the end of a cigar.

"Ya kin pay da 20 bucks over dare at da window," the little guy growled, holding up a ticket.

Handing his money though the opening, Dad wondered how that short fellow found him in the crowd. He patted the $2 in his shirt pocket. Just enough for refreshment. This day had turned totally around so fast. This could solve a thirst problem and give him a chance to share a few lies of his own.

Ma saw something large flash by the window. She hurried out to see Everet in front of the barn, dismounting a horse.

"What in the savior's sake is this?" she asked.

"This is a horse, Ma. His name is Tugger."

"Very good, but may I remind you, Mr. Paul Revere, that we have a farm to run."

"Very well, Mam," Everet said, pulling an imaginary hat to his waist and tilting forward. Tugger put out one front leg and bowed as well.

Ma huffed and stormed back to the house. What sort of advantage would a horse be anyway.

When Dad arrived, Everet had the old stall cleaned out, the young calves rearranged, and a big pile of hay moved to access the stall door.

At supper, Everet expounded on his grand plans for earning Tugger's position.

"He's not a work horse," Ma insisted. "He ain't built for pulling."

Dad knew she was right, but Everet had what every young man needed. A reason to stretch out.

Ma pulled the last few strokes of the brush through her hair and turned down the bed covers. "Still don't know what we need of a horse."

Dad pushed his trouser straps off his shoulders. "Probably don't," he said. "But logging off that steep section is a good idea. There's plenty of good firewood up there." He nudged the pillow and swung his feet into bed. "Everet's got a plan and I'm gonna let him try it. Should prove what kinda man he's gonna be. Winning or losing ain't the big thing here. It's how hard he tries."

Tugger adapted quickly to his new surroundings. Everet fitted him with a breast plate instead of a pulling collar. It was better suited to Tugger's strength and saved the hair on his front shoulders.

Using the old washout for a road quickened matters and soon the crew had a good pile of logs to work with. Dad marked and helped drop trees while Everet trimmed and cleaned. Tugger couldn't help much with the splitting and stacking. He stayed close by, nibbling at the grass. He was never very far from Everet. No need for fences.

That proved valuable one moonlit night. Dad woke up when he heard whinnering and stomping. Door slamming and gear grinding soon followed.

Ma yawned. "What was that?"

"Just the guard dog watching the wood pile out by the road," Dad murmured.

Ma sat up quickly. "We don't have a dog. Do we?"

"No," Dad answered. "We've got Tugger."

"Oh, yeah. I forgot," she wheezed and fell back down.

When Dad and Everet were out in the field Tugger hung around the yard.

If someone stopped to inspect their wood for sale, he hurried right over, closely supervising any activity around their hard work.

True to his word, Everet made the wood business work. He and Tugger harvested a good wage.

To continue through the winter Tugger needed better shoes. The farrier arrived with all his equipment tucked into a pickup truck. Dad walked around the vehicle several times. He always parked his old Buick out behind the shed. Buick never made a truck. His was a car with the back cut off and a wooden bed added. Wooden spoke artillery wheels identified its age.

"Used to be Mr. Pierson's horse," the farrier said when he saw Tugger. "Right smart animal," he added, pumping the forge. "His son was riding him. Even had a trainer. Advising him on how to do things, ya know." With one big foot between his knees, he held the nails in his teeth. It still didn't prevent him from talking. "Son contracted that tuberculosis stuff. Never did recover."

He set the last foot down. "I guess Mr. Pierson didn't recover either. Couldn't own the horse no more. Kept reminding him of his son." He closed down the forge and set his apron aside. "Too bad really. He's a right smart animal."

Everet handed the farrier his money. "What's so bad about it?"

"Well, being a show horse and all."

"Tugger's perfectly happy right here," Everet replied.

Dad just watched as Tugger nickered and shoved his head under Everet's arm.

That was one of the few times the farrier had nothing to say. All that was heard was the sonorous groan of gears as he drove away.

Later that night, during barn chores, Dad saw Tugger go out the stall door. "Ya left the door open. May have ta fetch your horse," he said to Everet as he passed.

Everet picked up his pail of milk. "He'll be back. Just gone down to the brook for a drink."

Dad stopped. "How do you know?"

"'Cause he's thirsty."

"How do you know?" Dad insisted.

Everet just shrugged and continued.

Later when Tugger returned, he put his head over the stall rail. Everet pulled out a rag and wiped his dripping chin.

As winter forced it's way into the area, the wood road got more defined. Deep snow made off trail cutting difficult so the team worked on their side road stacks. Finished product was sledded up from the main landing.

Dad observed the team efforts with a confident smile. Even Ma felt good about Everet's accomplishments. She used the kitchen window as a periscope to progress. The two of them coming across the field, swaying along, log in tow. She never said so or even hinted at it but she marvelled at how those two worked together. Tugger had no reins. Not even a halter, yet he knew precisely what to do.

Dad was cleaning the barn when he heard the big stall door open. Everet closed it behind them and hurried right by.

"Gotta call the vet," he snapped. "Tugger stepped on a branch and drove it into his foot."

Vilas leaned against Tugger's belly with one front foot tucked between his knees. Using large tweezers he probed around in the puncture wound. He felt the horses shoulder muscle twitch against his hip.

"That hurts," Everet said.

Vilas raised one eyebrow. How could Everet know that? He was on the other side of the stall. He couldn't possibly see.

A packing of salve and a fabric sock finished the job.

In the darkness, Dad escorted Vilas to his truck. Taking his money, Vilas stood there for a moment. "Do you really think your son can feel that horses pain?" His stern look demanded an answer.

How could he explain it? Would he tell him how they worked in the woods without saying a word? How Tugger didn't need a bridle? The numerous times they knew just what the other one wanted? This man worked with animals of all sorts. He should know. Surely he's seen this kind of bond before.

"Well, Vilas," Dad said, "was he right?"

Vilas tried to remain inscrutable. Never before had anyone dumped it back in his pasture. He could always dismiss or discredit an explanation with a huff or a scoff but now he lay under the microscope.

"Was he right?" Dad insisted.

Vilas closed the door and thrust his head out the window. "Let me know if any infection sets in."

Dad watched that new '49 Chevy pickup slip out into the road. "Don't worry," he muttered to the disappearing tail lights, "We won't."

Tugger took a week off and then the two were back in the forest. A good spring melt exposed a few stragglers. Dad warned of an icy trail but the first two trips went well. The team went up for one last load with a promise to be back for evening chores.

Dad hurried through the milking, grabbed the lantern and ran for the forest. Freeze thaw weather turned the skid road into an ice slide. Ma stared out the window at the closing darkness. The logging team was no where in sight.

Dad wasn't too far from the house when a big dark shadow came flowing toward him. It didn't have the swaying motion of towing a load. He was relieved to see Tugger but where was Everet?

Tugger walked right by him with an unusually high step. Everet lay on his back the wrong way. His head on Tugger's rump and no load behind. Dad slid open the heavy door and Tugger went right into his stall, dripping wet and breathing hard. When he pulled at Everet's arm to slide him off, Tugger leaned into him, pinning him against the wall.

"Okay! Okay!" Dad wheezed, "I won't take him off. I promise." He patted Everet's face. He was still breathing. He shook his shoulder. No response.

Ma came in the milk house door.

"Get the doc!" Dad yelled. *"And some blankets!"*

Ma ran with a fear she'd never known before. She feverishly dialed the phone. A slip on the front steps couldn't interrupt the mission. A sprained ankle and a bruised knee went unnoticed.

"Doc, come quick. Everet's hurt." Before the phone hit the cradle she was gone. On the way back to the barn she realized she hadn't told the Doc who or where she was. Why worry about that now. There's only one Everet in the area.

133

Dad untangled the harness, hanging it on it's hooks. What could possible bend the anchor rings like that. It would take a good team to tear those heavy tug straps. But there they were, ripped and dangling.

Ma dropped the pile of blankets on the salt bin. "Doc is on his way. Let's get him to the house.

"No," Dad said. "Moving him will cause more injury. Help me get him dried off."

Doc blew his horn and Dad ran to get him. Doc looked surprised to find his patient lying backward on a horse. He checked pulse, breathing and lifted an eyelid. "We'll have to get him to the house."

Dad was firm. "He stays right there, Doc."

A doctor doesn't take instructions from others. He grabbed an arm to pull and suddenly felt a huge hip squeezing him against the stall wall. "What in the horns of Halifax is this?"

"I told you, Doc. He stays there."

"How am I gonna work on him way up there," Doc wheezed, taking an inventory of his ribs.

They all watched in silence. Tugger pulled his legs under himself and sunk right down on his belly.

Doc was shocked. "How'd that horse know what I said?"

His knife slid up the back of Everet's shirt, exposing a heavy bruise in the lower lumbar area. The pants and belt fell victim to Doc's blade.

"Where was he?" Doc asked, massaging the bruise.

"In the woods," Dad admitted, trying to swallow his guilt. "Tugger brought him out."

Doc pulled off his stethoscope. "I find no blood in the lungs. Kidneys are still in place. There is paralysis in the legs. Right now he's unconscious. No apparent damage to the head so I don't know why. I can't tell any more without x-rays."

Ma's voice quivered. "Is his back broke, Doc?"

"X-rays," Doc repeated, closing his bag. "Watch that bruise. If it starts looking nasty call me. Til he wakes up, that's all I can do."

"What do I owe you, Doc?" Dad asked, holding open the door to his '48 Pontiac.

"How about a cord of firewood?"

"Consider it done."

That big straight 8 motor sounded smooth and capable, pushing a big car out into the darkness.

Dad would never forget that moment. Doc's face looked old and sullen in the pallid glow of the car's interior light. His soft slow words welded in his mind. "It's gonna be a long, hard road."

Ma covered her son with blankets. Arranging them carefully. She smoothed back his hair and for a moment She let her firm protective demeanor fold back. She kissed his cheek. Facing Tugger, she straightened his forelock and put her tear-stained face against his nose. "You know him so well. Tell him to stay with us. You tell him that, Okay?" She wiped her cheeks, and raised that strong inner spirit again.

She turned around and unexpectedly ran right into Dad's embrace. "What are we going to do?" She said settling against his chest.

"We're gonna have to wait. Just wait." She heard his voice quaver. "I should never have let them go up there."

Ma felt Tugger's nose against her back. "I guess he knows what we're saying."

"What makes you think that was Tugger?"

She looked up at Dad with renewed spirit. "Ya think that was Ev?"

"Message delivered. I'll take the night shift. You go take care of that ankle you're limping on."

For three days, Tugger never moved. Dad curried him down, inspected for bruises, changed his water, and put out grain to a cast statue.

That torn tow strap hung on the harness rack. How many times Dad stared at it, wondering how Tugger managed to snap it and free himself from the load. He inspected the accident site long enough to reenact the whole thing in his sleep. He couldn't tell if Tugger slipped or Everet bailed off, coming down that steep slope. Either way, the log landed across Everet's back and rolled over him.

By the way the snow was all torn up, Tugger must have laid down and pushed himself sideways, using his back as a plow to pile up snow. Then he somehow maneuvered Everet onto the pile and slid under him. It took a degree in engineering to accomplish the task.

Adding it all up, reinforced the fact that, in the face of tragedy, Tugger would not leave without him.

After numerous times, moving arms, repositioning his head, massaging his limbs, something happened. Those sleepless nights, imagining the worst, praying for the best, rewarded. The fourth day, Tugger moved forward and sniffed his oats. It had to be a sign and Ma responded with avid vigor. She soon had an arsenal of utensils and a supply of nourishing gruel, warm and ready. Her heart leaped when she spoke to him and he sighed. Dad hurried in to watch him raise his head and eat a few bites. He took a drink. A beacon of light in the consuming darkness. Finally, Tugger took an interest in moving around. Two days later Tugger delivered Everet to the front porch. He may have been able to sleep inside but Tugger insisted on a portion of the day where he could supervise the progress.

Then came the day a neighbor arrived in a station wagon to take Everet to the hospital for x-rays. Tugger put up big fuss, pacing around the car, interfering with every effort to load Everet. He wouldn't respond to Everet's reassurance of return.

When they left, Tugger just stood there, watching the big Packard disappear. There was no settling down. He paced the yard, round the barn, back to the road for another long survey. No one understood his anguish. They had taken his previous master away in the same manner. Even with persistent promises of return, he never did. Now it was happening again. Animals don't comprehend the need for hospital visits. His beloved master was gone. The correlation was real. Another spirit rupturing loss. If only he were human he could cry but he had only to pace and tread to manage the great storm within him.

Finally the car returned. Tugger heard it first. What a time getting Everet back in the house. They had to wait for Tugger. Who would argue with 1200 pounds of determination. He filled the entire tailgate. Sniffs, rubs, and hugs eventually verified his condition. With Everet inside, be assured that Tugger guarded the house constantly. No sudden disappearances during his watch.

Tests didn't reveal any verifiable damage but spinal injuries were unpredictable at best. Dad found a wheelchair so Everet could move out onto the new spring grass. It helped for a while but the reality of limited mobility soon eroded his spirit. With Tugger's encouragement, Everet cleaned up his school assignments for graduation.

A big party on the lawn lifted his spirit. His classmates came. He and Tugger wore silly hats and posed for photos.

Soon the sadness returned.

Ma watched him from the kitchen window, slumped in his chair. Tugger grazing beside him, contented to have him there. Many ideas of future prospects did inspire him for a short while. Dad could still hear Doc's voice saying, "It's going to be a long, hard road."

Returning from town, Dad stopped the old Buick right in front of the porch. Now that was unusual. He walked over to Everet with a big box in his hands. "Here's your next assignment. This is all the store receipts. This is the file and this is the ledger. The store owner complained about not having time to record all the transactions. I told him you had plenty of time and were willing to help. Pays a bit less than cutting wood but promises to be a lot safer." Dad turned for the house. "He wants it back tomorrow afternoon. I'll fetch your lap board."

He didn't want to look back because that would be preparation for disapproval but he did risk a glimpse. Tugger was nodding his approval.

The scheme worked, but it kept Dad ratcheting to and from town. Tugger seemed contented even though his exercise was limited.

Ma thought she kept a good watch on matters from her window until the day she looked out to see the chair on its side. One wheel turning slowly.

Dad heard her yelling, way up in the hay loft. She charged toward him. "They're gone! They're gone!"

For a moment he shared her panic. "Okay, so what do I do?"

Her arms flapped in all directions. "Go find them. Quick!"

"Calm down. Now think. What do I tell them when I

find them?" He looked into her wild, frantic eyes. "Who brought him home before?"

"Look there," he said, pointing toward the field. They both watched with fear and amazement. They wanted Everet to progress so what was the big issue? Had he made a bigger step than anticipated? It could be frightening and exciting as well.

Dad recognized Tuggers high step. The same one he used to bring Everet out of the forest. The mechanics of it smoothed out his stride so his rider felt very little bounce.

"Hi, Ma," Everet called out with more enthusiasm than they'd heard since the two of them met. "Tugger took me down to the brook."

Dad waved. "That's great son. Just stay around the house. Supper will be soon. And don't fall off!"

Ma's jaw dropped all the way to the bib of her apron. Dad swallowed hard. How did that animal know so much?

With Everet draped over his neck, Tugger pranced away with a ride smoother than a Cadillac. And easier to steer.

A saddle was now in order. One with a slightly modified, higher back support. Doc ordered a brace for added support. It had to be a girdle affair to be effective.

With all pieces in place, Everet took on a new vitality. He rushed through his accounting with Tugger anxiously waiting for duty.

Again Dad watched in amazement. But why should he be amazed. He saw Tugger do it when Doc first examined Everet. That horse just collapsed right down on his belly with his feet under him. Everet wheeled over, grabbed a handful of mane and pulled himself up belly first. With more squirms and grunts than an Olympic wrestler, he was in position.

139

The two of them spent a lot of time traveling the area. At supper, Everet would relay all the intriguing days events. Then one evening he announced that he and Tugger were going to the fall county fair. No surprise there, until Everet casually added that they were competing in the dressage competition. Dad almost swallowed his fork. Ma sat there, hypnotized by the salad.

Dad retrieved his fork and cleared his throat. He'd seen horse dancing once. He knew it to be very involved, disciplined, and difficult. "Have you considered the scope of this project? Do you know the movements?"

Everet Spoke with confidence. "Tugger does."

Dad's face instantly aged ten years. "It takes a lot of practice and precision."

"We've practiced it quite a bit."

"You're stepping into a very professional area of riding. I want you to be prepared for quick and hostile rejection. Competition can get aggressive. Especially when you're considered an intruder."

Everet nodded.

At bedtime, Ma thrashed around trying to rearrange the blankets over her. "You know he can't do that," she snapped.

Dad pulled at his socks. "Well then, why don't you go and tell him that. Those two have done some impossible things. I wouldn't put this out of their reach. Besides," he added, "I'm gonna be right there to make sure nothing gets out of hand."

Dad said practice and that they did. Out in the shade of the forest and at every available moment. The library was sparsely populated on the subject but determination produced some literature. A riding stick and a loop in Everet's boot allowed him to pull his leg up and over for a cleaner mount.

Just about the end of chores Dad would see the two ballet dancers coming across the field in a high step prance. It looked pretty good.

One afternoon Dad looked out and froze. When his heart finally verified what he saw he sprinted for the house.

"Ma!" Dad hollered. "Look!"

The two were coming across the field. Tugger limped severely, dragging one front foot. Everet, almost suspended by Tugger's neck, was walking. It was by no means a decisive step. He literally threw his hip forward to make a leg move. He looked like a string puppet but he was walking. How should they react to such a sight? Praise their son and lament the horse? And which one comes first?

Dad grabbed the chair and pushed it up to meet them. Everet slumped down, totally exhausted.

"Go get the vet," he gasped, wiping his tear-stained cheeks. Ma pulled out a clean cloth while Dad sprinted for the house. Tugger quickly passed him doing his stiff-legged short-stepped trot.

Everet changed color. In an instant, he went from chalky to crimson. "I've been set up!" Everet yelled. "You rascal!"

Tugger whinnered, bobbing his head. Dad broke out in unbridled laughter. It felt so good to have something go right. This horse truly had to be the best one in the whole world.

Ma, hands on hips, shook her head in disbelief. Tugger came over and put his head in Everet's lap.

"Why should I forgive you? Scaring me like that!"

That night, Ma pushed the pillow up in a pile. "Will that horse ever stop doing crazy things?"

Dad swung his legs in and pulled up the sheet. "I hope not."

141

It seemed like a fair trade and soon became an established routine. Tugger would work on his lessons and Everet would walk most of the way across the field. What started out as an extremely rigorous lean and swing maneuver refined into a hip sway that still relied on Tugger for the majority of the support. The two worked as hard on the walk as they did on the dance. You might say that Tugger was right there to support him every step of the way.

When fair time arrived Ma packed her choicest jar of pickles. That satisfied her end of the bargain. If Everet could work to compete, she could, too.

Dad waited with Everet in the registration line. A large well-dressed man appeared beside him. Dad tried to ignore him but who, on a day like this, would wear a suit?

"You entering the dressage competition?"

"Na," Dad said. "I'm just waiting to get some cotton candy."

The suited stranger completely ignored the sarcasm. "This used to be Mr. Pierson's horse. That's him over there in the grey fedora. He hired me to teach him the dance." He also managed to overlook how Everet supported himself heavily with Tugger's bridle. "He didn't need me anymore when his son passed away. Horse wouldn't work with anyone else. I'll see you at the show. Mr. Pierson should be there as well." With a stabbing wave, the suited stranger folded into the crowd.

Dad looked at Everet. They were both confused by the interruption. What did this guy want? There had to be some motive. Everet seemed unconcerned but Dad took it as a warning. Professionals can get protective when their title faces a challenge.

With grandstand tickets sold out, Ma and Dad, and many others gathered along the side rails. Dad's stomach soured when he saw the first performance. He'd never seen Everet's and Tugger's moves but these guys were good. How could his own advice to his son seem so out of place. "Don't consider the others. Just go out and do your own kur just as you designed it. Do your best and the judges will do the rest."

Everet and Tugger were the last ones called. Just as they entered the field, Dad heard a voice beside him.

"He has some stiff competition."

That stranger in the suit stood there. Couldn't he find someone else to persecute?

As the team waited for the music to start, Tugger stared at the audience. Was he looking at someone in particular? Someone he knew?

Tugger pranced to the swing of the music, slowed into a high-stepping trot, and then a trot in place. His diagonal step carried right into a double pirouette.

"Great execution, but the rider is too stiff." The suited stranger remarked. "He should flow with the horse."

Tugger loved to trot at a diagonal. The judges called them flexions. In mid course, he swapped to a double temp change that made him appear to be skipping like a child. He cantered into a full-body swivel that continued around in a full circle without losing a step or speed. The whole audience breathed a sigh. In a still stately standing position, Tugger started swaying his hind flanks to the beat of the music. At the drumbeat he kicked first one rear leg, then the other. A few in the audience stomped their feet in unison.

Then came the fox trot. One step forward, one step left. Then one step back and one step right. A springy step that brought applause. They finished with a high-stepping prance in a circle with his head toward the center. It looked like his feet were crossing over each other. Another well executed pirouette at a full trot brought him right up in front of the judges stand. The crowd burst into loud applause as Tugger bowed to the judges.

"Great show," the suited stranger yelled over the noise, "But he needs a better rider. Way too stiff and he didn't post with the pace. He won't take first place because of it."

Soon they announced the first place winner. It wasn't Everet and Tugger.

"See," the stranger remarked, "This team took last year's state championship. Naturally, the judges are on their side."

The first place team rode up to the judges stand. The rider dismounted and stepped forward to receive his blue ribbon. He pinned it on his chest, remounted and waved to the applause as he rode away.

Dad looked hard at Ma and turned to the stranger. "Is that the accepted method?"

The stranger nodded. "Proper protocol."

They announced Everet and Tugger as second place winners. They rode out to a voluminous applause. Tugger walked with a swing step, feet flailing in a wide arc. It was a cute stride.

"Oh no," Dad groaned. Ma held her breathe and stared.

"What's the problem?" the stranger asked.

"That's my son. He's paralyzed. He can't get off."

The stranger pulled at Dad's arm. "I'm sorry. I didn't know. I didn't know."

Tugger lined up in front of the judges. Tugger sunk down on his belly. Everet hooked his riding stick in his boot and pulled his leg up and over. Tugger turned his head so Everet could use the bridle for support. The audience watched in total silence. Even the speaker system that crackled with the wind, was quiet.

Everet stood straight and proud in front of the whole group.

The master of ceremonies snapped around, conferred with the judges, and returned to the microphone. "The judges have decided upon a tie for first place." He handed over a blue ribbon. Everet didn't pin it on himself. He hooked it on Tugger's bridle. Then laying on Tuggers neck, he hooked his boot and pulled it back up over the saddle. The straps of his back brace showed stretch marks in his shirt. Everyone watched in total silence. Tugger rose to a grand applause. He bowed to the judges, turned and bowed to the audience. This maneuver now became an accepted part of protocol and brought a standing ovation from both audience and judges.

"Now that's sportsmanship," the stranger yelled over the din.

"That's my son," Ma yelled back.

All the other contestants rode off the field. Tugger headed for the sideline. He passed right by Ma and Dad and stopped further down the line. Tugger turned his head. Everet released the blue ribbon and handed to the man in the grey fedora. "Tugger wants you to have this. He won it for you."

The stranger clamped onto Dad's arm. "You know that horse could win a lot of medals. With my help he could be a champion."

"I suppose he could," Dad said. "But what value is a cabinet full of medals and ribbons? You can't sell them and they're soon forgotten." He pointed toward the disappearing horse and rider. "What that horse has done will never be forgotten. He gave me my son back. And look over there at your former employer. What do you think is in his heart right now? That horse already is a champion. Wouldn't you agree?"

Dad took Ma's arm and yanked free of the stranger. "Let's go check on your pickles. I believe I have two champions in my family."

When Ma and Dad arrived home, Tugger wandered around the lawn, free of bridle and saddle. Everet sat at the kitchen table, deep in thought. Ma started rearranging the china in the closet to make room for her blue ribbon.

Dad sat down next to Everet. "Excellent work today, son. We're proud of you. You've made a lot of progress."

"Not enough," Everet said pushing a letter toward him.

With apprehension, Dad read the letter. "Why, this is a letter of acceptance to the college."

Ma almost dropped a precious piece of china. She recovered, faked a cough and smiled.

Dad cleared his throat. His heart couldn't take many more jolts like this. "How, how, how are you going to manage this? I mean how are you going to afford this?"

"I've applied for grants. With a small bank loan, I should be able to cover it."

Dad despised loans. They were far too risky. A difficult year could cause a man to go bad on his word. Unthinkable. Just unthinkable. Everet's injury forced him to hire help and dissolved funds set aside for a better car. "What about Tugger?"

"He'll come with me."

Ma's china tinkled again. She closed the door to avoid any further percussions.

With days passing quickly, Everet struggled with his walking. Tugger might be able to get him to the buildings but there were stairs and classrooms.

Miracles were still arriving on time. Everet found a tight

but neat apartment just off campus. A small empty shed in the rear cleared the way for Tugger. At least his residence off campus. A sizeable back yard lent room to move around and a stockade fence for entertainment. Tugger enjoyed looking out and watching the flow of life.

At college, Tugger got immediate attention. Enthusiasm for his presence bonded the entire freshman class. How, of course, could a horse of notoriety possibly avoid horsing around. He delivered his passenger with a high-stepping prance or a cute angled trot. Everyone watched whenever Tugger marched up to fetch Everet. It was as if he owned a watch, arriving right on time. He would lie down, let Everet mount, and march away with a plethora of intriguing steps that captured attention from all those around. Many planned their exit to enjoy his antics.

Since administration was mildly opposed to his presence, the students absorbed the challenge of keeping him out of sight during classes. Occasionally he would peek in a classroom window, disrupting everyone. Lots of giggles ensued but a sociable fellow just couldn't resist participation.

Many ingenious hideouts appeared where a horse could wait until classes ended and taxi his rider home. The camouflage project blossomed to upper class members and soon Tugger was the center focus of a campus Hide a Horse project.

Administration finally concluded that, even if it opposed the view of the student majority, It was causing a distraction. They met with the entire student body to clarify their position. During the Dean's address, a student jumped up and shouted, "He's our mascot!"

An immediate standing ovation dismissed all opposition. Tugger was now a student body elected member of this scholastic institution. A raffle and donation fund soon financed a suitable shelter for a 1200 pound mascot. Rides on Tugger added a considerable amount.

Warm summer days found Everet doing his work on the campus lawn with Tugger close by. Tugger's moves and wanderings usually went unnoticed but this time he nodded his head and nickered. He watched a girl pass by. She wasn't paying attention to him. In fact, she never gave attention to anyone. She always appeared to be in a hurry. They called her Mopsy because of her hair style. It looked like a dandelion puff. Not very becoming, but she didn't mind.

"A girlfriend?" Everet chided.

Tugger snorted and returned to the grass.

When football season arrived it was naturally necessary for the school mascot to be there. Everet rode onto the field dressed in uniform and helmet. Tugger had a drape of school colors and a custom made helmet with two holes for his ears to poke through. He lead the team onto the field with one of his dance steps. Just before game start he ran out to center field and bowed to the opposition.

Whenever his team made a touchdown, the band sounded the trumpet charge and Tugger reared up, both front feet punching the air. When the team got into a tough position it was natural to call a time out. Tugger would run out onto the field, put his head in the huddle, then run back to the sidelines. The plan always worked and the home team would surge ahead.

At half time, Tugger entertained the crowd with his numerous dance steps. He followed the band around the field, marching and turning to the music. Everet seldom rode. It was Tugger alone putting on his own clown show. He had a band-style hat and white booties to match the band shoes. After the game he pranced out to center field and bowed to the opposing team.

Soon the games were the talk of the town. Businesses closed at game time so everyone could attend. Why stay open. Everyone was at the field. Even the opposing team audience filled up with those who heard about Tugger.

Coach quickly became a celebrity and the college walked away with the state championship. A big celebration meant a team photograph. Everyone kneeled in a row with their helmets under one arm. The quarterback had his hand pinning the ball to the ground. Everet wore his uniform. Tugger had his helmet with his ears sticking out. They stood behind the quarterback. Just before the camera snapped, Tugger put his foot on the quarterback's shoulder. That special picture permanently resided on the inside cover of every yearbook from that day on. Tugger truly was a mascot, teammate and clown.

During spring break three of Everet's classmates went home with him. It was a boisterous three days with constant noise, activity, and competition. Who was first to the table. Who got the biggest piece of pie. First to the door and last to sleep. They sparred, jostled and joked about everything.

One day they were wrestling on the lawn. Tugger supervised all outside activity so he watched the proceedings.

One of them decided to involve Everet so he laid across him in what seemed to be a harmless position. Everet feigned a struggle. Tugger grabbed Everet's assailant by the britches and dragged him off. The tussle abruptly ended.

Tugger couldn't distinguish pretend from reality. That young man sat down rather slowly for supper. Tugger must have got a hold on a little more than the britches.

Supper involved pushing down large amounts of home cooking.

"Remember the time we hid Tugger in the bushes," one of the fellas chided between bites.

Another spoke up eagerly. "Yeah. Old lady—I mean Miss McAllister, took her botany class outside to show them all the flowers."

The first one swallowed hard and cut back in. "She was expounding on all their Latin names and derivatives. Tugger must've thought she was talking to him."

Not to be outdone, the third fella pushed ahead, giving the others a chance to take another bite. "Yeah! She turned around and met Tugger, looking at her through the bushes. The whole school heard it. Sounded like the fire alarm went off."

The first one added. "Scared her something awful."

"Scared her!!" The second one said. "Scared poor Tugger, too. He took off."

The third one muttered, "Boy, I'll say. You shoulda seen what he left behind."

Ma cleared her throat and introduced dessert.

When the crew returned to classes Ma and Dad felt the whole house settle back down on its foundation. They made a solemn vow never to be a teacher.

The next football season saw even more antics and even greater crowds. Town talk and business hovered around the games. Everyone knew the roster.

Tugger lead the home team onto the field. He had no rider. He was already clown enough and needed no encouragement. They lined up on the goal line. The opposite team lined up on their goal line. At the trumpet charge they ran toward each other, keeping their line straight. Right at center field they stopped abruptly, shook hands and filed off toward their sideline. Tugger stood there, looking both ways. Then he bowed to the opponents and trotted away.

Half-time antics were a celebrated feature. Baton swinging, the band marched onto the field. With a band leaders hat and a high-footed step, Tugger marched right along behind them. At midfield they stopped and split down the middle. Tugger marched right through the middle and continued on down the field. When he realized they weren't following, he turned and ran back. Coming up behind the leader, he started mimicking him. When he pumped the baton with his right arm, Tugger pumped his right leg in unison. When he changed to his left arm, Tugger changed legs. Soon the bandleader realized he was being copied so he pumped both arms. Tugger looked left, then right. Using his nose, he knocked his hat askew.

Tugger turned and the band leader mounted him. With a baton-swinging rider, Tugger marched away with the band in tow. He turned full circle and so did the band. He marched sideways, they followed suit. He skip stepped, and trotted in place. He turned to face the band and on the last note, the leader lofted the baton. Tugger held his foot in the air. They held that last note for a long time. Finally the leader tapped Tugger on the neck. Tugger dropped his foot, the baton dropped and the music stopped in unison.

Football couldn't be mentioned without reference to Tugger. Even Ma and Dad came to watch. Dad left the old Buick a good ways away and they walked in.

This game found the home team slightly behind at the half. When the band played the cheerleaders went out on field. Tugger went out with them, a pompom on each front foot. Mopsy led them out. She had never been part of the group before and neither had Tugger. He followed them rather well. When they shook a pompom he shook a leg. They swayed their rump, he did too. They threw their pompoms in the air, He looked over at the home bench and shook his head.

No one expected the next part. Not even Everet. Mopsy snapped the pompoms off his feet. Tugger sunk down so she could mount. She stood on his rump as he rose. After a short turn and dance, she dropped down into a riding position.

Leading Tugger down field with a high -step prance, the rest of the cheerleaders spread out. They knelt down and laid back on the grass, lined up like ladder rungs. Mopsy pulled Tugger around and pranced right toward them. The audience gasped as he ran right over them, stepping in be-tween. They all sat up, waved and lay down again. Tugger ran right back over them again. The crowd roared but all was not over. Mopsy steered Tugger over to the band, yelled something to the leader and trotted into the end zone. Just as they squared up on the field, the trumpeter sounded out the battle call and the entire band yelled, *"Charge!"*

Mopsy put her head up to his ear, sunk her heels in his ribs and said, "Prancer, git."

Those words burned into his heart. Tugger's blood turned to fire.

Not many had seen a horse race. Not many had seen a thoroughbred run but they were about to.

Tugger pulled both front feet, sunk on his haunches and lunged into the run. It felt so good to stretch out and he gave it all. Every muscle fought for more, demanded more. Mopsy pushed him faster. Come on more speed. Faster. More speed.

In five strides, he crossed the 50-yard line. They turned at the other end and the whole crowd shouted *Charge!"*

Tugger put his very soul into the run. Everything he had. Everything he could muster. The mind doesn't know exertion. It only calls for more.

They slowed for the end zone and trotted back to a huge cheering crowd. Mopsy searched the bleachers. There he was in the top row. A satisfied grin crowned by a grey fedora.

She slipped down, slapped Tugger on the shoulder and ran into the crowd. No one saw her run to Everet. No one saw her hook an arm around his neck, kiss him on the cheek, and say, "thank you."

No one knew it, except Everet. He just stood there overwhelmed. Watching that run made him feel exhilarated. His muscles felt challenged, as if he himself made the run. Now his cheek burned. It tingled with a sensation he'd never known before. This could be downright frustrating.

In the second half, the home team dominated their opponents, doing more than they thought they could. Everyone went away energized. Everet felt good but confused. What did this mean for his heart? First time experiences as potent as this were always confusing. He'd never been introduced to contact or touch. Especially from a girl that could ride like a windstorm. He hadn't considered himself desirable. He couldn't run or dance. Stairs required handrails and long distances required Tugger. Speaking of Tugger, how did he know her commands? That high-step prance right over those girls! And that vibrant run!

But wait. He'd been tricked. That's right, tricked. Centering on himself blurred the proceedings. That's why he had missed the obvious. "Tugger? Did you have anything to do with this?"

Tugger snorted and gave a little skip step.

"You rascal. Enjoyed yourself, didn't ya. Okay, I concede. I'll start running and dancing just like you do."

Tugger broke into a fast prance.

"Okay, okay, we'll practice. Especially with the dance coming up. As long as you don't get too flirty with the girls. I have enough to do without chaperoning you."

Tugger sunk down to let Everet off in front of his apartment. Then he dutifully strode through the side gate to his backyard respite.

"And someday," Everet said to a retreating rump, "you'll have to tell me where you learned to precision prance and step over five people. Remember, we keep no secrets."

It kept revisiting him without announcement. Her arm around his neck. The pressure of lips on his cheek. Things like this can interrupt one's concentration. Enjoyable but annoying, with all the accounts to record, class work, Tugger's exercise, and now dance practice. At least he didn't have stable chores as well. The neighbor willingly took care of that. He had the best garden around, with award winning produce to market.

Dance practice happened constantly. On the way to the bathroom. Getting dressed. Anywhere no one was watching. Everet felt he was ready but he wasn't sure for what. As long as the music was slow, he would survive.

Lights strung all over campus brightened the walkways littered with people. Music spread out over a large lawn populated with swinging bodies. Tugger followed Everet's wanderings among students and faculty. He strayed once to investigate some giggling in the bushes. Looking in, he was met with a scream. He quickly caught up with Everet.

154

The smell of alcohol wasn't pleasant anyway. Everet felt safe avoiding a crowd. Being at a distance, he could change directions if someone approached him for a dance. Besides, it gave Tugger room to move. The pair watched dancers sway to the lively saxophone.

At a quiet interlude, Mopsy appeared. She stepped right up to Tugger, shook out the cape she was carrying, and tossed it around his neck. Snaps in the front and a white carnation made him look like he was wearing a tuxedo. A stretch cord held on a miniature top hat. "May I borrow your dance partner?" she said to Everet.

She quickly spoke to the band and waved Tugger forward. A gap formed on the lawn when he moved toward her. A sonorous saxophone played a soul stirring Tennessee waltz. When Mopsy flowed toward him with raised arms Tugger lifted his chest. She swooped back, and he lowered his shoulders, raising his rump.

Everyone stopped to watch. Some even sang along. *I remember the night and the Tennessee waltz.* She step turned. He did as well. At her swinging arms, Tugger circled with a side step, keeping her in the center. The music pulled them together so close she put her head on his chest.

Everet shuddered. He himself felt the touch. He suddenly realized he was swaying to the music right along with everyone else. But to him it was more than that. He was dancing. He was dancing with her. It hit his ears hard enough to penetrate his heart. *I was waltzing with my darling the night they were playing the beautiful Tennessee waltz.*

The two bowed to each other just as the song ended. A generous round of applause provoked Tugger to bow to the audience and the band. Mopsy ran over to Everet with a skipping bounce, hooked an arm around his neck, whispered, "Thank you," in his ear and planted a kiss on his cheek. Not just a quick peck, but a lasting presence, and then she was gone. Her hair brushed his face. Her voice hung right on his ear.

One of his classmates landed an arm on his shoulder. "I didn't know your horse could dance like that." The young man appraised the silence. "You don't look so good. Is there anything I do? Maybe a shot of whiskey? Or a slap on the back to restart your heart?" With a quick laugh, he released his grip and strode away.

Everet remembered very little about the rest of the night. There in front of his little apartment he took off Tugger's hat and vest and guided himself inside. He hadn't been drinking so why did he feel drunk? He fell asleep with the music still welded in his brain. *I remember the night and the Tennessee waltz.*

There weren't many events left before graduation. Very few opportunities for Mopsy to carry out her sneak attacks. He'd have to be more prepared because Tugger wasn't giving him any forewarning. Duties flooded in and graduation day galloped right up.

A beautiful summer day demanded outside ceremonies. The football field bleachers were filled both sides. A stage and sound equipment occupied the end zone. Students lined the front of the stage, forming a solid block of school colors. Everet paid close attention to the call roster. There was the name he waited for. Helen Pierson. Mopsy was Mr. Pierson's daughter.

As a special amendment to the exercise, They awarded Tugger a diploma for leadership and sports participation. Draped in school colors and a mortar board with his ears sticking through, he trotted up to accept his diploma.

As the band played, Tugger skip-step trotted beside the

line of parading students. Audience applause encouraged a dignified bow before he rushed to catch up with the group. Everet mounted and Tugger hurried through the crowd. Everet wasn't sure what his destination was. Or what he was pursuing with such determination.

There she was. Tugger ran right up and put his head against her back. "All right," she conceded, pulling off her mortar board. She kissed him on the forehead and rubbed his nose. "A graduation present."

"Helen," Everet said. "Helen Pierson." The words felt smooth and rhythmical. "You must know Tugger well. You've run with him, danced with him, and graduated with him."

"I knew Tugger before you did."

Why, yes. How foolish of him not to recognize the name. He hadn't considered the history of Tugger's previous owner. "So where are you going from here?"

"Home, I guess. Why?"

"I thought you might like to meet my folks." That sounded too much like a date. Easily declined. There must be a valid reason for such an offer. "Since they're related to Tugger, you know."

Now that sounded even more ridiculous. This is how one makes an obvious fool of himself.

She paused and shrugged. "They're probably the other side of campus by now."

He had a definite maybe. At least it wasn't a total rejection. Why was he so slow at thinking? So illogical? "You could ride with me?" Everet's demeanor sagged. "I guess that's kind'a crazy with you dressed the way you are. Sorry. I'm not thinking well at all."

"Don't be so certain," she said pulling at her robe. It fell away to reveal a plaid blouse, jeans and riding boots.

Everet stared. *What's next? Should he scoot forward? Would it be too much weight for Tugger? What should he say?*

Tugger took care of the details. He sank down and rose again with ease. Her arms were around his waist. His heart rate doubled. Surely she could feel it pounding.

"Let's go, Tugger," Helen said, pushing her heals into his ribs. "Take us to Everet's Ma and Dad."

Tugger confidently strode away with a gentle walk.

"You must be an accomplished rider," Everet said.

"Not really."

"That run at the ball game told a different story."

"My brother spent all his time with dressage so my Dad and I would invent duties and distractions for him. Then I'd get a chance to take Tugger out for a real stretch. He loves to run but his heart won't allow extended exertion."

They caught up to Ma and Dad before they got to their car. Dad felt good about that. Helen wouldn't see his rugged old makeshift truck. Small talk and hand shakes alerted them to Everet's future interests.

"Gotta go," Helen said. "My ride is expecting me."

"Can I take you back?"

"Oh, no. It's just around the corner over there. Thanks for the ride." Wrapping her arms around his neck, she kissed him long and hard, right on the mouth.

When she stepped back, Everet almost fell over. "Graduation present," she said.

Everet was trying to regain his internal balance as she giggled and skipped away.

Again she ran away, leaving him confused and flustered. Every time a bigger shock. Every time an emotional tsunami.

Tugger nickered as she disappeared from view. "I totally

agree," Everet said. But considering the circumstances, and how all this just happened to come about. It mimicked the same pattern of the last trick. "You set me up again, didn't you? You rascal."

Tugger snorted and turned his head away.

Armed with his CPA license, Everet took on several new clients. He rented the entire lower floor of the residence he was staying at, and hung out his sign. A bigger living area meant room for an office, files and a window out into Tugger's yard. Lots of things fit nicely into place. He enjoyed watching Tugger graze and occasionally look out over the fence to ponder social movements.

Why was he bobbing his head? He was inviting someone over for a visit. Why, it was Miss McAllister, the teacher he frightened. Students called her a spinster but she was a fine looking lady. Tugger thought so too and now they were making friends. Another person closed in on the conversation. It was Mr. Pierson. He paused for a cordial greeting. Tugger collected his acknowledgments and watched the two of them trace a course for the coffee shop.

"You rascal," Everet muttered, sliding back in his chair. He pulled out a ledger with all the figures and calculations. It would be tight right now but with business expanding he was confident about his plan. He whistled to Tugger, patted him on the nose, and walked toward the center of town.

He slid into a chair and waited for the bank manager. Appraising the customers as potential clients, there was definitely the need to learn a new skill. That of interviewing applicants for expanding his own staff.

The bank manager stiffened. "Well, we don't regularly lend this much on such a tight margin."

Through the glass partition of his office, he saw Mr. Pierson pass by. Recognizing Everet, he looked at the bank manager and nodded.

"But I believe you have a firm grasp on your situation." He pushed the ledger back to Everet. "I'll have all the documents waiting for you in the morning."

That Friday afternoon, Tugger and Everet rode home for the weekend. Saturday morning, just after chores two vehicles drove in the yard. Dad met the owner of the Ford dealership just as he got out of the new 1954 pickup truck. He handed Dad the keys and waved to the man in the rear vehicle.

Dad didn't see the men wrestle that big box out of the back. He didn't hear them negotiate the porch steps. Cardboard and crate in hand, they got in the second vehicle and created a dusty trail toward town.

"Dad, look at this!!" Ma exclaimed.

"I am," he said, touching the door handle as if it were a newborn. A steering wheel with no cracks. Seats so smooth. A shiny black spare tire anchored to the side of the bed. It had a chrome wheel cover, too. He closed the tailgate. It latched firmly. He shook it to be certain. Sky blue with a white top. He could hardly breathe.

"Dad!" Ma yelled. "You gotta see this!!"

His hand reluctantly left the V8 insignia on the hood.

With the old wringer washer pushed over in the corner, a brand new breed of machine occupied its position. Sleek square cabinetry with no protruding lever. A stylish rear control panel with "set it and forget it" features.

Ma took all afternoon to read the owners manual and move the controls. She wouldn't plug it in until she understood the cycles. There was a chance of setting something in the wrong position and causing damage.

An exciting weekend made the soft slow Monday ride back to work memorable. With cooler weather arriving, Everet set up a table in the back yard, keeping his records and being with Tugger. He recognized that intuitive little nicker as Tugger moved toward the fence. Helen came down the street and Tugger's bobbing head invited her over for a visit. Everet set his work aside, guiding her across the street to the coffee shop. Her schedule allowed only a brief visit but it gave him time to study her new hair style. A chance to see her walk away. *God, she was beautiful.*

Everet took Tugger for a walk around campus. It would be regaining its hyperactivity soon. They stood side by side, watching the football tryouts. Dusk invited them back through town. Some turned to watch. Most didn't. They were accustomed to Tugger's clop clop clop step. If they did look, it was just to verify the source.

The mailman left Everet off at his Ma and Dad's home. He walked in just as they were finishing breakfast. "What brings you home son?" Dad asked, reaching for his coat.

He was casual and disciplined, cementing his composure. "Tugger passed last night."

Dad just stood there, one arm in his jacket, like a plaster statue, frozen in time. Ma sat at the table rubbing a spot on her apron. It wasn't soiled or wrinkled. She just kept rubbing that spot. Her lower lip trembled. Everet put his hand on her shoulder. It was the first time he had ever touched his mother.

"He was at peace," he said.

"Well," Dad said, staring at the ceiling. "I guess we have some work to do." His voice quavered only once.

"Everything is arranged. Tugger will be interned beside

Mr. Pierson's son. His first owner. Helen and I thought it appropriate."

Everet helped Dad with chores. Then he stood there for a while in Tugger's stall, touching all the events of the past. This is what Tugger felt like when he lost his master and friend. Before he and Everet met. Maybe someday, Everet thought. Maybe someone will come along and buy him and absorb this crushing pain.

Even if it was a grey day, it didn't rain. Dad parked his truck right in front of Everet's office and they all walked over together. Businesses were closed everywhere. The college canceled classes so all could attend. No one questioned why a memorial for an animal could shut down an entire town. Anyone who knew Tugger knew why.

Mr. Pierson set a special headstone with a carved relief of a prancing horse. Both names Tugger and Prancer were there. Miss McAllister braced herself on Mr. Pierson's arm. Helen looked very disciplined. She made eye contact with no one. Not even Everet. She kept the servants alerted to special needs, managed traffic flow, flower arrangements, and monitored her Dad's condition. For the majority of the services, he concerned himself with Miss McAllister's needs.

Days flowed by and activities carried on as usual. As usual as they could. Something felt out of balance. Like a picture puzzle with pieces missing. Everet found himself glancing out the window to check on a now vacant spot. A habit that would be hard to overcome.

Loud stomping feet on the front steps grabbed Everet's attention. The football coach stormed in, planted himself in front of the desk, and dug knuckles into his hips. "Have you seen what's happening? Something has to be done," he demanded. "The team has totally lost interest. They're gone with the wind." He waved at the ceiling. "The bleachers are empty. A junior varsity high school team could easily beat us." He raised his arms as if offering a sacrifice. "I can't inspire them at all. This next game we face one of the toughest teams in the state. We're gonna look like a bunch of drunk monkeys." His arms dropped but he dared not turn around. "We need Tugger."

Everet swallowed hard. "I have an idea. Let's go talk to the dean."

A few days later signs appeared all over town. Tugger will be at the game. The next day they were all over campus. Even under heavy interrogation coach feigned ignorance.

Bleachers filled. People crowded the area. In the locker room coach eliminated his pregame pep talk. "Well guys, I promised you Tugger. Well, here he is. Tugger 2."

Two guys came in. The first wore a horses head, complete with helmet and two ears sticking up. The second had his head buried in the back of first man's waist. A blanket of school colors covered the difference.

Everyone laughed. All fell silent when Everet came in wearing his uniform. "Why do you laugh?" He asked. "Isn't he still here? You did it then and you can't now? He encouraged me to walk. He taught me a lot. What did he teach you? Let's go show them what we learned. And remember Tugger."

Tugger 2 ran out onto the field in a sideways canter. The crowd fell silent. The team lined up both sides of him and bowed to the opponents. They turned and bowed to the home crowd and the trumpet sounded the battle call. Everyone yelled, *"Charge!"* Tugger 2 raised his front feet and pounded the air. Then he ran off the field and the game started. Both teams fought hard.

At half time Tugger 2 imitated the cheerleaders. When they laid down in a line he came charging at them, stopped and stepped over each one carefully. Then he went charging away doing a turn and dance.

The audience loved it and the home team went on to hold their opponents scoreless.

Now, with only one minute left in the game, the home team controlled the ball. They were 60 yards from the goal line. Time for one more play. Would they try for a long pass or attempt kicking a field goal? The opposing team sent two players back to cover any long pass.

Coach called time out. Tugger 2 ran out to join the huddle and add encouragement. "Okay," the quarterback growled. "You end men, run like you've never run before and remember Tugger."

The huddle broke and Tugger 2 ran off the field.

The captain of the opposing team noticed that Tugger 2 lacked the coordination he had when he ran onto the field. There was a man with a clean jersey in the backfield. They tried sneaking in a kicker. He waved the two deep men forward into the line. "Get the kicker," he yelled just as the ball snapped. The would-be kicker threw himself at the first wave of assault. The quarterback had only a few seconds. Backing up he set the ball. Hardly time to aim. He yelled *Remember Tugger.* Then with strength beyond himself, he launched it away.

Everyone gasped. The ball was in the air. Wherever it landed was game end. Coach stood ramrod straight, fists clenched, gritting his teeth. If willpower could keep the ball in the air it would never come down. Both teams stopped blocking, shoving, pushing. They just stood there and watched the ball rise. Everyone, except the end man. He ran for all he was worth. Just like Tugger, he himself

164

was making that mighty charge down field. The ball was coming down. It was beyond his reach. He needed more speed. Faster. Run faster. *Remember Tugger.*

He didn't remember stepping into the end zone. He didn't remember stopping. He turned around to see the referee's arms go up and the end of game horn sounded. Then the home side of the field exploded. People were jumping and shouting. Coach was deeply involved in a serious match of shadow boxing. Tugger 2 had both front feet pounding the air. He looked down. The ball was in his hand.

Everet surveyed the wild crowd in the bleachers. There was Mr. Pierson waving his grey fedora high in the air and Miss McAllister stitched to his arm. Helen was with them, bouncing and waving. What a beautiful smile. She waved to him. She said something. He could read lips. Those three words. His heart started punching holes in his ribs. He'd never heard these words before.

He walked by his Dad's pickup parked there in the front row. Down into town. Down the desolate streets by his office. Tugger's presence was still here. At the game. In the players. Even here in this yard where he used to look out at the passing world. He inspired, invited, tempted everyone to exceed their own limits. He himself being a prime example. How could he get over losing such a beautiful friend.

A special display case was being set up in the foyer of memorial hall. It wasn't finished but who would mind if he took a sneak peek. There were trophies, students handiwork, and photos of memorable faculty members. Those who gave special effort to the school. The entire back panel was a full stretch photo of the football team, all lined up, kneeling. Tugger stood behind them wearing his helmet with is ears sticking out and one foot on the quarterbacks shoulder.

A click of the door latch meant someone else just entered. Everet didn't mind. He knew all the faculty and security. He worked closely with the dean on this Tugger 2 project. Even the cleaning staff were all friends.

His heart swelled, crowding his lungs. Toward him walked the most beautiful girl in the world. "What brings you here?" He choked.

"Looking for you. Your Ma and Dad left without you and you weren't in your office. I figured you'd be here where Tugger was."

When she got close, he stiffened and backed a step away. "Are you gonna run away?"

"No," she said, looking confused.

"Every time we meet, you touch me and then run away." His voice quavered. "I don't think I can take two losses this close together."

Helen turned toward the display case. "I'm sorry. I had to do that. When brother died, Dad went into deep depression. He lost mom, then his son, then Tugger. I was the only one left. He was so afraid I was going to find a fella and leave him all alone. I had to be careful. That's why the crazy hair style. So I wouldn't be attractive. If he found out I was interested in you, he might've had a relapse."

She turned back toward Everet, Looking into his eyes. "Did you see him at the game today? He's never waved his hat like that. Miss McAllister showed up this morning with a coffee cake. They went to the game together. When I got home, they were in the den. Dad was telling her about his childhood escapades. Like the time he fed beer to the neighbor's chickens. They were laughing like grade schoolers. I left to give them room."

She stepped up close to him. "I believe Daddy is okay now. I don't have to be careful anymore. I can be with you." She reached for his hand. "If you want me."

He took her hand and she sunk into his chest. The smell of her hair. The warmth of her embrace. She wasn't going to get away again.

This must be how Tugger felt that day at the fair when he and Everet first met.

"That night at the dance?" Everet confessed. "When you danced with Tugger? I danced with you, too."

"I so desperately wanted to be at that dance. I had to be certain no other girl got her talons into you. I assured Daddy that I would only dance with Tugger. I made that neck tuxedo to convince him of my intentions."

"You made that? I still have it in my office."

"Yes. I made it. A girl has to have skills if she wants to be a wife."

She snuggled in deeper. "The blue ribbon you gave Daddy sits on the fireplace mantle right beside brother's picture."

"And the time you were a cheerleader. Your ride down the field," Everet sighed. "You looked like an expert." He glanced over at Tuggers picture. That rascal was smiling. He left them with so many things to remember him by.

Everet's stomach wrenched. "At the game I saw…" He heard her breathing. So soft. He swallowed three times to get that sticky lump to go down. "Helen, I love you."

There! He did it. Tugger would be proud of him.

Her voice vibrated against his chest. "Everet, I love you."

They both swayed together. They were dancing. Yes, they were dancing. Softly singing.

I remember the night and the Tennessee waltz.

Later, they would learn that Mr. Pierson, Helen's father, donated a statue for the front entrance of the college. A larger-than-life granite statue of a football player kneeling. One hand pinning the ball to the ground. Standing behind him a stately horse wearing a helmet with his ears sticking out and one front foot on the player's shoulder.

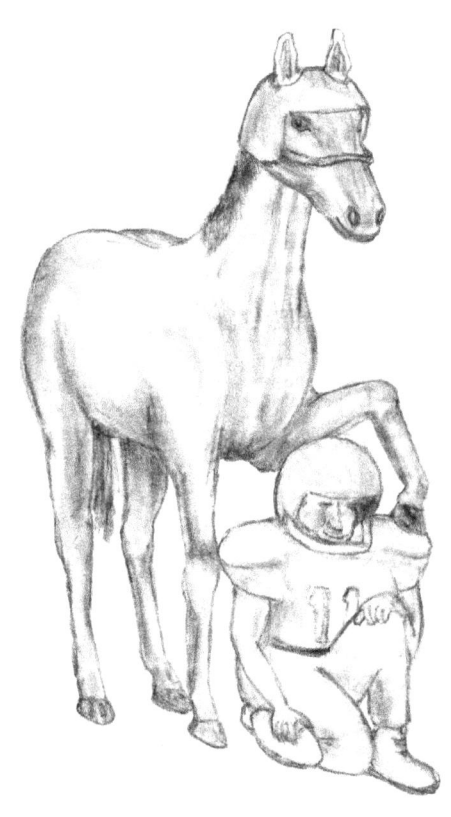

Last Trip to Town

CLANKING OF THE kitchen stove griddles below him sounded a morning alarm. Avery knew what to expect by the thick layer of frost coating his bedroom window. His toes curled up like sled runners when they hit the bare linoleum floor. He grabbed his clothes and hurried through the curtain at the top of the stairs. Any remaining heat in the parlor stove made dressing far more bearable. He had to be quick. If his mother caught him she would call him Tiny Whiny.

Avery wasn't small for his age. He could do a lot for twelve years old. Dad didn't mind if he used the stove to warm up his clothes, why should his mother. After all, their bedroom was downstairs right off the kitchen. Avery knew that his house was going to have a stove in the bedroom. And a big thick wool rug on the floor, too.

With the stoves chunked up, Avery and his Dad headed for the barn leaving Ma to rise and prepare breakfast. Anything left on the back porch was frozen, including their boots. Ma didn't like them inside. They smelled and left wet stains. One pair of socks and waxed bread wrappers didn't afford much protection. Fortunately the barn would be warm.

Bitter cold air burned the back of Avery's throat. Snow under foot had a crisp crunch. Maybe it was complaining about the cold as well.

"How cold is it, Dad?" he asked.

"Oh, 12, maybe 14."

That had to be below zero. Dad was a man of so few words that he rarely finished a sentence. But like any farmer he was a good weather reader. Living with the land meant being in constant touch with the elements.

Dad's casual glance toward the north corner of the barn suggested what the day's task would be. He had built a new wood delivery sled last fall. It sat there, tongue and end stakes sticking out of the snow like sentinels waiting for duty call. All that seasoned wood down across the swamp could be accessed easily with the swamp frozen solid.

They both hurried into the gratifying warmth of the barn. Only bitter cold could force Dad to do that. No smoking in the barn for fear of fire and no smoking in the house for fear of Ma required a slow transit between. He'd snatch a match from a pocket of his green plaid trousers, strike it with his thumb nail and coax a puff of smoke from an unwilling pipe. This morning didn't witness any of that.

Barn chores had a way of easing a person into a demanding day. A scoop of grain aroused reluctant cows to their feet. Clanking stanchions, shovel scraping gutters, clicking milk pail handles, warm milk hitting the pail. All pleasant sounds of a daily routine. The aroma of fresh hay and an opportunity to warm up cold boots. How could this be called chores?

Dad carried the milk to the house, one big shiny steel can in each hand and left them on the back porch for Ma to process after it cooled. They left their boots out there, too.

She had the stove roaring and breakfast ready. Ham, boiled potatoes and thick pork gravy. A working man's meal and an early heart attack. Avery loved the bread—thick bread slathered with rich salted butter. Breakfast was a good time for thought that could override Ma's complaining about the cold, lack of dry fire wood, or how much butter Avery used on his bread. He had to come up with a method of keeping his boots warm on that cold porch. Rocks behind the kitchen stove hadn't worked very well. Dad said they wouldn't but he had to try. Ma wouldn't allow them on the top burners. Besides, they'd get too hot. Behind the stove worked well but they cooled off long before morning. A long sturdy sock filled with sand should work. If it filled the whole boot it might hold enough heat. Then to put it in some strategic spot near the stove so it wasn't in the way. Aunt Nellie wore big heavy socks all winter. She might have a worn out pair he could work with. She was always a warm bubbly person. He liked visiting her. All the questions she asked him made him feel important.

Ma was sputtering about the days chores, stopping only to take a bite. She certainly made up for her husband's reticence. Dad finally conceded that he was going to take the cord wood out of the swamp.

"Froze well," he said.

"Good," Ma replied. "Finally get some money coming in. Hope that sled holds up. You spent enough on it. Ought to be made of gold."

Dad was a carpenter by heart and a farmer by compromise. He cut and fashioned the runners during the fall wood cutting. Every separator had to be notched and pinned. Two cord of beach logs weighed three ton. Dad robbed the iron from his previous sled to brace the tongue and reinforce the stake pockets. New bolts and stay chains were the only things he bought.

They put on their coats and boots, leaving Ma lecturing about the waste of money.

Tom and Jerry knew something needed their attention

when the stall door behind them swung open. With high steps, they backed out and lined up at the harness rack. Three-quarter-inch long studs on each shoe were great for traction on ice and snow but didn't work well on the wooden barn floor.

Dad dressed them with blanket, harness and collar, adjusting the straps and mane. These were his working partners. He talked to them more than he did the rest of his family. Jerry weighed a ton and her brother Tom weighed a ton-fifty pounds. A pair of titans worthy to operate a farm with.

Even the team didn't like the brutally cold morning. They pranced and stomped while Dad loaded the sled with chains, binders, axe and shovel.

The sled slipped along almost silently, following the two swaying bodies. Their feet pounding the snow with heavy thuds. When they reached the ice the thuds turned to sharp pops, leaving a dotted white trail. Bunches of swamp grass stuck out of the ice forming tiny tepees. The swamp looked like a miniature Indian village on a crystal plain.

Beach logs were heavy and rolling them on took strength and skill. Avery helped by blocking them when needed. Most of the time he just stayed out of the way. This gave him opportunity to walk up the tongue and adjust the harness or blanket on the team. Or was it a chance to put his hands underneath for their warmth.

Dad chained the load, checking all points carefully. This load was going to Charlands firewood distributors. He wanted no breakdowns on the way to town.

The team heaved into the load. Wood creaked and leather stretched. Dad rode the front tongue while Avery walked along beside the sled. He alternated between breathing through his mittens and hiding them under his armpits. It must be hard to be a horse because they could do neither. The team blew frosty breath as they chugged along.

It was going to be a good day despite the fierce cold. Avery warmed at the thought of seeing Charland's new Walkashaw saw mill. He'd heard about them replacing the old steam-powered flat blade with a new circular saw unit. Dad didn't like it because the gasoline engine made a lot of noise that frightened the horses. All the trucks moving around made them nervous.

That's what Avery wanted to do someday. Operate a mill. Or maybe the crane that unloaded the trucks. Or maybe both for that matter.

Dad stopped the sled next to the porch. He carried the processed milk to the shed and fetched his lunch box. Ma followed him out. "Now don't be stopping at the store, ya hear? There's plenty to do here. No sense wasting time jabbering and buying tobacco. *No spending money on tobacco!*"

Dad tugged his hat down hard. That was the signal. End of conversation. He had to be quick or the sled would freeze down. Even on ice and snow, heavily loaded runners warmed up enough to make water. Just one word, "come," and leather groaned.

Avery walked along behind the sled watching his Dad's pipe smoke waft over the load.

When Scribner's hill came into view, Avery ran ahead. A car or truck coming down would force quick action and put the team in jeopardy. One slip on this hard pull could cause an animal to fall and the load would pull them backwards. Dad had brake pins set in the front runners. Any emergency and he'd step on them, nailing the sled to the ground, taking the pressure off the team. A downed horse could mess up a lot of harness.

Tom and Jerry leaned into Scribner's hill, shortening and

173

synchronizing steps in unison. They were two years old when they came to the farm. A first anniversary gift from Dad's father. After twenty-two years of service one knew the other's every mood and move.

Avery waited for the sled at the top so he could follow it down. A pile of brake chains lay coiled up on the front of each runner. When the load started pushing the team, Dad would give the pile a kick. They stretched out under the runners, grinding into the ice, creating a friction brake. The ring on the end of the chain fit over a pin on the rear of each runner. When brakes were no longer needed, another kick of the front ring released the chain, the sled ran off them and they stretched out behind. Twenty feet of chain was heavy but Avery managed to gather it and pile it up on the front runner as the sled continued on.

Hills were always unpredictable and dangerous. Traffic ruts made odd width tracks for a runner to follow. The team was the only steering wheel so getting out of a prominent rut left a challenge. Colliding with frozen chunks sent shudders through the entire load.

No time to rest. Avery grabbed a shovel and ran ahead. Tyler bridge had to be snowed down before the load arrived. Wooden runners on a wooden bridge didn't slide well at all. Cradling the shovel in his arms, he breathed through his mittens.

Things weren't going to go smoothly now. Mort Allard's team was stuck on the bridge. His hired man, Willey, tried to make the bridge without snowing it down. Now he sat close to the other side, his team thrashing with the locked-down load. He only had on a cord-and-a-half load of stove-length wood but Mort's light team just wasn't up to it. So there, beside an exhausted pair of horses, Willey stood in his green plaid wool trousers. The same kind of trousers

Dad wore. Avery knew that someday he was going to have a pair of those green wool trousers. Maybe even two. They had to be warm at nearly three dollars a pair. And a pair of those fur-topped boots, too.

Avery quickly grabbed snow with his shovel and scattered it on the bridge. Dad would be here soon and expect the job done.

He heard the frustrated "Whoa," and the pounding of heavy hooves stopped. Dad stepped off, lit his pipe and went up to evaluate the situation. He never asked why Willey was all alone. Mort knew better. A man can't snow down a bridge and drive a team, too. Now a thin layer of ice bonded the sled even tighter.

Together, Tom and Jerry couldn't squeeze by the locked sled so they had to be uncoupled, led by and joined again.

"Just hitch on the end of the main shaft," Willey said.

Putting the teams in tandem was dangerous. They weren't accustomed to pulling in unison and they didn't respond to the same commands.

"Pull the tongue right off," Dad responded.

"Not a chance," Willey replied.

Reluctantly Dad complied, fastening his evener to the tongue. Tom and Jerry had just leaned into their collars to measure the load when Willey yelled, "Giddap." All lunged forward and *pow*, the tongue severed from the pivot plate.

Dad yanked his hat down. A quick brake loose like that could cause an animal to trip or misstep, hurting his partner. A bad jump or catch step with one of those huge feet will drive a sharp shoe cork into their own shin, lacerating the leg or tearing off a shoe. An injury that would take weeks to heal. Fortunately no damage was done to the animals.

He turned to Avery. "Get a brake chain," and motioned Willey and his animals aside. With the chain wrapped around the front crosspiece, Dad dropped his pin in the loop. He stepped in front of his team, adjusted a collar, smoothed a mane, tugged at a shoulder strap. They knew what this meant. Then he turned his back saying, "Come."

The team moved up against the harness, measured the load and leaned into it. The sled ripped loose with a soft thud and followed the horses over to the side of the road. They came up behind Dad. Tom nudged him in the back with his huge head.

"Leave ya with the chain," Dad said, lifting the pin. "Need it back tomorrow."

Avery finished snowing the bridge while Dad returned to his own load. It was well frozen down.

Again, Dad positioned collars, straighten straps, pulled on a top knot. Preparation for the task. Athletes take deep breathes and shake their arms. Horses, too, must focus their energy and synchronize. Now came the decisive moment, this measured a team and their owner. This is what people paid to watch.

The two treaded a bit, getting a solid footing, waiting. Then came the command, "Come." They slowly leaned into the collar. The pull had to be even or they would go into a worthless see-saw action. Shoulders bulged, necks lowered, front feet lifted off the ground in unison. Muscles strained and shuddered. Everything stood still for the longest moment.

Dad never looked back. He just kept walking away. Then came that slow groan and the sled started to move. The horses grabbed another footing and another. As the runners quickly shed their ice, the sled moved easier.

Dad stepped onto the tongue as they passed. Once off the bridge he lifted a hand, "Tomorrow."

Willey never answered. He just stood there in his green

plaid wool trousers watching Dad's pipe smoke wafting over a disappearing load.

Charland's big yard was ablaze with activity and equipment. It overflowed with trucks. Some being loaded. Some being unloaded. Conveyors spit firewood into large dump bodies. Cranes grabbed logs like big hands. Their cables lifted them with ease.

There were so many things to appraise. So much going on. Avery tried to study everything all at once. He didn't realize he was walking along beside the sled. He could've stepped into a cavern and not known it. Only when the sled stopped, did he awaken to his position. They were in front of the unloading ramp.

Dad stepped off and went to find Mr. Charland. Avery climbed the sled tongue and adjusted the horses' blankets. He stretched to see the cutting area. The whine of the big saw and roar of the trucks made the horses nervous. They looked so small and strange amongst all this equipment.

Dad was speaking with Mr. Charland when suddenly he yanked down on his hat and walked away. Mr. Charland followed and soon they were close enough to be heard. "Can't pay you more."

"Sell it myself," Dad replied, mounting the sled.

"You don't have a buyer for log length."

Dad took the reins. "Burn it myself." Then with a huff he said more than he'd said all day. "Your price ain't gone down. Why should mine?"

Avery drew back the blankets and jumped down. This may spoil his ever getting a job here. All this fabulous machinery may be just a vision of what could've been. It also meant a long walk home. He wouldn't be riding an empty sled. The horses were tired, too. A hard pull home wasn't something to look forward to.

A long moment of uncertainty passed.

"All right," Mr. Charland conceded. "Ten dollars. But this is it. *No more.*"

Dad released the binders and went to collect his money. This certainly was it. Dad's sled and team were the last to pass through the yard. Commercialism had embraced gas and steel.

Tom and Jerry strutted out with a high step, announcing the proud end of a fine era. A time when muscle and sweat were honor and dignity. A time when accomplishing a task, procedure carried just as much importance as the finished product. Only the eventuality of matters would prove that profits for pride is such a poor trade.

They were the only team in front of Driscoll's store. Everything else was iron. Every customer greeted the potbelly stove first. A saving grace for Avery's feet. A few glanced at his small frame in that big chair, his feet aimed at the loading door. Dad picked up his tobacco and a plug of chew for his best friends. They loved the molasses in it. A fine treat for a good job done.

Dad was catching up on the latest news when Avery left the stove long enough to appraise the jackknife case. He weighed the four cents in his pocket. Knives were ten cents. Well out of his reach. Further down the aisle, on a long shelf stood the fur-topped boots. The most beautiful footwear in the whole world, lined up like a platoon of soldiers ready for a parade. Temptation to touch overwhelmed him. He checked. It looked safe. He plunged his hand down inside one. Yessir, that fur went all the way to the bottom. Now that was luxury.

When all money matters were settled, candid old Mr. Driscoll spoke. Folks knew he wouldn't abandon an opportunity to address a matter even if it did alienate a customer.

'What's seen is louder than what's heard' was his motto. "Mighty cold out there," he said. "Your hired hand there tugged a lotta heat out of my stove just warming up his feet. Those old barn boots don't look hardly adequate."

Avery shrunk, unaware of being observed. It would be years before he noticed the mirrors over each aisle.

"All your wife spends on paper and paint," Mr. Driscoll continued. "Seems she could suffer for some well-deserved boots for a hard worker."

Dad never looked around. He yanked down on his hat and left with Avery in tow.

The road home was a quiet one. Dad on the front of the sled, hugging a brace with one arm and the reins with the other, Avery on the back, clamped to the rear stake. This was one of the few times he was allowed to ride. Log work had it's inherent dangers. Sledding did, too. No one could know that this time next year Avery's older brother Courtney would fall victim to a sled load of logs. Coming down off a hill and he somehow slipped off the front. Horses couldn't hold it back.

Dad crowded the edge to let a milk truck go by. Avery waved and watched him pass quickly out of sight. That's what he wanted to be. A truck driver. It would be warm up in that cab. He liked Tom and Jerry but iron was welded in his very soul.

Dad lit his pipe. A good long slow ride home left time for a man to ponder matters. Dad knew he was getting old. The horses were getting old. This way of life was getting old. With their other son's leaving the farm for reasons little to be explained, and Avery tracing the same trail, it left an unquestionable destination for the farm. Small farms just couldn't survive any longer. Carpentry jobs on the side were far and few between. Dad talked about a job at the

179

plywood box mill. He'd need a car for that. The buggy horse, Molly, left last fall. The team here filled in for her but not for daily trips to work. Lots of changes. Lots of uncertainties. Lots to think about.

They could see it in the distance, barking out a frustrated roar and blowing steam into the afternoon air. Silas got too close to the edge and dropped one whole side of his milk truck into the ditch. Dad stopped the sled well back and walked up to appraise the situation. Silas yelled out, "Can ya pull me? I gotta chain."

Dad looked things over, searching for a hitch point and pull direction. Things had to be done right you know. Proper procedure meant success.

Silas came forward with a chain. "Got a good load on. Gonna be a hard tug but I can help with the motor."

"Turn the motor off," Dad ordered. When all was quiet, he brought the team up, attaching the chain with care and caution. Silas pushed his head out the window. "I can start her up and help ya out."

Dad made the running board in two steps. "Want me to pull ya?" Silas nodded. "Then just steer."

Then came the routine. A tug at the cheek strap. Adjust the collar. Dad stepped back and said "Come."

They stomped and set their rear feet, then leaned into the collar. The truck slid forward in the ditch.

Silas said, "Ya know I can…"

That's as far as he got before he recognized Dad's nasty glower. This team pulled rocks and stumps in the field. A double try was nothing new.

"Gee," Dad said and the horses stepped left in unison. "Gee," again and they took another side step. Dad patted their cheeks, turned his back, said, "Come," and walked away.

They measured the load and took their stance. Tom thumped Jerry on the shoulder with his head. Then with acute precision they balanced each others strength. Tug straps creaked. Tom took a quick breath and Jerry matched him. Front feet tucked right up to their chests and they hung there. Rump muscles bulged and shivered. Avery swore he heard the chain biting into the whippletree. They hunkered down till their belly's almost touched the ground. Neither one would back off.

It sounded like ice crushing when the front of the truck lifted up into the road. The team grabbed another footing and heaved again. Sucking in air, they pulled again. Dad never turned around. He had set the distance and they didn't stop until they reached him. Jerry shoved him in the back with her head, pushing him a full three steps forward. Tom shook himself in approval.

Silas jumped out to help with the chain. "By golly, that was a good'un. Didn't think ya had it there for a while. What da I owe ya?"

Dad shrugged and took the two quarters Silas held out. Then he motioned toward his sled. "Don't start the motor 'til I'm back there."

The horses backed up to the sled when the truck roared to life. Dad and Avery watched the truck disappear into the distance above two swaying rumps. A frustratingly slow way of travel but it still felt good. Once more muscle ruled over metal.

The temperature went down right along with the sun. Twilight left them with the groan of leather, a rhythmic thumping of heavy hooves and an occasional grunt from a log runner crushing a chunk of ice. Chores were waiting and a warm stall for his team. They always earned their keep. Fifty cents for the rescue paid for tobacco. What a saving grace. Dad would've heard about it for days.

But things were changing rapidly. Giving up this way of life certainly wouldn't be easy. Some of it would be downright heartbreaking. But everything moves on. Yessir, things were going to change.

Old Gus

HOWARD SLAMMED THE cover down on the milk can with his forearm, tied a rope to the handle and lowered it into the well. It slid down beside the other two cans in the cool water below. Tomorrow would be a trip-to-town day.

Gus knew the routine well. Every third day, Howard hitched him to the wagon and loaded three cans of cold milk from the well. A click of the tongue and Gus shouldered the load out between the two stone pillars' marking the drive. A wide swing into the road and Gus ambled along toward town.

Those pillars were put there by Howard's Dad as a solid marker. Never again would this entrance fail to be recognized.

Howard was only five years old, but the memory will always stay with him. It was a clear winter's day when he and his father were returning from town. The sled made crispy crunching sounds as Roxie pulled it over the frozen roadbed.

Either Dad miss-estimated or Roxie was slow to respond. She missed the drive and went right down into the road ditch. The sled stopped suddenly and the front of the horse disappeared.

Dad panicked. He unhooked the sled and pulled it back. There she was with her front feet in the ditch and her head in the snow on the opposite side. Her hind legs and belly were still in the road.

Dad pushed the snow away from her face while Howard ran for the shovel.

It was no use. Even with the snow removed all around her, without her front feet hitting something solid, she couldn't move.

"She's gonna freeze! Go get Mort," Dad wheezed.

Thinking about it now, it seems kinda risky sending a child on a two-and-a-half mile trek in the extreme cold, but it made sense at the time. In his oversized pants and galoshes, five-year-old Howard felt up to the challenge.

It took him the better part of an hour. He kicked at the front door because his hands were so cold he didn't want to take them out of his pockets.

Soon Howard was hugging a warm stove and saying what he could with shaking limbs and a dancing jaw.

Mort seemed reluctant to help. "Just cozying up for the evening," he replied.

It took what seemed like an eternity but with tears and whimpering Howard finally convinced him that Dad needed help. Or Mort finally concluded that this kid wouldn't leave without him.

Mort moved just as fast as the weather. If ambition were measurable, Mort would have a hard time registering on the chart.

It felt cold, but good to be headed back.

Dad had Roxie covered with stable blankets. He was down in the ditch massaging her front legs. Mort hitched onto her harness and pulled her out. She didn't come straight out like she went in, but rolled up on her side and slid out.

After she got on her feet, Dad continued to rub her front legs, loading her back with blankets.

Mort watched for a while. When he figured his silence wasn't working he made numerous comments about "getting back," and "didn't need him anymore."

Dad came to the conclusion that this wasn't going to be a neighborly good deed. From the bowels of an old worn wallet, he pulled from concealment a well-creased, sweat-stained dollar. It must've been his emergency fund and this incident must have qualified. He gestured it in Mort's direction.

Mort took very little time covering the extra acreage to fetch it. In an instant, he was on the trail toward home. It was getting toward dusk. Maybe he was afraid of the dark.

Early that spring, Dad put a big stone pillar on each side of the drive. He called them an insurance policy. Even though a tragedy was averted, Dad never stopped lamenting the loss of that dollar.

Howard got to reminisce about a lot of things on these slow and easy rides to town. He didn't have to do a thing. Old Gus stopped to pick up Harland. That was part of the routine. Harland was a millwright in town. He walked to town every week day. Riding the milk wagon gave him a reprieve and a chance to talk to a neighbor.

By the time Gus arrived at the creamery, he had eight cans of milk and four passengers. Everyone left Howard a nickel. It worked out well for all.

Gus always stopped at the local store to allow Howard to purchase a tin of tobacco. He didn't chew, but Gus did. It was his treat for the trip.

When they got home, Gus got his chew while Howard removed the harness. Gus was the only horse around with an iron band reinforcing his collar right where the main ring attached. It was the only way the leather wright could repair it.

Howard stood there with his hand on that harness, thinking. He hated winters. This was just another reminder of how dangerous cold weather can be. He managed to escape another unavoidable event that trumpeted tragedy. Being older and aware of the sudden dangers that bad weather can cause, one should be prepared for adversity.

It was just last year. He and Gus were coming back from town when a severely cold wind rushed through the area. A sudden snow squall turned Basset Flats into a sea of blinding white, piling up a huge snow drift. Howard considered turning back but Gus lunged right into the waist deep pile. Howard tried to stop him but he kept throwing himself into the harness. Releasing the wagon was out of the question. A man could quickly lose a hand. With a light jacket, no gloves, and no hat to shield the pelting white snow, all Howard could do was get behind and push. How could Gus see where he was going?

Basset Flats seemed endless, but Gus kept right on pounding at it. Finally the wagon moved steadily forward. Howard collapsed in the back. Thankfully the milk cans were empty. Otherwise, the milk would've been butter. He worried about the pillars marking the driveway. How would Gus find them? Would he go right by and they become a victim of this blizzard? Or would he collapse before he got home? Howard tried looking over the side of the wagon, shielding his face with his bare hands. Where were those markers?

The wagon stopped. Howard slipped out and felt his way forward. Gus was still standing. Now he could unhitch if his hands could find the pin. Bare flesh sticks to cold steel. He backed into something solid behind him. It was the barn. Gus brought them right up beside the barn.

He cleared the door and brought in a horse totally covered with snow. Harness removed and in a warm stall, This strong-willed animal thoroughly enjoyed a rub down and a good chew.

After the storm settled, marks in the snow clearly showed that Gus hit the bull's eye, bringing the load right between those stone pillars.

Howard knew that was when it all started. Maybe it was the strain of pushing the wagon. Maybe it was the fear of the situation. Even though it had been a year, anything strenuous brought back that pain in his left arm. It worried him to be in such a hard place. He liked farming but felt compromised. A man wasn't considered a man if he couldn't handle his own load. That included unloading his milk cans at the creamery. They weighed up toward ninety pounds and a man should be able to unload and carry a full can in each hand. It was an unsaid universal standard. With no children and no hired help it put a big question mark on the rest of farming duties.

He left the harness rack and finished the evening milking even though he didn't feel well. Loading the cans the next morning brought back that the pain. Still manageable but for how much longer. How many more times. Unfriendly decisions were closing in.

Harland wasn't out waiting for his ride to town. It must be Saturday. Howard didn't pay much attention to the calendar. Knowing the month was close enough.

Now this was unusual. No one at the creamery either. Unloading those eight cans of milk took a lot longer than usual. He put them in the cooler and left a note with his can numbers on it. No money in the jar today but he had ten cents with him. That would buy Gus's tobacco.

The store was closed, too. A sign in the window said

"Happy holiday." Well, it wasn't a fine holiday. No chew for Gus and an empty money jar. Things looked mighty disappointing.

When they got home, Howard tried pulling the hitch pin on the wagon but Gus kept pressure on it so it wouldn't come out. This was the usual time he got his chew. No amount of coaxing changed his mind. Howard tried a little chopped hay dipped in molasses. Gus ate it but he wasn't fooled. If this horse wouldn't give up during that snow storm, he must be a large part mule.

Howard told his wife Elsie, where he was going and set his mind to a two-and-a-half mile walk. He knew the man that bought Mort's farm chewed tobacco. He'd seen him go by occasionally. Even from a distance, the turn of the head and thrust of the jaw made it obvious.

That farm had been sold at least twice since he'd been up there as a child. This upcoming generation was more inter-ested in making money than building a reputation.

From a long ways off, Howard saw him up in the field loading hay. He followed an old fence and cut across the meadow.

"Hi. I'm your neighbor," Howard said, approaching from the opposite side of the wagon.

"Kevin McGuire. Irishman, ya know. What brings ye up here?"

Howard pointed to the dent in his shirt. "That can of chew in your pocket."

"Ya chew, do ya?"

"No, but my horse does. He gets a treat for his trip to town and everything's closed. Would you be selling that tin of tobacco in your pocket?"

"Canna do that. Empty. I might 'ave a spare at the house," Kevin said, pushing up a fork full of hay.

"Oh, okay," Howard conceded, looking at the extra distance he had to cover. "I'll go down and talk to your wife."

"Canna do that. She's na there."

"Well then, come along. You must know where it is."

Kevin swung another dusty jag of hay up onto the wagon. "Canna do that either," he said, turning away from a cloud of chaff. "Be late for chores." He stabbed into another pile. "No sense in goin' down empty-handed."

Howard stood there for a while appraising the situation. He eyed the extra pitch fork attached to the wagon. It was a long walk to go home empty-handed and who knows how long this Irishman could stretch things out.

Howard snatched the spare fork and leaned into the job. He tossed the bundles, even if it did make his chest hurt. Besides, it may be just a pulled muscle.

When Kevin stopped the wagon next to the barn, Howard expected him to draw a path toward the house, but he didn't. Kevin scaled the load and threw down several bundles.

Howard realized where this maneuver was leading so he just leaned on his fork and watched, suspecting that Kevin wouldn't say a word.

Soon enough, Kevin came down off the load and commenced carrying the bundles into the barn.

Now Howard mounted the load and threw down the bundles. This was the easy position and the controlling one. When Kevin didn't move fast enough, Howard tossed another fork full right on top.

"Ya could be a little slower," Kevin complained.

"You don't wanna be late for chores, do you?" Howard chided.

He kicked the chaff off the wagon bed and eased down onto the ground. "Now we get that tin of tobacco," he said with force.

"Ya kin wait here," Kevin said, mounting the porch.

"Why?" Howard asked, holding the door open. This was the same door he kicked at once before. He didn't want a reason to do it again.

Kevin's request to wait outside was well-formulated when Howard saw his wife at the dry sink washing vegetables. Kevin disappeared for only a moment. He slapped down a tin of tobacco on the table. "That'll be ten cents," he said, keeping his hand on top of it.

"What happened to the tin in your pocket? The bulge is gone," Howard growled.

"Told ya t'was empty. I threw it away."

"You want twice the price for it. I suppose my help was of no value."

"Never asked ya for yer help," Kevin replied.

Kevin's wife stood there, frozen at the dry sink, with her back to the tense transaction.

Howard knew he had to be careful. At least until that tin was in his own hand. He rubbed the two nickels in his pocket. Drawing them out slowly, he laid them on the drying bench, well out of reach. That Irishman would have to take his hand off the tobacco to reach the money.

This room kindled old memories. The warm stove he stood in front of, shivering and whimpering while others formulated ways of benefitting from the circumstances. Groans and sighs, conveying an unwillingness to interrupt their own comfort. That same energy still pervaded.

Finally, Howard stepped back to the door with the can surrounded by his big hand. He looked. Yes, the paper seal was still intact. He was almost out the door when he heard Kevin's wife call.

"A wee moment," she said, sailing to a nearby cabinet. She pressed a jar of jelly into his hand. "For yew and yer pleasant wife." It had a ribbon around its metal band and a flower painted on the lid.

Howard stared into her apologetic eyes. They were young eyes surrounded by the strains of worry. "Regards, Mam," he said with a gentleness even he didn't recognize. It just came out all on its own.

Feet couldn't take him away from there fast enough. That jar certainly lightened his load. His step would've been a frustrated stomp without it. Now it was plain why his Dad always lamented the loss of that dollar. It wasn't the financial loss that mattered so much as the feeling of being swindled. A neighborly good deed of little effort shouldn't produce harsh feelings. Maybe it was the land here that affected the owners. Maybe it was something in the water. Whatever the cause, Howard vowed to walk all the way to town rather than return here again.

"Ya should'na done that," Kevin growled as his wife returned to her vegetables.

"Yer quite right," she replied. "I should'na tried ta save ya. After all, ya have such a grand way of building a fine relationship with yer neighbors. The last time it cost us the barn and a good jag of hay. We had ta move here because of yer reputation." She turned to face him, holding the knife up in front of her. Her thumb coursed across the blade and her voice turned as hard as the steel in her hand. "Twice is enough. If we have ta move again, I'll not be goin' with ya."

Gus hadn't moved very far. Just enough for a few nibbles of grass on the lawn. He thoroughly processed his treat while Howard attended to the milking.

The last can of milk slipped into the well. Howard snubbed the rope and drew a course for the house.

The jelly jar sat right in the middle of the kitchen table. He turned it slowly, watching a sunset's pallid light expose a strange iridescence. It almost glowed within itself.

"That may've eased the feelings toward your Irish neighbors," Elsie said. "But I'd be letting the dog sample it before slathering it on anything."

Such a thought startled him. How could something so clear and warm be harmful? No! Absolutely no! He couldn't justify such an idea.

Three days later, Howard was loading cans from the well into the wagon when the pain came back with a vengeance. It hit him in the chest hard enough to take his breath away. Getting up into the wagon proved a bit awkward, but Gus waited. Thankfully things had settled down by the time they arrived in town and all went well. Howard bought an entire pack of chewing tobacco. He wasn't about to get caught short again.

He was pretty cautious for the next few days. An old roller winch and a makeshift tripod from the tool shed would take a lot of the strain off getting the cans up out of the well. Another few days and he'd have it installed.

This time he couldn't ignore it. With the third can loaded, he managed to make it back into the kitchen. He sat down at the table and passed out. Elsie tried to rouse him but couldn't. She scribbled a note, stuffed it into the jar, tucked it under the wagon seat and sent Gus on his way. The horse didn't seem to be concerned. He ambled up the road with casual routine.

Howard woke up to Doc's prodding. "What's this all about?"

"You," Doc scolded. "That's what it's all about."

Howard looked around. Elsie had managed to get him

on the couch in the parlor. "Gotta get Gus into town."

"You ain't going anywhere," Doc replied.

A sudden crushing pain pushed him back down onto the couch.

"Gus has been to town already," Doc said. "The boys at the creamery took care of things. They gave me Elsie's note and sent Gus home. He's back and everything has been taken care of so you just stay right where you are."

Doc shuffled into the kitchen, plunked a bottle on the table and wrestled with his coat. "Keep him still for a couple of weeks if you can. No hard work. And a teaspoon of that when he's got pain.

Elsie pushed a jar toward him. "What about this, Doc?"

He studied the small remainder of jelly, watching light pass through it. He took a dab of it and let it simmer on his tongue. "Where'd you get this?"

"Neighbor up the road here," Elsie replied. "McGuire gave it to him."

Doc closed his eyes to let the full sense of taste blaze a pattern on his memory. "Now that's heaven. A few years ago my wife and I went on a special trip to the state fair. A young lady up there was selling this stuff. One jar like this would fetch a good day's wage. It took all four blue ribbons."

Doc cast her a glance. "You don't think this is the cause of Howard's problems do you?"

He watched her stiffen, eyes darting around the room, looking for a place to rest. "Maybe there's something he ain't telling you. A good while back he stopped by my office in town with this same complaint. I wanted to do a complete exam but he wouldn't spend the dollar and a half. So I gave him a bottle of laudanum and sent him on his way. That there on the table is a refill." Doc finished wrestling with his coat. "It's his heart, Elsie. It won't take a lot more strain. The next spasm could very well be his last."

A cool night breeze rushed in through the open door. "You send Gus to town as usual," Doc said. "I'll tell the creamery workers to handle things in there." Doc pulled at his collar and attacked the darkness.

In the days that followed, Howard assembled the winch and cradle over the well. Another winch hitched in a near-by tree lifted the load into the wagon. Then Gus set off for town unassisted. He stopped for his riders as programmed. The creamery men handled the product, dutifully recording transactions and depositing the money in the jar. Gus stopped at the local store where the storekeeper checked the jar and filled any orders. He took payment and replaced the remaining funds. With goods packed and loaded, all he had to say was, "Okay, Gus, go on home."

Gus made many trips alone. It would appear to be a very vulnerable situation. Anyone could apprehend the horse along the way. Such a thing wasn't even considered among the residents. Everyone knew Howard and Elsie. Everyone knew everyone. Very few strangers trod the area. And even if they did, it would be difficult to escape local folk's scrutiny. People just did what was right and honest. Gus did as well. You might say he fit right in as a good citizen.

After a few weeks of convalescing, Howard took a seat on the wagon ride to town. He caught up on local news and gossip. Allowing the men at the creamery to handle the load would take some getting used to.

Gus took Howard to the store for his treats. That's when Howard saw them through the window. Their firm stance and stiff gestures alluded to an intense disagreement. Howard eased the door open just enough to avoid the bell.

"I'll not be goin' all the way home and back for thirty-five cents." Mrs. McGuire snapped in her Irish brogue.

The storekeeper threw one arm in the air. "It took a quite a while to get my money the last time. Now I'm not a bank."

"That was me husband. I nere knew about it. And what bank is goin' ta loan me thirty-five cents."

"Look," the storekeeper reasoned, "why don't you just put one small item back."

"When I come in here, I only buy what ah needs."

Mrs. Thorpe was coming and Howard didn't want to be suspected of eavesdropping so he charged right in, sending the bell into a frenzy. "Came for my pack of a chew," he announced, totally oblivious of anyone else's presence.

The storekeeper fetched a ten-pack of chewing tobacco and tended Howard's outstretched dollar. A half dollar clicked on counter and slid toward him. Howard looked down at it. "I hear there's a well-respected jelly maker somewhere in these parts. Some say a jar of that brew would fetch a good days wage."

The storekeeper cast him a bewildered look, while Mrs. McGuire kept her back to the proceedings.

That's when Howard leaned over close, pushing the coin ahead of him. He spoke softly. "Will this cover the discrepancy between you two?"

The storekeeper nodded sheepishly, glancing at Mrs. McGuire's back.

Howard strode toward the door. Even though her back was to him, he touched the brim of his hat. "Sorry about the intrusion. Regards, Mam."

"Okay, Gus. Let's go home," Howard chirped. He felt good about his actions. Things were looking up. At least for now. He got a chance to say no hard feelings. An opportunity to demonstrate what this town was all about. A little forgiving and a lot of living. Yes sir, things were looking up.

Something To Crow About

HE NEVER HAD a name. Didn't need one. They just called him Crow. Grandpa said we didn't choose him. He chose us.

Crow flew in one spring day while Grandpa was fixing fence. He sat there on one of the newly driven posts, cocking his head side to side.

"What'n hell ya doin?" Grandpa said. "Surveying the job?" Answering a gentle whistle, Bess pulled the wagon up to the next post hole.

A while later, riding on the cool spring breeze came a metallic tapping sound. That pesky crow was assaulting Grandpa's lunch box. "What'n hell ya doin?" Grandpa barked. "Git away from there."

The crow flew off toward the forest.

Appraising the sun's position, he realized it was about time so he steered Bess over to a shady spot beside the brook and pulled out his lunch.

Just about then, that pesky crow swung in and sat down right on the rump strap of Bess's harness. Grandpa braced for a reaction but none came. Bess looked back with idle indifference and returned to the new fresh grass. Crow strutted back and forth on that strap, studying Grandpa's progress with his lunch. Grandpa finally conceded and tossed out a piece of bread.

All that day crow enjoyed his commanding position on

Bess's harness. Grandpa didn't see any harm in it and Bess accepted the extra company. Even the swaying ride to the barn didn't disturb him at all. Crows are used to branches swaying in the wind so a horses rump would be a normal ride.

When they reached the barn, crow took up residence in the apple tree. That evening, when Grandpa came out of the barn, He saw the crow picking at something near the manure pile. "What'n hell ya doin?" Grandpa said, tossing out a handful of corn. "No self respecting bird should have to resort to that for a meal."

It soon became an established routine. Crow bivouacked in the apple tree. In the morning when Bess went, crow went. Crow was the time keeper and the lunch box was his dinner bell. His only deviation was the farm machinery. Whenever Grandpa got on or off the machinery crow moved up to the hames work. Humans could get close but not too close.

It may have appeared to be an odd group but it worked pretty well. They dined together in the shade of a tree or down by the brook, sharing a cool breeze, a cold drink and a chunk of Grandma's soft bread.

Grandma, however, didn't have the same view of matters. Crows were scavengers, always looking for a handout. Even though Grandpa assured her that they had a purpose she still placed them in with thieves and loafers. She scoffed when Grandpa took a piece of meat or other table scraps out to crow. "Do the same for your cat, Mew," he'd say. "Is she a beggar, too?"

That morning promised to be a good dry day and the downed hay only needed a little tedding to make it ready for the barn. Grandpa backed Bess up to the tedder and dropped the hitch pin. Hooking his lunch box beside the

197

lift lever, he took his seat and gently dropped the reins. "Hup" he said. Bess didn't move. Confused, he shook the reins again. "Hup." Bess shook her mane and let out a low whinner. Just then crow came swooping in, landed on the rump strap and straightened his feathers. Bess looked back to check on his position and promptly set off for the field. "Bess," Grandpa said, "You'd better have a talk with your teammate here about being late for work."

In the heat of the day, the crew stopped for lunch near the edge of the field. This time Grandpa brought a sugar cube for Bess. While he poured himself a drink from the thermos crow flashed in and snatched the sugar cube. "What'n hell ya doing?" Grandpa declared. "That's for Bess."

Even Grandpa admitted that what happened next is something very few get to see. Crow cut around and landed right in front of the horse. Bess lowered her huge head, rolled her lips back and took that cube right out of crow's extended beak. That bird wouldn't take it out of a person's hand but he'd give it to an animal with a mouth big enough to swallow him, treat and all. This again set up a routine. From then on any treats for Bess were delivered by airmail.

With the haying done and cold weather setting in, Grandpa wondered what crow was going to do for shelter. Maybe a small house in the apple tree would do. But who knew what crows do for wintering over. The three of them were spreading the last loads of the manure pile when crow answered that question. That night, when Bess went in the barn he flew right in, too.

"What'n hell ya doing? Taking over the place?" Grandpa asked.

Crow flew up and lit on the stanchion beam over the cows. He strutted back and forth, looked at Grandpa and said. "What'n hell ya doing?"

Grandpa laughed in amazement and crow mimicked him with a raucous "haw haw haw."

So this was crows new residence. He drank from the cow's water bowls, picked grain from the manger, and slept on Bess's back. Of course accommodations didn't come without assigned duties. Crow readily accepted the duty of pestering any cow that refused to get up for morning milking. He took any treats left for Bess from the top shelf and personally delivered them. He also assumed the difficult task of harassing the cat, Mew. Anything that moved was a target for crow's antics.

Mew tried to take naps during the day but crow would sneak up and pull the hair on her tail. Then quickly fly away, laughing, haw haw haw. She had to hide under the barn to get a decent undisturbed rest.

One evening Mew was enjoying her nightly treat of warm milk. Crow flew out through the open window and returned with a pebble. He carefully measured the conditions. Eyes closed, Mew was licking at her dish of milk, content with the situation. Crow took to the air, swinging around, he dropped the pebble. Mew got a shocking face full of her own supper. And crow got a big laugh from his perch. Another well-executed contrivance, haw haw haw.

These tricks went untold. Grandma would surely look down on crow antics, no matter how well conceived and inventive they were.

No matter the circumstances, pay back is always inevitable. Even if not contrived. Who would've guessed that this bright winter day would possibly be a great opportunity. Such a day was perfect for fetching more wood for the constantly dwindling pile at the house. Bess broke trail with the log sled in tow. Crow contentedly surveyed their progress from his usual position. Bess bowed her head to pass under a low, snow-laden branch. The hames hooked the branch. It snapped back, dumping a cold surprise. Crow coughed and shook. Cleaning himself off, he looked at Bess and said, "What'n hell ya doin?" Bess nodded her head and snorted. It would be hard-pressed to tell if that was a laugh or an apology.

As the day went on and the sled filled with fire wood, a winter wind gathered force. Crow strutted nervously up and down Bess's back. That was all the warning Grandpa needed. He pulled the pin on the sled and the trio made a charge for the trail home. Everything quickly turned blinding white. Without a sled to ride on, Grandpa locked his hand into Bess's side strap and stumbled along to her lead. She would surely know the way better than he.

Grandma paced the porch, barely able to establish the shape of the barn. Finally she recognized the outline of Grandpa holding his collar, trudging along beside a snow-covered horse. She screamed at them and heard something indiscernible in return.

It wasn't too long before she heard big feet stomping across the porch. Warm clothes were hanging in front of the stove and steam trailed from the tea pot.

"Why is your shirt so wet when you had this coat?" Grandma asked, draping it over the rack. A small black feather floated to the floor. "You used your coat to cover that ridiculous bird didn't you. You could'a froze to death."

Grandpa snuggled into a warm shirt. Would'a done th th the sa sa same for Mew. Besides' he war war warned us about th th the storm."

Grandma huffed and fussed over all that horse hair on his coat. And why was he risking his life for some carrion-eating scavenger.

He couldn't tell her the whole story but it made him

smile to think of it. All that snow piled on Bess. It didn't look like there was anything under there. When he pushed it off and lifted the coat there was crow, hunkered down, dry and safe. He stretched up and announced, "What'n hell ya doin?" Now how could a man ever forget something like that?

There were lots of things he couldn't tell her. Like the time that summer when another bird landed in the hay field, evidently surveying the territory. Crow stretched and bristled to the intrusion. Apparently this new arrival wasn't any relative that crow wanted to introduce to his team-mate. Bess looked over, stomped one foot, shook her mane and snorted. The visitor sized up his welcoming commit-tee, and promptly left. He must have notified others about the hospitality because no one else attempted to visit. Crow and Bess were an analogous team that needed no additions.

Or the time Grandpa left an empty can of bag balm up on Bess's treat shelf. Crow flew over for a close inspection. Far too large for him to pick up and a definite violation of space, he quickly devised an admirable use for it. Here comes cat. Off goes can. There goes cat. It must have cost Mew at least two of her nine lives.

It didn't become evident until later that this snowy cold event and Grandpa's coat had apparently instilled in crow enough trust of humans to stop jumping up to the hames whenever Grandpa got off his equipment. He stayed on the rump strap. Allowing humans to get that close was a big concession for a bird of his stature.

Not much happened on the farm that winter. At least nothing to exceed the usual routine. Days were consumed by repetitive tasks that left little to talk about except the weather, what needed repair, and a list of supplies for the next trip to town.

The biggest and best alteration were visitors. A new and captive audience to tell old stories. But this was even better. With their daughter's second child soon to arrive, their four-year-old Grandson, Levi, would be staying with them for a while. Grandma started preparation immediately. Besides the room and fresh bedding, other important things needed attention. The rocking horse had to be retrieved from the attic and properly positioned in the room. a full stock of flour and sugar were needed for entertaining a youngster. Enough to make every kind of confection any reliable recipe book could hold. That paled to the stack of books and puzzles assembled. Of course, there were other intriguing things to occupy a youth. Cooking on a wood stove, laundering with a wringer washer, planting a garden, sitting on the porch, and eating fresh apple pie.

Don't put aside special events like hiding under the porch with the chickens, studying all the jars of preserves in the cellar, taking naps on the cool grass, climbing the apple tree, finding the holes in the barn foundation that Mew used for hiding places, and helping with the barn chores.

Grandma fretted about that last one. Grandpa did as well. He didn't want Levi going around with a new descriptive term to display. It might be a little difficult to explain where such an adjective came from. And how would one convince a youngster that a crow could use such a term but a person shouldn't.

As much as Grandma loved consuming Levi's attention, a boy will eventually succumb to the attraction of animals. Grandpa was captured by the chores and didn't notice Little Levi venture in.

Pacing the stanchion beam, crow appraised the new arrival. He'd seen him outside but this was an opportunity to evaluate matters in close quarters. What kind of tricks could he invest in with this opponent?

After a long staring session crow opened with, "What'n hell ya doin?"

Levi pointed up. "Grandpa, that bird just–"

Crow swooped down and right back up to the stanchion beam. He turned around with Levi's hat in his beak. "Haw haw haw."

"Took my hat," Levi whimpered.

Since the cat was wise to his tricks, crow needed a new target and what self-respecting bird would pass up an opportunity like this?

Grandpa chuckled. "Oh, he'll give it back." Hopefully crow wouldn't drop it in the gutter.

Crow soon left it on the grain bin.

As Levi followed Grandpa around, he tried to mimic crow's laugh. He never repeated crows talking, but his hat was always pulled down tight.

Levi assumed duties in the barn as well. He filled Mew's dish with warm milk, gave the cows a scoop of salt and swept the manger. One evening, as he swept, he sung a song Grandma taught him. He swung the broom to the simple tune. When he looked up crow was swinging around on his perch as well. Levi sang louder and swirled faster. Crow turned and strutted as well. Finally Levi fell down, dizzy and giddy with laughter. Crow looked down from his perch and added his usual "Haw haw haw."

Grandpa assigned Levi another task. That of putting a sugar cube on the upper shelf. Then they watched. Crow flew over, took the treat and delivered it to Bess in her stall. He landed on the top rail and she always reached up and took it from his beak.

"I wanna give Bess a treat, too" Levi begged. He carried

his little prize over to that ominous looking wall called a stall. With measured caution he negotiated the slats, moving upward, careful not to drop his reward. With elbows locked over the top rail, he held out the cube, eyes closed to avoid witnessing approaching pain. The cube disappeared from his grasp. Back on the floor, Levi beamed with delight. He had overcome his fear and rose to the challenge. Even crow added his approval with "Haw haw haw."

It was the next night during chores that Grandpa said, "lets have a little fun." He gave Levi a small chunk of chewing tobacco to put on the shelf. They watched as crow flew over to snatch it, but stopped. He looked at it. Picked it up and dropped it several times. Then he strutted and paced, measuring the chunk, contemplating the possibility of a trick. Finally he grabbed it and took it over to Bess. Instead of handing it to her, he dropped it in her grain bin. That way if Bess didn't want it, his loyalty wouldn't be questioned.

When she ate it he flew away contented that it was a worthy treat and not a prank after all. It was nothing he approved of, but Bess liked it.

One morning, while Grandpa managed farm machinery, crow saw Grandma hanging fresh laundry out on the line. He glided over and landed on the clothesline post. "What'n hell ya doin?" he said.

Grandma sneered at him. "You mark my laundry and you'll be soup by tonight," she growled.

Crow laughed, "haw haw haw," and returned to the apple tree. No doubt a friendlier place to wait for the day's work to get organized.

Later that evening, Grandpa went out for his usual visit to the out house. He was concerned about Bess's foot so he doubled back to the barn to check on it. No need to turn on the lights with a full moon out. When Grandpa entered the stall, crow went out to join the cows.

With Bess's foot between his knees, Grandpa heard the soft squeak of the barn door. Through the slats of the stall he saw Levi walk over and look up at crow. "Mr. Crow," he said. "Please be careful of Grandma. She doesn't like you. I don't know why cause she likes everybody else. I heard her say she was going to make you into soup. All of us would miss you a lot so you just stay here in the barn where it's safe okay?"

The barn door closed softly leaving Grandpa in turmoil. What adults say as an inflated threat can be taken quite seriously by a youngster. They have a vivid imagination that's not to be trifled with. He well-remembered how he felt as an adolescent when he found his pet chicken torn apart by a fox. Openly voicing her contempt was a concern and now it effected little Levi. He couldn't make her accept crow and he wasn't about to get rid of him either. Bess liked him and it was no different than having a dog.

Good weather brought the team out into the field. With days like this it should be a pleasure to work but Grandpa was in anguish about the situation. There seemed to be no reasonable way to handle this predicament. He was so deep in thought that he hardly noticed crow flying away toward the house.

Looking out the kitchen window, Grandma saw him. There was that despicable vagrant and he was harassing Levi. Dive bombing him as he lay there on the grass, wrapped up in his blanket, taking a nap. Levi no doubt rolled up to protect himself. This had to be dealt with promptly.

Just as she reached for her broom something strange occurred. It had to be a vision because it happened years ago.

But it seemed so real. She could see her uncle sitting there at this very table. His big booming voice telling about the time when he was young. He loved to lay on the lawn and roll up in his blanket. He'd stay in his little cocoon until he couldn't breathe any longer and then he'd unroll quickly, pulling in huge gulps of cool air. One day when he tried to unroll and the blanket flap didn't release. He rolled and rolled in desperation. Finally the flap released. He found himself way down next to the fence. Just a couple more rolls and he would've been locked inside forever.

Just as quickly as the vision appeared, it was gone.

Grandma yanked open the kitchen door and crossed the porch in one bound. She snapped the blanket and Levi spun out like a top. He lay there limp and ashen. She shook him and yelled, "Levi!" No response. She sat him up and in total desperation slapped him hard. "Levi!" His head rolled back and he gasped for air. She pulled him to her and together they cried.

Gathering him in her arms, she stood up, and there was crow watching intently from the tree. For a long time she stared into those inky black eyes. "Okay," she said. "You can stay."

Crow lifted off the limb and returned to the field.

That night proved to be a boisterous one as Levi related the events at the dinner table. Grandma was slow to respond but she did concede it was crow that alerted her to the situation. Grandpa felt a great load lift from him. Things might just settle down now.

Morning proved cool and field work waited. Grandpa weighed his lunch box. It sccmcd heavier than usual. "What's this?" he asked, looking inside. Grandma didn't answer.

"Something extra for crow?" He chided.

Grandma just turned to her duties. He smiled but said no more. How appropriate, to have crow make Grandma eat crow. It must be difficult enough without him forcing her to do it all in one swallow.

Days passed quickly and Levi had to leave. He took with him a generous supply of indelible memories. So many sweet and simple things that bring pleasure to the present and comfort to the future. Life is filled with complications. Pleasant memories of enjoyable moments bring a person back to the basics. They are a guide to what is of real value.

The farm had it's constant duties and soon the days were back to normal. Grandma was doing her usual mundane duties and staring out the kitchen window when she saw him. What was he doing here and where had he come from. Mew saw him, too. The warm porch steps were no protection from a big dog so she sprinted for the barn. Opportunity knocked and the dog immediately stepped up to the challenge. He passed the porch just as Grandma came out the door. Her shouting and whirling broom was no deterrent.

From his command post in the apple tree crow could see that Mew wasn't going to make it. Maybe it was something about an intruder. Maybe he was just being territorial. Or maybe it was the challenge of a good trick.

Crow dropped from his perch, using gravity to gain speed. When his talons bit into the dogs neck he changed his mind. When a beak pinched his flapping ear he changed his course. With wings beating him on the side of the head he changed his attitude.

When one can't access their adversary the best strategy is to retreat. And swing a wide arc to avoid a swirling broom.

At the edge of the lawn crow dismounted his howling victim and returned to the tree. He strutted along the limb, adding his usual "Haw haw haw."

"That's right crow," Grandma said, pumping her broom at the dog. "And don't come back or I'll sic him on you again."

Grandpa came around the corner of the barn to see what the fracas was all about. Grandma pointed her broom at the retreating dog and then at crow. Grandpa nodded and went back to work. Bess whinnered slightly as he went by.

"Just crow," Grandpa said, "Putting another feather in his cap." He adjusted his hat and picked up the shovel. "Oh, remember when I told you to speak to your partner about being late for work?" He swung another scoop into the wagon. "Well, forget it."

It was the next fall and the trio were working on the last of the winters hay supply. Hot dry days made good hay. Bess seemed nervous and Grandpa hurried to finish the load and get her in the shade. Crow lifted off her back, circling to gain altitude. As soon as he returned he pecked her on the rump and without orders Bess started for the barn. Grandpa didn't question horse sense. He threw the fork on the load and followed. Bess leaned into the load and got it up to a fast walk. It wasn't a heavy load but the field made it roll hard.

They reached the hay shed just as the wind picked up. It was a cold wind. A threatening wind. Unusual for a hot day.

With the hay under cover, Grandpa pulled the pin and opened the barn doors. He wrestled with the wind to close them as a heavy hail pelted the area. Just then he heard the door at the other end of the barn slam shut by the wind. Had he left it open? Had the wind torn the latch?

Grandma hurried down the aisle. He stared in amazement. She hadn't been in the barn in so long he had to search his memory.

"Are you all right?" she asked. "Yeah," Grandpa replied. Hail rattled the barn as he stripped the harness off Bess.

"I saw crow fly up high. When he came down quickly I went and took the laundry off the line. This wind would've spread it all the way to town."

Grandpa wasn't paying attention. "What's wrong?" she asked.

"Bess," Grandpa said. "I think she's overheated." He soaked grain bags in water and spread them over her as she fought for air. The hail stopped as abruptly as it started so he hurried outside and filled a sack with chunks of ice that littered the ground.

By chore time, Bess had settled down to a stall with fresh bedding and a big helping of grain. Crow watched every maneuver from the top board of her stall.

It was right then that Grandpa resolved to reduce Bess to light work and lots of field rest. He had all winter to measure his options. He may even cut back himself.

Really though; how does a person go from a one-horse farm to a no-horse farm. This would take some heavy deliberation.

Early the next morning things weren't right in the barn. Grandpa could tell just as he stepped in the door. Bess was laying in her stall, breathing in shallow gasps. About mid morning Grandpa made the trip over to Halsey's place to get help. They used the tractor to haul her out of the barn and onto the stone boat. It was a long sad trip down across the pasture. Crow flew overhead.

That noisy smoky tractor dug a big hole in a shady spot near the forest where the trio enjoyed many lunches. With the dirt pushed back the tractor left. Grandpa stayed there for some time. He had a lot of reviewing to do. Here lay his workmate, comrade, companion and friend. They understood each other through a crude, unwritten language of moods, motions, whistles and clicks. He really didn't have anything to say. Nothing Bess didn't already know. They had said it all very well in their days together.

Crow watched the whole procession from a nearby branch.

When Grandpa finally left, he turned back. "Ya coming crow?' The bird didn't move. He just stayed there hunkered down on that branch.

Chores went slowly that night. The barn felt so vacant.

Before sunrise Grandpa was up. He headed down across the field with food for crow but crow was gone. Both he and Grandma hoped he'd come back some day but he never did. Grandpa said that he probably went and found some other horse to ride on but in his heart he hoped he hadn't.

From then on, whenever a crow gave his raucous caw they would look up to see if that crazy black vagrant had returned to pull another prank.

Pondering Stone

WHAT THIS MORNING seemed like a worthy endeavor now felt rather silly. Spending all day driving around on old back roads following some sketchy directions.

Mom told me all she knew. The new owners moved it. They gave it to some guy from Peacham. A tall slim man with a constant smile. She said they lived on some hill in the area. Bask Hill, or something like that.

I went back to the farm. The new owners certainly changed it. The house glittered like some sequined dance hall girl. New windows, plastic shutters, numerous additions, and four color paint.

Dana's marker tree was gone, too. The victim of a landscaper's axe. It no doubt would've shaded the new guest house patio.

I stopped to ask about it. That was a brave maneuver. I guess I shouldn't have. Someone who had no respect for a marker tree certainly wouldn't consider a big stone of any value.

Maybe it was what I said.

"What happened to the big stone that used to be over there? Yes, right where you put that useless curve in your driveway. That's right, I'm interested in a big rock. The previous owner used to sit on it."

That look of distant thought soon turned into sinister distrust. I left before they had a chance to question me any further.

I didn't feel comfortable asking local business owners if they knew a tall slim man who smiled a lot and lived on Bask Hill, or Mask Hill, or something like that. They would no doubt think I left my snow shovel out in the rain. Then I'd have two people thinking I was a bit tipsy. If they got together, who knows what they could convince the authorities of.

So now I'm on my own, cruising the area, steadily losing confidence in my better judgement. Why would I think a tall slim man would take a big rock with the intent of putting it out right next to the road. A backyard ornament or landscape boulder would be more appropriate. Some obscure spot that would make it far from obvious.

Wait! There it is! In the middle of someone's lawn. That had to be it. The central motif of a flower garden. It seemed a lot more useful when it served as "a chair in the open air." That's what Grandpa called it. There was the brown stain on the side where Grandpa drummed out his pipe.

I pulled over to the shoulder and stopped. One of those lonely old dirt roads. No need to worry about traffic.

The stone looked so much smaller. Of course, I was just a youngster when Dad went up to help with the haying, mending and painting. To me that stone was a mountain offering the world's best view. Why, a young man could almost stretch up and touch the sky. And it was sturdy enough to keep even the strongest adversary at bay.

Grandpa called it his pondering stone and after supper he would sit on one corner of it and smoke his pipe. During our summer visits, evenings would find him leaning back on that sun-heated portion, collecting thoughts, plans, and memories. Visitors didn't interfere with his ritual. They could wait inside or join him and listen to his stories.

Weather played an immensely important part of a

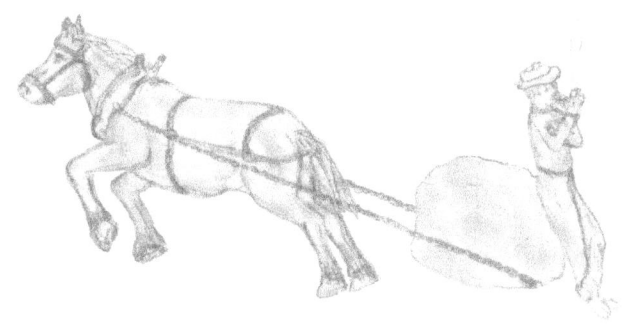

farmer's daily routine. Every task or duty hinged on the weather. For many subsistence farmers, their very existence depended on it. Without much prodding, Grandpa would expound on all sorts of objects or actions could be used to forecast the weather. Just about everything from the length of his thumbnail to the fur on the dog acted as a barometer. Grass or leaves told of rain. Drifting smoke from a chimney signified a cold spell. Grasshoppers, caterpillars, plants of all sorts, skunks, and even squirrels indicated the severity and length of winter. Hog's fat layer, chickens eggs, or the cat's sleeping position prognosticated springs arrival.

Everything had its logic but no documented reliability. A few indicators actually contradicted each other. But that wasn't important. Life was unpredictable so it didn't matter what lense you looked through. The outcome was the same.

When I got older, I helped Grandpa during high school summer vacations. Actually, he showed me where the tools were and added encouragement. He sent me up the ladder to repair the barn roof.

"What's this?" I said. "No nails?"

"Use the ones you pull out," he said. "Just straighten 'um and put 'um right back in. They're still fit and willing."

His tool shed had a battalion of glass jars with nails of

213

all sizes ready for another enlistment. Paint brushes were cleaned, combed, and trimmed. Axes and sickles were worn thin from sharpening.

While I was captive on the roof, he told of the year he moved the barn back away from the road. "Had to wait for a dry summer so the ground was nice and hard," he bragged. With an ingenious series of rolls all roped together, he and Dana pulled it onto a new foundation. "Just the two of us," he added. "Back when we was fit and worthy."

After evening chores I'd join him on the pondering stone.

"Everything has a purpose. And every job has a method," he'd say. "Take this stone here. It came from the field over there," he said, pushing his thumb in the general direction. He would point to the area he was referring to but seldom looked that way. "Was just a nuisance over there in the field, so Dana and I towed it over here." Had to build a cradle so when we got it up on the sled it wouldn't roll off the other side. That would be a waste. Used what they call a rolling hitch. Procedure is just as important as product. The method makes the matter."

A long lazy column of smoke rose from his cheeks. "Course, Dana couldn't pull that load over soft ground so we had ta wait for a good freeze. No sense in doin' it wrong, then havin' to do it over."

"Grandpa? Is there anything that doesn't need a method?" I asked.

He turned his head to determine wind direction. Drew a match. Inspected it. A thumbnail on the head lit it first time. Putting the spent match in his pocket, he released a long puff of smoke, and watched it drift away.

"What doesn't need a method, Grandpa?"

"I'm thinking," he replied.

It was during those last few summers I figured out why

Grandpa didn't turn or look in the direction he was referring. His arm waved to a spot on the left. "Over there next to that big pine tree is where we buried Dana. First horse I had on this farm. I planted that tree to mark the spot."

The big tree succumbed to a heavy snow storm. I cut it up and hauled it away earlier that spring. A small pine tree pushed new roots into that area. I planted it as a replacement marker.

"That area will look a little different until that new tree puts on some size," I said.

"Not to me it won't," Grandpa replied

He had an immutable mental picture branded into his memory and there was no need in looking that way to verify it. Or maybe it was his way of not having to deal with unwanted changes.

I was away at college when Grandpa died. Grandma followed soon after and the farm was sold. Life became so cluttered that I hadn't thought about it until recently.

A voice next to my car window startled me. "Help ya?"

He leaned over and put a big smiling face right next to my shoulder.

"Just admiring your flowers." I said.

"Wife does a good job don't she. Even had me bring in that big rock special. Came from a farm a ways from here. Almost owned that farm. Got out bid by some outa-stata. Wife talked him outa that rock. Just up and told him he wouldn't use it and she would."

"Everything has its purpose," I muttered.

"What'd ya say?"

"How'd you get it here?"

"One of them big front loaders from the town gravel pit. Brother-in-law works there. Just snatched her up and drove over here."

215

After a brief appraisal he said, "You from around here?"

"I used to work summers on a farm not too far from here."

He gave me a satisfied nod and a brief wave as I drove away.

I felt better. My search wasn't some frivolous excursion. It was another lesson from the pondering stone. There are times, when trying to link the present with the future, we have to reconnect with the past. Occasionally we all should look over our shoulder to see where we've been and get our bearings.

Yes, stop and take account of matters. Think about what really matters. Sit for a while on the pondering stone.

Foreigner

No ONE SAW him come into the logging camp. All of the men were in the forest with their horses dragging out logs. Odors of food drifted from the chow hall so he aimed in that direction.

It was Jessop, the kitchen boy who saw him first. He came out for more stove wood and ran right into him. Jessop froze when he saw only the man's belt buckle. He looked up, and up, and up further. The stranger, if it was human, had no face. A thick crop of hair, crowded down by a tight hat, met bushy eyebrows. A big burly mustache hid any vestige of a mouth. An ample beard was tucked into the front of his shirt. Sharp black eyes and two weathered cheeks, and a pudgy nose that sat on top of the mustache, were all that showed.

Jessop backed away slowly, fearing that some monster had come out of the forest to eat him.

The two cheeks pushed apart, tugging the mustache with them and a mouth appeared. "Job," the stranger said.

He couldn't speak so he jabbed a finger toward the side of the chow hall where the manager's office was located.

The mouth turned into a smile and the stranger walked away.

The manager watched him duck and turn sideways to get in the door. He tried to keep his composure. "What do you want?" he asked with a commanding voice.

"Job," the stranger said. "Job."

"Do you have a team?" After a long silence he paraded two fingers on his desk in a puppet fashion. "Horses. Do you have horses?"

Nodding, the stranger motioned toward the door. "Lou," he said.

The manager pushed a pencil toward him. "Okay. Your job is to drag out logs the cutting crew left. Bring them over to the railway. You get paid by the board foot. Pays five dollars a week, room and meals for you and your team, if you meet the weekly minimum quota. Sign here."

The signature looked like someone shuffled the alphabet. The last part strained the English language. "Okay, aaah, aaah, sir," the manager said. "You can start this morning."

"Ees good," the stranger replied.

"Jessop," the manager barked. "Show this man around."

Jessop ran in, sidestepped the stranger and hurried out the door. He wanted to stay out of range of this giant.

The manager watched them leave. That's when he saw the stranger's horse: 1600 pounds is a decent size for a pulling horse. A 2000 pound horse is an exceptional animal. A team that size is a real asset. This horse was just like the stranger. Huge. It could weigh in at 2500 pounds. Extra large front shoulders crowded the pulling collar up close to its ears. The usual leather tugging straps had been replaced with chains wrapped in leather to protect the animal's skin.

"Hey," the manager yelled. "Hey, Stranger."

The stranger stopped and looked back.

"You're supposed to have two horses. Two," the manager said holding up two fingers.

The stranger nodded and pointed to his horse. "Lou," he said, making the sign of muscle. "Ees good."

"Yeh?" The manager replied. "We'll see about that when you meet your quota."

Jessop raced to the bunk house. "Sleep," he said, putting his head on his pillowed hands. He pointed to the stable. "Horse sleep." He gestured toward the chow hall. "Eat." Then to the forest trail. "Work."

Jessop's guard relaxed when the stranger motioned to his horse and the pair went up the trail. Why did the man carry the evener bar and chains? All the other teamsters strapped it up under their horses tail so it wouldn't hit their rear legs. The others had reins and this man had none. Not even a halter. The horse followed along without question.

By supper time all the teamsters had seen or heard about him. Some saw him when they went by. Others watched him pass by with his horse a few steps behind, pulling a respectable load. A few met him at the rail drop, checking their load.

With the animals in the barn, all the men led a course toward the chow hall. Everyone noticed the stranger coming out of the forest with his last load. No one questioned what they'd heard. He certainly was huge and a little frightening with just his eyes, cheeks, and hands exposed.

Dropping the load and putting his horse away made the stranger a little late for supper. All conversation stopped when he literally ducked in the door.

Scooping his meal from the pots he looked for a place to sit down. Tables were barely past his knees and chairs were for adolescents. The stranger went outside and returned with a heavy old gnarly piece of stump that defied any splitting maul. It was short and sturdy enough for his frame.

Never had the chow hall been so quiet. Slowly the room emptied, man by man.

When the stranger finished, he washed his plate in the sink and put it on the drain board. He was the only one to do that. Then he looked in the kitchen. "Ees good," he announced.

The bunk house was chilly. No one wanted to invest in splitting the wood for the stove.

"What ya think, Luke?" Mike asked, pulling off his boots.

Luke slumped down on the hard bed. "Don't like it one darn bit."

"That's one heap of horse he has," John added, inspecting a hole in his shirt. "Wonder where it came from."

"Wonder where he came from," Luke replied. "And why he's here."

Mike stretched out on his bunk. "Probably to earn some money."

"Well, I don't like it," Luke grumbled. "Some furner comin' over here and stealin' our work."

Mike adjusted his pillow and crossed his legs. Didn't you say your Grandpappy came over here? He must've been a furner. What woulda happened if he'd been denied a job?"

"That's different," Luke huffed.

"Hey, guys, you gotta see this," one of the teamsters interrupted.

They all took turns looking out the window, watching the stranger split wood with one hand. No one said a thing when he came in and filled the wood box with one arm load. Starting the stove required that he get down on his knees.

Surveying the bunks made it obvious. Nothing would fit. The stranger grabbed his sack and squeezed out the door.

"Where's he goin?" Luke asked.

Mike lit a cigarette. "Probably the barn. Only place big

enough to hold him. Lucky guy. He won't have ta listen to you snore."

"Don't need no furner round here anyhow," Luke complained.

From that time on, the stranger stayed in the barn with his workmate, Lou. He would check his ears, dress his hoofs and comb him down. Lou always had a clean stall, fresh bedding and plenty of water.

In the early hours of the morning, a few light sleepers in the bunk house heard the stove door squeak open and a fresh chunk of wood tumble onto the dwindling coals. A light click of the bunk house door meant rising to a warm room and dry clothes.

None of the teamsters complained about the warm room or the dry clothes. Many were amazed how a big man could slip in so quietly. Just a light squeak of the stove door and a cool breeze when the door closed marked the event. They deliberated about when he slept. Whenever someone went near the barn they'd see him rubbing Lou, cleaning stalls or oiling harness.

Jessop slogged into camp before dawn. He always arrived early to get the kitchen stove hot and the coffee on. It was a mile and a quarter to his house. Quite a walk for a youngster but it kept him and his Ma going. They supplied the camp with bread and eggs. A load he carried in his back pack every day. Already tired, he set his pack down in the kitchen. What a surprise to find the days supply of wood all split and stacked next to the stove. The most hated and strenuous job grinned at him in the pallid light of dawn.

From that day on, the stove wood box at the kitchen and the bunkhouse never emptied and Jessop saw to it the stranger's coffee cup never emptied.

It was Mike who finally asked. He went to the manager. "What is that man's name?"

"What man?" The manager asked.

"The furner," Mike replied.

"You don't wanna know," the manager said, scratching his head. "Looks like someone scrambled the alphabet, then tried to put it back together with a shovel."

"So where's he from?"

The manager went back to his papers. "Guess you'll have to ask him."

Frustrated, Mike drove his team into the forest. That guy took care of a lot of things around the camp. He used wrapped chain for harness. And even with that one horse he met his quota.

Then Mike realized he always saw the furner go by him with his load. That meant he was taking the logs that were further in and further to drag out. Why hadn't he noticed that before?

Rain had cut a ravine in this part of the skid trail. Mike snapped the reins on his team to speed them up so the logs would slide right over the ditch. Unfortunately the horses stopped on the other side of the ditch to catch their step and the load quickly took advantage of the slack. With good momentum and no lifting force, his logs stabbed into the opposite bank. His team strained to lift it but nothing worked. Tugging only improved it's grip.

This was going to be a lot of strenuous work. A narrow trail meant separating the team and rejoining them on the back side of the load. No doubt the logs would only come out one by one which meant breaking down the load. Then reassembling the load, separating the team and lining them up in front again. Hopefully, a second try would clear the ditch.

Mike stood there, lamenting his situation, when he heard the familiar sound of wood scrubbing on dirt, accompanied by heavy breathing and a faint sound of someone humming.

The stranger was passing along on a side trail far too narrow for a team of horses. He stopped and so did the horse. The stranger came over to access the situation.

Mike didn't know what to say. The only thing he could think of was to hook on the front in tandem and hope the chain held.

The stranger pulled the pin on his own load, shouldered a length of chain and said, "Lou."

One horse easily maneuvered between trees, following his master to the rear of Mike's load. The stranger snapped a chain around the lowest log, attached the draw bar and set the pin. He motioned Mike to back up his team to give some slack.

Mike could only watch for he realized the force it would take to free the entire pile at once. Even his heavy team wouldn't attempt that.

The stranger said, "Lou" and the huge animal leaned into the hitch. It strained but nothing happened. Fetching a rope, the stranger tied it to the butt log, threw the other end over his shoulder, leaned into it and they both pulled. Nothing happened

Mike figured they'd tried and it would be time for the stranger to leave him with the problem. Instead, with a straining voice, the stranger said, "*LOUU.*"

Mike had never seen anything like it. That huge animal humped his back, put his front feet almost beside his rear feet and leaned into the hitch. His front shoulders added the force of another member.

The two of them hung there. If the hitch broke they would both plant their faces in the dirt.

Finally the bottom log slid back in the slack of the wrap chain. That broke the adhesion of the entire load and all the others slid back out of the hole. Mike's heart jumped so hard he let out a hoot.

Slapping his animal on the shoulder, the stranger pulled his pin and released his chain. Then he motioned Mike to put his team at an angle to the ditch. When the logs entered the ditch, instead of plowing in, they slid up the other side and continued on their way. Mike waved and yelled "Thanks." He would never forget that image of a huge man standing beside a gigantic horse, waving. "Ees good," echoed through the forest.

Everyone listened when Mike told about it in the bunk house that night. "Yup," Mike said. "That furner sure knows what he's doing."

The name set and from that day on the big man was known as Furner.

When Furner went to town, children ran and adults stared. Everyone stopped to look out the window. That gigantic horse was always a step or two behind him. Where Furner went, Lou went.

The post office clerk whistled when he saw the address on his letter. "Gonna take 30 cents and a month to get there. Probably have'ta go by boat."

Every Sunday, Furner went to church. He went in just as services were starting and sat in the back on a low bench against the wall. Youngsters fidgeted in their seats, trying to look back without getting reprimanded.

He'd put his quarter in the box and leave quietly during the last song. Those tall church doors were the only ones he didn't have to duck for.

People could see him through the windows, going back up to the camp with Lou following close behind.

Since the logging camp quartered horses, it needed hay for the winter. Local farmers entertained the profits.

One evening, just as the teamsters were leaving the chow hall, a young man drove in with a wagonload of hay and stopped next the barn loft. He waved to the men that walked by but no one paid any attention. "Least they could do is help," he muttered, scaling the load. At this height the first few fork fulls went through the hatch doorway easily. But as the pile diminished it would get much harder.

The hatchway filled quickly. He slid down, went in and climbed the ladder to the loft. Now he had to move each pile to the rear of the loft and pile it again. Why would his Dad send him up here alone? Especially this late. He'd be going home in the dark. His horses didn't like the dark and neither did he. Just an owl hoot made them nervous and hard to handle. They felt vulnerable hitched to a wagon.

Chores were waiting and each fork full got exponentially heavier.

He was about to go down to throw in more when a big pile flew in through the hatchway and slid almost back to him. Someone out there had decided to help and they had a good arm. He put that one away and another slid right back to him. There had to be two men out there. He was so relieved he wanted to cry. His dread melted and in between the strains of lifting he whistled a little tune.

He was still whistling when he dismounted the loft ladder. Stepping outside, he almost swallowed his tongue. His lips stuck in the whistle position but no sound came out.

Right next to him was the giant they called Furner. He'd heard about him but put little stock in their intentional exaggerations. He had to swallow to open his throat for air. This man was so huge a pitchfork looked like a toy in his hands.

Furner smiled. "Ees good," he said turning toward the barn.

The young man hurried out of there. He was a good distance away when he realized he should've thanked Furner for his help.

A few days later, Luke approached the drop station with his load. Furner was just finishing up so he had to wait. He didn't approve of Furner's presence from his first arrival and wasn't about to be swayed by the others. Delays were especially perturbing.

Furner picked up his chains and called for Lou to step forward.

Luke snapped the reins and his team pulled the load up into place. He kicked the top log to loosen the tow chain. Releasing the grab hook, he tossed it over the pile. It hung up on the lower log instead of sliding down to the ground. A chain had to be laying flat on the ground to slip out under the load without catching. Luke stepped around to free his chain.

At that crucial moment one member of his team thrashed. The chain tugged, jostling the pile and the top log tumbled. It hit Luke just above the knees. He went down hard. The sound of wood colliding with wood sent chills through him. How quickly his mind snapped back to that horrible moment when his father lay there in his arms. A renegade log had rolled over his own father. He could even hear his father's last words. They were labored and gurgly. "Never turn your back on the load son. Never turn your back on the looo…"

Now it was his turn. Another second and he would be hit with a spine crushing blow.

For some reason it delayed. He rose to his hands and knees, scurrying out of the way. Relieved, he stood up and brushed away the dirt. Some miraculous stroke of luck had spared him.

He turned to get back to work and what he saw jolted his very soul. There was Furner, legs braced, holding the butt end of that log in his lap.

Furner dropped the villain with a stomach wrenching thud. "Ees good," he said walking away. "Lou," he called and the horse followed him back into the forest.

That night at supper, Furner was the last one in. He tended to Lou first.

Everyone watched him scrunch down for the door. He filled his plate, descended onto his tree stump chair, arranged his legs under the table and bowed his head in prayer.

When Furner looked up Luke was standing in front of him with a full cup of coffee. He set it down next to the plate and looked right into those sharp dark eyes. "Thanks, Furner," he said. "I'm liken you being here with us."

Another story was told at the bunk house that night. After Furner had filled the wood box, he loaded the stove and left for the barn. Luke sat at the table, slowly turning a deck of cards in his hands. No one interrupted. No one made a sound. Luke told of his father's death. He told about the feeling he had when that log hit him and what went through his mind on his way back into the forest.

"Don't know where he came from or how he got there. First, he was headed up into the woods and then he was standin' over me. He has to be a connection. Has to be a connection 'tween him and the Lord."

When Saturday, payday arrived, everyone took their receipts into the pay office where the banker exchanged them for money. Then the men piled into a wagon and headed for town. Mike stood in line outside when Furner came up, counting his tickets. Mike watched him count out six.

"Wait, Furner," he said. "You only need five."

Furner nodded and went back to put the sixth one away.

Mike was about to board the wagon to town when he saw Furner hurrying out of the barn.

"What's the matter?" Mike called.

Furner looked confused. He held out the sixth ticket. Then he opened his hand to reveal only four dollars.

Mike hollered to the others, "Hold the wagon, I'll be right back." He motioned to Jessop to follow him.

The banker looked confused when three sizes stormed into the office. Little Jessop, medium Mike and huge Furner. His confusion turned to fear when Mike snatched his cash box and sorted through the receipts. Only four of Furner's receipts showed.

"Where's the fifth?" Mike snarled.

"He gave me four," the banker replied.

Mike put his finger in the bankers face. "I watched him count um myself. Are calling me a liar?"

The banker grabbed the extra receipt from Furner, handed him a dollar and closed his cash box. "See? He had it with him the whole time."

Mike stood there pinning the banker behind the desk. "You're gonna get searched. You got that ticket on ya. You're cheatin him."

"That's preposterous," the banker said, his voice shaking.

"Jessop," Mike growled. "Get the others and then fetch my rope."

Sweat beaded on the banker's face and his breathing

228

quickened as the room filled with men.

That's when Furner shoved the cashbox into the bankers chest and guided him toward the door. The crowd melted out of the way.

The banker didn't need further instructions. He vaulted into his carriage and snapped the reins, allowing the jerk of the carriage to slam him into the seat.

"Don't come back here," Mike yelled at the retreating rig. "How long has he been cheating you Furner? Probably since you got here see'n as how you brought six tickets in the first place." Mike motioned toward the wagon. "Come on with us."

"Ees good," Furner answered, waving them on. He'd go get Lou and the two would walk to town.

Noise and laughter rolled out of the bar as Furner and Lou passed by. At the post office he came out with a letter. A precious piece of news. He bought a lantern at the store, then sat on the steps outside to read his letter. He read it and tucked it away. Then took it out and read it again.

Looking out the window, the storekeeper huffed. That huge man right there on his front steps would surely scare people away. Maybe it was a good thing. He wanted to close early any way. All his help was over at the bar and he just received a big load of stock. He locked the front door and flipped the closed sign. He stared at it through the back entrance. A whole big wagon load of boxes, bags and barrels. A man his age shouldn't have to handle all that alone. Must be four ton of stuff there. He couldn't leave it on the wagon so vulnerable to thievery.

It took several grunts to get the first bag up on his shoulder. Some day he'd have a ramp made. Something heavy enough to handle a hand truck.

Suddenly the heavy weight lifted off his shoulder. His heart jumped. Every muscle tightened. How stupid of him. What a perfect setup for robbery. The back door wide open, cash in the register, and everyone over at the noisy bar. How could he have left himself so open? He winced, ready for the blow to the back of his head.

Through squinting eyes he saw Furner lean forward and go in the back door. He had a 100 pound sack in each hand. Not under his arm, but in his hand like someone would carry a lunch bag. When he came back out, he motioned toward the door and pretended to write on his hand. The storekeeper gladly obeyed and fetched his checklist.

Barrels of pickles, soda crackers, sacks of grain, bags of seed, boxes of Salvatore and canned beans came in so fast the storekeeper could hardly keep up. He just pointed to where he wanted it, read the label and checked the order sheet.

With the last item tallied, he scanned the pages. Order complete. Not a piece missing.

Where was Furner? He looked out back. Just an empty wagon. He ran out front. There in the distance he saw a big man going up the street with a horse following him.

Monday morning at breakfast, one of the teamsters noticed his friend didn't look well. "Where's your appetite, Stoney?" he asked. "You're so thin we can see both sides of you at the same time, as it is. If you don't eat you won't even cast a shadow."

Stoney jumped up, threw his food in the trash and stormed out.

Mike broke the tense silence. "Don't take no offense. He's mad at himself. The paymaster brought up a letter for him Saturday. He was in such a hurry to go to town, he put it on his bunk and left. Seems he got hooked into a card game and a couple card sharks cleaned him out."

Mike sipped his coffee." When he got back, the letter said his son is going in the hospital for an important operation on Friday."

"Why don't he just go home?" One of the men asked. "Manager should understand."

"He ain't got the dollar and a quarter for the train ticket," Mike added. "That's why he's mad at himself. He got suckered in."

"Why can't we loan it to him?" one of the teamsters suggested.

"Tried that," Mike replied. "Says he's not gonna be beholdin' to nobody."

"He's only hurting himself," Luke added.

Mike gulped the last of his coffee. "I know, but a man's got a right to run his own affairs."

Everyone filed out to harness their horses. Stoney was already driving his team up the forest trail.

That evening, when Mike came in the bunk house, Stoney was sitting on his bed, slowly turning that letter in his hands. "I know it's kinda tough. Worrying about your son and all."

Stoney held up the paper. It wasn't a letter at all. It was two train tickets. One for going and one for coming back.

"Where'd they come from?" Mike exclaimed.

Stoney looked up at him. "You don't know?"

"I can truly say I don't," Mike answered, holding up his daily quota ticket. "Somebody had'ta go ta town ta get um. It wasn't me cause I made my quota. Can't be in town and in the woods, too. Don't know of anyone that went ta town today."

Just then, Luke walked in.

"Did ya make your quota today, Luke?" Mike asked.

Luke held up his ticket.

"It warnt him either," Mike said. "Know of anyone that went ta town today?"

Luke shook his head. "Nope. Why?"

"Stoney's son is in the hospital," Luke said. "He found these train tickets and don't know where they came from."

"Well," Luke drawled, waving toward the door. "Can't be any of them other fellas. They're all comparing their tallies. Can't be Furner cause he don't know what we're saying. I'd soon say the good Lord provides. Won't do any good fussin' about it. I suggest you get your sack packed and head for town. Cookie might let Jessop take you in with the wagon."

Stoney pondered a while, then reluctantly complied.

Jessop drove the wagon to town a little slower than usual so they'd arrive close to departure time. He didn't want Stoney going in and asking the station agent who bought the tickets. It meant getting back to camp real close to dark.

On the way back to camp he went by the road to his house. Three-quarter miles back to camp the road was wide and clear. Not as scary in the dark as the narrow, closed-in trail to his house. It had a thick crushing sensation that darkness multiplied.

Just a little further and there was Furner standing in the road with a lantern in his hand. He gave Jessop the lit lantern and motioned him toward his house. Jessop watched him take the horses halter and lead it off toward the camp. He never rode. He always walked. Maybe he couldn't fit in the seat.

Whatever the reason, Jessop made a quick sprint home, avoiding those spots that purposely hook your shoe. Put

232

there by some ghost that delights in scraped hands and dirty knees.

The next morning Jessop tried to return the lantern but Furner refused. Days were getting shorter and that lantern would always cast a warm light of friendship and concern. He couldn't believe this man frightened him just a while ago. And now he had a genuine desire to hug him.

When snow arrived, it made log skidding more difficult and dangerous. Wet clothes hung everywhere in the bunk house. Short days led to short tempers. Everyone was a grouch. Everyone except Furner. He stretched out in the barn with only himself to deal with.

One morning, Furner looked out to a thick blanket of wet, heavy snow. He kicked his way to the bunk house and loaded the stove. A couple men felt a rush of cold air enter. It was settling to know warmth would be waiting for them to awake. Back at the barn, Furner threw a blanket over Lou and led him out into the predawn chill.

Jessop filled his sack with bread and looked outside with dread. Even as much as he hated to go, duty called. The cook would be angry without fresh bread and a warm stove to prepare breakfast for a bunch of ornery men. Pushing through heavy knee-high snow tired him quickly. Even hard working muscles couldn't overcome the penetrating cold that dampness brought. His pants were soaked, his hands were numb. He stumbled on, hoping the camp road would be easier.

There it was ahead. Just as impassable, just as consuming, just as discouraging.

Wet and shivering he looked back toward home. He was at the half way point. A pushed path was the only advantage in turning back. Could he even manage that? His legs were like frozen logs. He was so tired even his arms didn't want to hold frozen hands up under his armpits anymore. He couldn't feel them anyway. His only driving incentive was what would his mother do without him? She really couldn't survive alone.

He heard a rushing wind. No, it was different than a strong wind. It was a thrashing sound. Or was it heavy breathing?

A big shadow appeared through the snow. Someone was here. It was Lou.

Huge hands lifted him up and laid him on that wide strong back. A blanket covered his shaking frame. Then came that familiar voice. "Lou." He felt the rhythmical movement of strong muscle under the grateful warmth of a heavy blanket.

His spasms had finally stopped when the blanket lifted. There was Furner's big hairy smile. Jessop knew an angel could not have looked any better.

The kitchen stove glowed. He and Furner hugged tin cups of hot coffee when the cook staggered into the kitchen.

"Well," the cook said yawning, and pulling up his suspenders. "I see ya made it. What cha doin' sittin' around? Git the coffee goin'."

Jessop held up his cup.

"Well, then," the cook growled, "fill the wood box."

Jessop gestured toward the stove.

"Then git out in the kitchen and slice up some bread."

Jessop held out a plate of hot toast. "Want some?"

The cook stormed out and Furner smiled. "Ees good, eh?"

Snow storms continued to plague the area. Skid trails were difficult to keep open. Distance to the rail head increased as good trees diminished. Horses worked harder and so did the men. Very few met their quota. Log quantity went down but expenses didn't. By spring the lumber company closed the operation and the railroad closed the spur.

Most of the men took their horses and went back to farming. Some went out searching for other operations. Furner decided to stay.

Since the company abandoned the operation they didn't care if Furner used the buildings. He cut and sold firewood, hired out to clear fields and helped with haying. He stopped by often to help Jessop with winter wood and fence building. Things were sparse for everyone.

People saw him come to church every Sunday and return to camp with Lou following along behind. Most Sundays he'd stop to help Jessop. Payment was a good meal. Theresa always made a big stew for the two men. Jessop was sprouting into a fine young man.

Doc made a late house call. He didn't get back to town until dark. Pulling the carriage up in front of his office, he could see a big dark form in front of the post office. It was Lou. Furner sat there on the steps. Doc moved closer. He was slowly turning a letter in his hands.

"You all right, Furner?" he asked.

He heard a low growl. Then the big man got up and walked out of town. Lou followed along behind.

It was two weeks later when Doc came into town. He stopped his carriage in front of the church. The Pastor finished talking to his parishioners and came over.

"Seen Furner lately?" Doc asked.

"Ain't seen him in a while," the Pastor said.

"I see you haven't been watching your flock," Doc chided.

The Pastor threw back his shoulders. "Well, move your butt over and let's go check."

They met Jessop on the way out of town. "Seen Furner lately?" Doc asked.

Jessop shook his head.

"We're going to check on him," Pastor added.

"Me, too," Jessop replied, jumping on the back of the carriage.

On the way there they passed a big pile of rocks near the side of the road. No one had to ask why it was there.

The barn door swung open easily. Lou's empty stall faced them, clean with fresh hay. Furner lay on a large bunk in the next stall. He had converted much of the stable into a camp kitchen with the chow hall stove and parts of the bunk house.

Doc lifted one eye lid and listened to a raspy breath while the Pastor fumbled through a few meager belongings. "Look at this letter here. Has more stamps on it than a dog has fleas. Must be from family."

Doc laid down a limp hand. "We'll need it to notify next of kin. He doesn't have much time left."

Jessop stood there horrified. What could he do? His Ma had nursing skills. She wanted to be a nurse but home duties denied her that advantage. Just maybe. He had to try.

Jessop threw wood in the stove and lit a match. "You get this fire going. I'll be back in twenty minutes." He burst out the door and ran down the road like death was chasing him. Because it was.

He didn't even feel his feet hitting the ground. His mind covered the years he'd known this man. He saw the big pile of rocks coming up, then disappear behind him. When he cut the turn from the camp road he wasn't even breathing hard. Now sixteen years old and a far cry from that little lad Furner rescued there in the snow.

Trees and bushes flashed by. There was the fence Furner

helped him build. There was the field they hayed together.

He crossed the porch in two bounds. "*Maaaa.*" He snapped the door open to see his mother's frightened look.

"What's the matter?" She stuttered.

"It's Furner. He's dying."

Her face turned ashen, with a blank stare of disbelief. Assembling the situation in her mind, she rushed to the stove. "Harness Betsy. I'll be right out."

Jessop set a record. He pulled the carriage out of the shed alone. Betsy stepped obediently between the shafts. Ma loaded hot broth, blankets and herbs.

Betsy ran heavy footed. Like she was carrying an extra load. Maybe she drank too much water and had the bloat.

When Jessop arrived the Doc and Pastor were gone. The stove was hot and Furner was still breathing. They'd taken Furner's shoulder satchel. Maybe they were going to notify next of kin.

Theresa started with stove warmed blankets and an herb mist inhalant. His breathing sounded like dried beans shaking in a tin can. She suspected pneumonia and hypothermia. Jessop gathered firewood for the hungry stove. He could visualize Furner splitting wood with one hand. That heavy maul looked like a little hatchet in his hand.

Later in the afternoon, he went home to set the fires and fetch preserves.

Theresa fussed with the blanket shrouding Furner's head. It held in the warm herbal mist. Then she smoothed back his thick curly hair. It was the first time she touched him.

Her soft hand must have triggered a distant memory. She heard him whisper "Natasha?" He was delirious.

"Theresa," she said, checking a weak pulse.

"Theresa," he whispered, squeezing her hand.

She pushed the hot blanket up under his beard. He was on his way back.

When Jessop got back, he put Betsy in Lou's stall for the night.

In the early hours before dawn Furner coughed. Jessop snapped awake. He studied Furner's breathing. Raspy but steady. Through the dense mustache he found a lower lip and dumped in a small spoonful of broth. "Be careful now. Swallow this."

It disappeared without incident.

"I know Lou is gone," Jessop said. "But I'm here and so is Ma. She thinks a lot of you and so do I." He pushed back a recalcitrant lock of hair to expose a seldom seen forehead. "I know you can understand me. You knew what Mike said when he told about Stoney and the train ticket. You sent me to town to buy them. I had a hard time keeping that secret. Stoney suspected me but I never told."

Jessop tipped up another spoonful of broth. "The first time you came into the camp. I thought you were a monster coming out of the woods to eat me. And that morning of the big snow storm. You and Lou saved my life. I wouldn't have made it home. I don't know how you knew but I'm glad you did. I like to think I'm the only one to ever ride on Lou's back. He sure was a loyal friend."

In the lamplight, Jessop saw a small tear squeeze out of the corner of his eye and trace a path down a bushy beard.

"I never had a Dad," Jessop continued. "He died in a drinking bout when I was very young. We would'a been all right if he'd been sober. Ma has all sorts of nursing skills. She's read all the books. Studied enough to be a doctor but never could afford the exams. Maybe it's a good thing she did cause now she gets a chance to practice on you."

"Theresa," Furner whispered.

238

Jessop's heart jumped. "That's her name and she's gonna get you better." Jessop teased in another spoon of broth. "Who knows, maybe someday, you can be my Dad. I'd like that. Then I wouldn't have to split all the wood alone."

Ma rose slowly from her pile of blankets. "How's he doing?"

"Four spoons of broth," Jessop replied.

"Ees good," she said and fell back asleep.

Doc and the Pastor returned the second day. Jessop was home tending the barn chores when they arrived. Doc was pleased with Furner's progress. "He has a severe case of pneumonia but seems to be on the mend. Mighty tough man, mighty tough man. We'll get him in to town as soon as he's able."

Doc turned to Theresa. "Think you and Jessop can handle a few more days?" He sniffed the herbal formula simmering on the stove and passed it off as food. Theresa heard them coming and removed the shroud. It looked like a table linen, draped over the only chair.

"I sent a telegram to Boston," the Pastor announced. "Lots of churches there. Someone there should recognize his language."

"Why?" Theresa asked.

The Pastor looked confused. "If he's gonna die on us, who should we notify and how?"

Theresa stood defensively. "He's not gonna die. He's a big man that wants to be left alone. You should be able to honor that. If he wants you to know more, he'll tell you."

The Doc and the Pastor left quietly.

She was replacing the shroud when Furner said, "Theresa." His temperature climbed rapidly. The fever set in hard. He thrashed and mumbled. When Jessop arrived he

239

helped apply cold compresses to Furner's head and chest. "It's gonna be a hard night," she said.

Finally, after hours of struggling, Furner relaxed. Jessop collapsed on the pile of blankets. When he woke his Ma had a huge hand in her lap and her head on Furner's shoulder. He quietly moved closer to see that big chest rise and fall. He made it again.

Four days passed before Furner could sit up. Jessop and his Ma crutched him to the wagon. They made a long slow trip to town with their patient wrapped in every blanket available. It was the first ride anyone had ever seen him take.

Betsy had a very interrupted stride. Jessop worried that she may be going lame.

Furner ducked and squeezed into Doc's recovery room where an enlarged bunk awaited him. A dose of laudanum and a bowl of Theresa's hot broth convinced the big man to rest.

When Jessop came out of Doc's office, the livery man had released Betsy from the wagon. He had her by the reins, leading her away. "I'll take her home," he said, wondering what the infraction was.

"Won't make home," the livery man replied. "Lucky if she makes my stable."

His lumber camp job gone. No work in the area. Trying to run a farm. Caring for a sick man and now the horse. It wasn't that difficult to understand why Furner felt it easier to end it all.

Ma's reassuring arm dropped on his shoulder. "We can walk. You have a little red wagon. We'll pull it together. We don't need this big wagon. We'll sell it." She threw her shoulders back. "Furner always walked. Why, this was probably the first wagon ride of his life."

"Yeah," Jessop sighed. "And our last."

"Come on," Ma suggested. "Let's go tend to Betsy. Maybe that livery fella knows someone who needs a good sturdy wagon."

It was four days later, when Theresa was coming out of the recovery room. The Pastor and a stranger were waiting in the main office. "The doctor's out right now," she said.

The Pastor gestured toward the stranger. "This is Reverend Moss. We've come to talk to Furner."

"What about?" she asked. "He never says more than three words."

"I speak his language," Reverend Moss replied.

Theresa stood her ground in front of the recovery room door.

The Pastor apologized. "We don't want to intrude. The Reverend here is from Boston. He answered my telegram. We want to know more about him."

"Like why he wanted to die?" she snapped. "He's a big man that lost his job and his horse. It broke his heart. What else is there to know?"

Reverend Moss tugged a letter from his pocket. "This letter is from his family."

Theresa stiffened. "No one knew he was married. In delirium, he whispered the name Natasha."

"That's his sister," Reverend Moss replied.

Theresa's heart settled back. She opened the door. "I'm staying with you in case of a bad reaction."

Reverend Moss pushed a chair over close, inspected the size of this man and sat down. He leaned over even closer and in Furner's native language said, "Stanislous Mahallovich, can you hear me?"

Furner's head rolled toward him and one eye opened just a crack. "Who are you?"

"I'm Reverend Moss from Boston. I've come to help."

Furner grunted and looked away.

"You have suffered great losses," the Reverend said. "I have read the letter from your family."

"I have nothing left," Furner whispered. "My God has abandoned me."

"I think not," the Reverend replied. "Your diary has some beautiful words in it. You write well. I know of a publisher in Boston that works with this type of material. You could go there, translate your words and publish them in a book."

"I have nothing," Furner muttered. "Am I supposed to walk there and live in the street?"

He laughed under his breath. It was a light chuckle that detonated a succession of coughs and gasps.

Theresa rushed in, "Enough," she said, pushing him upright and stuffing pillows under his back.

Reverend Moss and the Pastor left the recovery room just as Doc came in. They explained their presence. Then the Reverend interpreted the letter from Furner's family abroad.

The Doc sunk into his chair. "That explains it. I saw Furner there on the post office steps late one night. No doubt why he went home looking so dejected. Found out his Ma and Pa and invalid sister all died in a plague. No doubt that was where he was sending his money. To help them. Then to lose his horse that same night. Who could question why the man feels broken."

Theresa carefully finished closing the recovery room door. She laid her head on Furner's huge chest. Tears soaked into his shirt. "I didn't know," she cried softly. "I didn't know."

A big hand encircled her soft hair. "Ees good. Ees good," he whispered.

The Pastor and Reverend Moss left, discussing a plan.

That Sunday just before services ended, the Pastor made an announcement. He told his parishioners of the need to raise money to send Furner to Boston. "We could put a special contribution box in the rear for those who so desire. This is your church so you people decide. Is it something you approve of?" After a short pause and a few mutters, someone in the back boomed out, "Ees good," and the whole congregation broke out in applause.

Over the next few days people casually came in to show their appreciation for Furner's help in their behalf. Even the devout atheists like the storekeeper braved the excursion.

Later in the week, when the Pastor and Reverend Moss were counting the proceeds, the banker stepped in. "Got enough for the trip?" he asked.

"Not quite," the Pastor lied.

A ten dollar bill dropped on the table in front of him. "This aught'a help."

Under lifted eyebrows, the two of them watched him walk out.

"There's always room for reform," the Reverend breathed.

"Room," the Pastor wheezed. "He'd take up the whole front row." He tucked the money safely in the sack. "Furner must've saved his life to warrant this."

Furner was recovering well. He was able to be up and dressed so after the next Sunday service, the whole congregation followed the Pastor down to Doc's office. Even the storekeeper came out to join the gathering.

The Pastor and Reverend Moss found Furner sitting on a low bench at the table. The Reverend handed him the envelop and spoke in his own language.

"Train tickets and money to go to Boston. You did it for Stoney. Now your friends have done it for you." He gestured toward the door. "They're waiting for you outside."

Furner stared at it in disbelief. He looked out to see the crowd. "How did you know about Stoney?"

"Jessop likes to brag about you," the Reverend admitted.

After along silence and a few sighs, Furner rose and squeezed through the door. He appraised the group, then raised his arms. "Ees good" he bellowed. "Ees good."

After a long bout of cheers and applause the crowd slowly dispersed. Very few noticed Furner staring at something coming up the street. He stood there, paralyzed by what he saw. Jessop led his horse Betsy up in front of him. Along beside her stood a two week old colt. As young as it was, it had the discernible features of its father. Large front shoulders, short neck and wide flank.

"Little Lou," Jessop said.

Furner almost stopped breathing. His lip quivered. Kneeling down, he kissed the animal on the neck. "Litta Lou," he exclaimed. "Litta Lou." He kissed him on the forehead, rubbed that big chest and wide back.

Standing up, he gestured toward heaven and spoke in his own language. It was more than most had ever heard him say. Even Betsy nickered in response.

Reverend Moss broke the silence. "Wow," he muttered. "The man truly is a poet."

"What'd he say?" The storekeeper asked.

"He thanked God for sending him a savior and a prince." Reverend Moss replied.

"Yeah?" The storekeeper drawled. Being an atheist and skeptic he saw room for sarcasm. "What'd the horse say?"

"Amen," the Reverend replied and walked away.

Furner appraised the colt for quite some time. Betsy didn't mind the attention she got for her role in the project.

Monday morning found Furner sitting on the front steps of the barber shop. When the barber showed up he gestured for a hair cut. He absolutely wouldn't fit in a chair so the surgery took place right there on the front steps. Hands flashed as they communicated length and procedure.

Soon a forehead appeared. Then a nose showed up. A shortened and trimmed beard exposed a mouth and two cheeks. Finally bushy eyebrows weeded out around soft dark eyes.

After cleaning up a whole bucket of trimmings, the barber accepted Furner's offer of thirty cents. Twice the price of a standard hair cut but well worth it.

Later in the day, Theresa came in with Furner's meal. She stepped in on Furner and Reverend Moss talking. They spoke in their own language so she didn't feel intrusive. She divided a hefty soup between them and went outside to wait.

"You know their language," the Reverend said. "Why don't you use it?"

Furner tested his soup. "People are suspicious of strangers. They ask fewer questions and demand fewer answers. I came here for a job. That is all. People fear my size. If I shared their language they would fear my motives as well." He stirred his soup in slow contemplation. "You are from the old country?"

"My father was," the Reverend replied. "He insisted I speak his language. He would talk in no other."

Furner dipped his bread in the broth. "Smart man. See how much you have learned? When you give up your language, you give up your voice. Values are lost. Your heritage is lost. Languages are beautiful. Like a fine uniform that identifies a soldier and his nation. It demands a great responsibility and a pride that should not be allowed to diminish."

Reverend Moss wiped the bowl with his last bite of

bread. "I'm going to enjoy working with you in Boston." He pushed away from the table. "I must be going. Thank Theresa for me. She is a fine lady."

"Ees good," Furner replied as the door closed.

A little ways down the street Theresa intercepted the Reverend. "I need your help." She struggled with the words to describe her intentions. "I want to know his words."

"That's a big task," Reverend Moss replied.

"Well," Theresa said looking down at her hands.

Reverend Moss noticed someone approaching. "And I thank you for the soup and bread," he announced. "I'd like to buy a loaf for myself. Would it be possible for you to bring it tomorrow? I'll stop by to retrieve it."

He watched the passerby retreat. "Now, what were you about to say?"

She handed him a small note. "Can you teach me this?"

He drew a long slow breath.

She stared at him. "Is he?"

"No," the Reverend interrupted. " He handed back the note. "I'll help you. We'll get together on this. Ees good." He shook his head. "He's even got me saying it."

Theresa felt at ease with her decision as she watched the Reverend walk away.

He whirled around. "And I'm serious about the bread."

By week's end Furner was ready for the big adventure. He waited quietly at Doc's table.

Theresa nervously assembled all the things she had used for cooking and caring for this big man.

He motioned her over and reached out for her hand. Inspecting the rough side, then the smooth side, he pressed ten dollars into her palm. He motioned toward his mouth. "And Litta Lou," he said.

Yes, he ate a lot of food and the colt would need attention. Funds were tight even if she was working for the Doc full time now.

Her heart raced. She was standing in front of him. He was holding her hand. Couldn't he feel the heavy pulse? She looked into those dark eyes, drew in a full breath of courage and spoke in his language. "Stanislaus Mahallovich, I love you."

He never flinched. Just sat there staring at her. He swallowed several times and smiled.

They both saw Reverend Moss approaching. Furner released her hand. "Ees good," he said squeezing out of the office.

Theresa stood there, watching them walk away. She had cooked for him, laundered and mended his clothes, tended to him for weeks, cured his illness, held his hand, even cried on his chest and he just walks away. She probably touched him more than any other woman on earth and he just walks away. She threw her heart in his lap and he walks away. "I hate men," she growled. "I hate men." She went into the recovery room, threw herself on that big bed and sobbed.

The Pastor watched the train melt into the distance.

"Well, sir," the ticket agent said, stepping up beside him. "We've seen the last of him."

"He'll be back," the Pastor replied.

"Why?" The ticket agent added. "Ain't nothin here. This is the last stop to nowhere."

"What are you doing here?" The Pastor asked and walked away.

Furner sat sideways, wedged into a three-person bench

area. Reverend Moss enjoyed the bay in front of him.

"Did you say goodbye to Theresa?" The Reverend asked.

Furner nodded.

"So what did she say?"

"You pretend," Furner grunted. "She could only learn those words from you."

"So what did you tell her?"

Furner spoke slowly. "When a man proposes marriage he must be able to pay the bride price. I cannot. Her first husband lied to her. He promised to be a support and died in a self-gratifying drunken stupor."

The Reverend shrugged. "Maybe he had good intentions."

"Don't be like the others," Furner growled. "People can justify anything. Good intentions are still a lie if the truth is ignored. Leading her on without a solid foundation for support is a lie. It only leads to failure and broken trust."

"Do you love her?" Reverend Moss asked.

Furner stared off into the distance. "Yes."

"Then why disappoint her?"

Furner was tired of talking. "Disappointment or failure. Which one would you rather have?" He said pushing down in his seat and propping his head up with one arm.

It was almost dark when Furner spoke again. "You have asked me many personal questions. Now I can ask you. What financial gain is there for you in this endeavor?"

"What do you mean?" The Reverend asked.

Furner looked at him hard. "My words are straight. You come to me, stay many days, lead me to Boston, help me with a book without some sort of gain?"

Reverend Moss shrugged. "I'm a Reverend."

Furner nodded. "And how long have you owned a publishing company?"

Reverend Moss broke into loud laughter.

Boston posed many challenges. Carriages were too small. Restaurants were too small. New clothes were too small. Beds were too small. Hotel clerks just stared or hid under the counter and refused to come out. Children ran and adults avoided him. Furner ignored it all.

One day, while enjoying a walk in the park, Furner and Reverend Moss entertained a brief rest on a bench looking out over the river.

"One of your poems speaks about a bench in the forest," Reverend Moss said.

"It was a bench I built for my sister," Furner reminisced. "I used to carry her up and let her view the lake far away. She would watch the birds and the butterflies. It was peaceful and comforting for her. It gave her a sense of mobility. From there she could travel the world in her mind. She was frail in body, but strong in spirit."

Reverend Moss felt the afternoon breeze on his cheek. "Do you wish you were back there?"

"No," Furner replied.

"Where would you like to be?" Reverend Moss asked.

"In a warm stable next to Lou," Furner said, looking away.

Winter proved to be a harsh one. Even a late spring couldn't seem to push it out of the way. Jessop pitched the last bit of hay into Betsy's feed tray. Mice picked at the few scattered oats around the empty bin. There wasn't much he could do about it. The banker didn't want to see him around. He owed him too much. He didn't like going to town anyhow. Everyone avoided him. He owed them all.

The banker had suggested selling Little Lou. Less than a year old and almost as big as his mother, he'd make good breeding stock.

Jessop cringed at the thought. It was just too much to

consider. That maneuver would haunt him forever.

Little Lou paced and whinnied. Must've read Jessop's thoughts. Just as he lifted the latch to his stall, Little Lou bolted out.

Jessop stepped out the barn door. Maybe he wanted to find a fresh blade of grass or drink from the brook.

Then he heard it. Faint but recognizable. "Litta Lou. Litta Lou."

The horse ran like a storm wind, thrashing and kicking up his heels.

Furner dropped his cases and met him like a long-lost playmate. He laughed so loud the neighbors could hear it. Little Lou bounced and whinnied and snorted. He just couldn't stand still and neither could Jessop. While the two frolicked in the road, he ran for the house.

"Ma. *MA*," he yelled.

She met him at the door. "Is the barn on fire?"

"No," Jessop gasped, pointing toward the road. "It's Furner."

Her heart stuck in her throat. She couldn't breathe. There he was coming up the road in a fine suit carrying two large cases, talking and singing to a perfectly crazy acting horse.

When things finally settled down, Furner sat at the table on his low designated stool, sipping a hot cup of coffee. Jessop just couldn't stop smiling.

Theresa served a turnip and a few soft potatoes from the bottom of the bin. That's all they had. She filled Furner's coffee cup and sat down.

Under heavy eyebrows, Furner stared at Jessop.

"I'd better put the horse back in the barn," Jessop said.

Furner reached over and took Theresa's hand. Then he said in his own language, *"Theresa, I love you."*

She recognized the words. They were galvanized on her heart.

Furner pointed to her, then himself and locked his hands together.

Theresa stood up and turned her back on him, arms folded in front of her. "You can say it. You can say it so I can understand it."

Furner coughed and fidgeted, but Theresa stood firm. Finally Furner put a table napkin on the floor, knelt on it and drew a deep breath. In plain and accurate English, he said, "Theresa, will you marry me?"

She turned to face him. With tear stained cheeks, she said, "Yes."

Just at that moment, Jessop burst in the door. Kicking up both heels, he yelled, "*Yeee haaa.*"

Furner returned to town with only one case. The other one was full of all sorts of finery a bride needed. Somehow a suit for Jessop managed to slip in there as well.

That Sunday the Pastor made the announcement from the pulpit. "We now have a published author in our midst and he's getting married. Everyone in town is invited so ya better be here."

Furner smiled and waved to the congregation as they all turned to see him setting in the rear.

He walked out in the midst of the crowd. The children were no longer afraid of him. They laughed at how many could fit their hands on just one of his. He would have at least three dangling from each arm. When he leaned forward, one brave little one rubbed his beard. Seeing the safety in it, they all wanted to try. Furner held out his hand and one courageous lad sat down on it as if it were a chair. His eyes swelled when Furner lifted him up as high as he could reach. When the safety of the ground showed up again, he walked over to his group. "See, I was higher than him," he announced. "I could see the ocean from up there."

Everyone in town wanted to shake his hand. Furner would gesture toward the farm and flash some money.

"Oh, Jessop?" The person would say. "He owes me for fourteen bales of hay. Maybe fifty cents."

Furner palmed them a dollar. "Ess good. Ees good," he'd say.

Furner finally came to the storekeeper. He stacked up grain, potatoes, salt and flour. Then he motioned toward the farm.

"Jessop owes me eight dollars," the storekeeper announced. "Total comes to nineteen dollars and thirty cents."

Furner dropped a twenty, took a few pieces of licorice and said, "Ees Good?"

With the wagon loaded, Furner started up the road. "Litta Lou," he said. The horse followed along. Not a halter, not a bridle, not a rein.

Saturday came hot and dry. It was the first time Furner had been in the front of the church. Collars were tight and sticky.

Everyone stood while Jessop brought his Ma up the aisle. The banker was there in the crowd. People said he'd rather be locked in his vault for a week than be seen in church. Even the storekeeper was there, trying to hide in the group.

Theresa looked so short next to Furner. She didn't quite top his elbow. Before the Pastor started, Furner pulled out his handkerchief, put it on the floor and knelt on it. Now she came up to his shoulder. He motioned the Pastor to proceed.

The Pastor cleared his throat. "Do you Stan, ahhh, Stan."

He tapped the Pastor's bible. "Furner," he said.

"Oh, yes," the Pastor continued. "Furner? Do you take this woman for your wife?"

"I do," Furner said.

"Been practicing I see," the Pastor chided. "Do you Theresa take this man for your husband?"

"I do," she said. "And if you ever take to drinking, I'll throw you out of the house myself."

When the laughter subsided Furner grinned. "Ees good."

"Well, I take it you both agree to the terms and conditions," the Pastor announced. "So I pronounce you man and wife."

Then the Pastor gestured to the side and out of the crowd stepped Reverend Moss. No one expected or even anticipated his presence. Even Furner was shocked.

The Reverend raised his hands and spoke in Furner's native language. "Stanislous Mahallovich and Theresa Mahallovich. May you have God's eternal blessing."

"Thank you, Reverend," Furner said. "My God has blessed me with a savior, a princess and many true friends."

"Well," the Pastor added. "You may kiss the bride."

Theresa jumped into his arms and for the first time their lips met.

Furner picked up his handkerchief and put it back in his pocket. "Ees good," he said to a thunderous applause.

Outside, he lifted his bride up into the wagon as if she were a youngster. Then he held out his hand. "Jessop, my son."

"Litta Lou," he said. With his new family following in the wagon, Furner walked out of town waving to everyone. "Ees good. Ees good."

The Pastor and Reverend Moss watched them go. "Ees good," Reverend Moss sighed.

They lived a good life on a little farm with a big horse. And so it went with a man who frightened children, awed adults and found good in everything. Shortly after he died, they changed the name of the town to Furnersville. This sign stood by the road at the entrance:

Welcome to Furnersville
Named after the Biggest Man
this area has ever known
Ees Good

About the Author

Rusty Clark DeVoid grew up in Vermont listening to his family's stories. Company visits were special times. Interactive things took place. Sitting around watching TV was as insulting as falling asleep.

Grandparents visits were always exciting. He'd listen to adult conversation instead of being chased outside to play with the others. Everyone sat around and talked about family, friends, neighbors, the weather, ailments, or work. A man's work was a measure of accomplishment and a good source for conversation. The events they described revealed who they were and what they were. It displayed the things they enjoyed and what challenged their pride and tenacity. What a way of viewing the world through someone else's eyes.

Grandpa's prideful accomplishments usually involved his horses. They were his workmates, loyal friends, and members of the family. Elevated to center stage, he would embroider his stories with details and descriptions that amounted to an oral education. Animal traits, equipment, materials and methods, were part of the curriculum. He put more work in the story than the event.

Dad would occasionally add his experiences or be prompted later to include his portion. Such treasures are a family album in themselves. More valuable than any picture for they tell of the inner person. Life is as much a patchwork as the first blanket we were wrapped in and deserves to be recorded. These tales rescue a fascinating time period for you and me.

Even though I've never worked with a team of horses I feel that I've been there. That era passed by too quickly. It was a hard and unforgiving time, salted with pleasurable moments.

Thanks to my folks and their folks for sharing their numerous experiences. They no doubt felt an explicable need to tell about them, just as I do now.